My Torturess

Middle East Literature in Translation
Michael Beard and Adnan Haydar, *Series Editors*

Other titles from Middle East Literature in Translation

Arabs and the Art of Storytelling: A Strange Familiarity
Abdelfattah Kilito; Mbarek Sryfi and Eric Sellin, trans.

Beyond Love
Hadiya Hussein; Ikram Masmoudi, trans.

Chronicles of Majnun Layla and Selected Poems
Qassim Haddad

The Emperor Tea Garden
Nazlı Eray; Robert Finn, trans.

Monarch of the Square: An Anthology
of Muhammad Zafzaf's Short Stories
Mbarek Sryfi and Roger Allen, trans.

A Sleepless Eye: Aphorisms from the Sahara
Ibrahim al-Koni

The Story of Joseph: A Fourteenth-Century
Turkish Morality Play by Sheyyad Hamza
Bill Hickman, trans.

Tree of Pearls, Queen of Egypt
Jurji Zaydan; Samah Selim, trans.

My
Torturess

BENSALEM HIMMICH

Translated from the Arabic by Roger Allen

SYRACUSE UNIVERSITY PRESS

Originally published in Arabic as *Mu'adhdhibati* (Cairo: Dar al-Shurouq, 2010)

For a listing of books published and distributed by Syracuse University Press,
visit www.SyracuseUniversityPress.syr.edu.

ISBN: 978-0-8156-1047-2 (pbk.)   978-0-8156-5317-2 (e-book)

Library of Congress Cataloging-in-Publication Data
Himmich, Ben Salem, 1947–
  [Mu'adhdhabati. English]
  My tortueress / Bensalem Himmich ; translated from the Arabic by Roger Allen. — First edition.
     pages cm — (Middle East literature in translation)
  ISBN 978-0-8156-1047-2 (pbk. : alk. paper) — ISBN 978-0-8156-5317-2 1. Extraordinary rendition—
Fiction.   2. Torture—Fiction.   I. Allen, Roger, 1942– translator.   II. Title.
  PJ7832.I445M8313 2015
  892.7'36—dc23   2015001670

Manufactured in the United States of America

Dedicated to the souls of
Sa'ida Laminbahi and Dris Binzikri

"When you enslave people whose mothers have born them free"
'Umar ibn al-Khattab (the 2nd Caliph of Islam)

Philosopher and writer, **Bensalem Himmich** (former Minister of Culture in Morocco) is the author of a number of works (in both Arabic and French). Four of his novels have been translated in many languages. He has won a number of prizes and distinctions, including the Naguib Mahfouz Prize (the American University in Cairo, 2002), the Sharjah-UNESCO Prize (2003), the Diploma and Medal of the Academic Society of Arts and Letters (Paris, 2009)—for his works as a whole, the Naguib Mahfouz Prize of the Egyptian Writers Union (2009), and the Prize of the Academy of Floral Games in Toulouse, France (2011). His novel, *My Torturess*, was nominated for the International Arabic Fiction Prize (the "Arab Booker") in 2011.

Roger Allen won the 2012 Saif Ghobash Banipal Prize for his translation of *A Muslim Suicide* by Bensalem Himmich (Syracuse University Press, 2011). He has also translated two other novels by Himmich: *The Polymath* (2004) and *The Theocrat* (2005). Allen retired from his position as the Sascha Jane Patterson Harvie Professor of Social Thought and Comparative Ethics in the School of Arts & Sciences at the University of Pennsylvania in 2011. He is the author and translator of numerous books and articles on modern Arabic fiction, novels, and stories.

Contents

Foreword   ⋆   *xi*

1. The Shock and Terror Cellar   ⋆   *1*

2. Spending Time in My Cell   ⋆   *7*

3. Before the Investigating Judge   ⋆   *11*

4. A Wounded Man on My Bedcover   ⋆   *23*

5. How Can I Write My Report about Myself?   ⋆   *28*

6. In the Clutches of the Investigating Judge's Secretary   ⋆   *37*

7. Yet Another Wounded Man on My Bed   ⋆   *42*

8. My Session with Both the Investigating Judge and His Secretary, Nahid al-Busni   ⋆   *47*

9. A Prisoners' Soccer Game   ⋆   *57*

10. My Worst Night of Torture   ⋆   *62*

11. These Are My Injuries, and Then They Cut My Hair   ⋆   *74*

12. With the Investigating Judge and His New Secretary   ⋆   *78*

13. The Letter That Is a Gleaming Light, and I Witness Executions   ⋆   *89*

14. Another Torture Session   ⋆   *98*

15. From the Crazy Block to the Shop
    for the People Practicing for Judgment Day · 107

16. Between My Walls: *The Christian Fayruz* · 116

17. Appointment with the Disciplinary Committee · 124

18. The Condition of My Leg Worsens
    and the Block Starts to Sway · 132

19. Another of the Judge's Whims: *My Appointment
    as Mufti* · 137

20. From the Hospital to My Involvement
    in a Communal Burial · 147

21. In My Torturess's Bed: *A Night
    of Debauchery and Terror* · 153

22. I Have No Choice but to Sleep
    and Wake Up to the Vestiges of a Fire · 162

23. From the Penitents' Wing to a Debauched
    Nightclub · 166

24. A Final Meeting with the Judge,
    Then the Dormitory with No Sleep · 176

25. The Major Soirée and Its Disgusting Surprises · 188

26. My Return to My Beloved Land · 201

27. Conclusion · 204

    Afterword · 215

    Glossary · 223

Foreword

"Dear Hamuda,

It may well prove difficult for you to turn into a hired hand, some-one at the beck and call of tyrants with all their fiendish schemes—professional spy, double agent, hired killer. In that case, you'll need to come up with a solution, one that may save you provided you learn to do it well. You have to pretend to be crazy, mentally ill. You should pepper your interrogators with all kinds of crazy talk. Threaten your torturers by coughing all over them and infecting them with your sickness. Maybe, just maybe, they'll give up and send you back to your country or somewhere close, drugged with opium. You'll eventually come round to find yourself with an electronic belt around you and a bullet aimed at your head, to be fired if you should so much as breathe a word of your story to a living soul or raise a complaint against forces unknown . . ."

Oh yes, my gracious Na'ima, may God be gracious to you and comfort you!

That note that you sneaked into my pocket and begged me to destroy after I had read it, that precious note, I've memorized it by heart. I fed its paper and ink to my stomach for it to digest. I can vouch for the fact that I owe my rescue to it, emerging alive from the dark recesses of a horrendous prison. But for that note, I would have spent still more years under relentless guard watch and enduring never-ending torture sessions, all supervised and directed by that truly barbaric and expert hang-woman of evil memory and repute known by the name "Mama Ghula."

Now that I've come back to my bookstore and my home, where vermin and insects have fouled everything during my long prison term, how am I supposed to go out into the streets, squares, markets, and mosques in Oujda without bumping into people and chatting with them? How can I use them to salve my wounds and breathe in the sweet zephyrs of my recovered freedom by contacting them and getting together? Am I supposed to be able to travel to Ouad-Zem to look for my mother and find out whether she's still alive or has died and gone to meet her generous Maker? If I did that, how could I explain to the small number of people who still remember me why I've been away for so long, why I look so dreadfully emaciated and the hair on my head and beard has turned grey? If the clever ones managed to get me to talk about what happened to me, would I be expected to talk about it all under the banner of truth and honesty, or indulge instead in all kinds of deception, falsification, and duplicity? Whichever route I chose, I would find myself between a rock and a hard place: a bullet to my head or an electric charge to my heart, neither of which could possibly miss once they were fired. Either that, or else a tissue of lies and deceit, along with all the self-hate and remorse that goes with it.

Alternatively, silence may be the solution, relying on the inexorable passage of time, which would also involve always staying at home. But both those requirements will inevitably morph into two other types of prison, as the time period grows ever longer and the space is so confined. When we are talking about someone like me who has been traumatized by a barbaric incarceration, any kind of prison, however light its burden may seem, will provoke a nervous attack and twist the knife in my wound.

So take things slowly, I told myself, till the multiple layers of hesitation and despair gradually peel away and the feeling of depression lightens a bit.

In the early days I thought I could meet people in public places, albeit taking all necessary precautions and adopting all manner of concealment strategies. For example, I would regularly avoid going out in broad daylight when exposure and visibility would be at their maximum. Even when I ventured out at night, when it was likely to be pitch dark, I would put on a reinforced metal helmet and bullet-proof vest that I had made myself out of iron and steel and concealed inside my leather jacket, something I had bought from a stall downtown that I had visited in disguise at dead of night.

As I walked along streets and alleys, there was much less movement at night; the lights would be either turned off completely or kept low. Peering eyes used to stare curiously at my outfit but without attracting too much attention. Maybe they assumed I was a motorcyclist; I had left my bike, was now walking on foot, and had forgotten to take off my helmet. In stores, cafeterias and cafes customers became more and more curious about my general appearance; they kept nodding in my direction and cracking malicious jokes. Children and teenagers went so far as to stand in my way and call me "cosmonaut"—all of which made me decide to strike those particular spots from my list of regular haunts.

Apart from those few spaces where no people were to be found, the only places I could go were the city mosques. I started visiting them in rotation just before evening prayer time, all in the hope of avoiding prying eyes and people's attention. But, as the nights rolled by, things started to go awry with the worshippers in the mosques, some with shaven or uncovered heads, others wearing skullcaps and turbans. For no particular reason they were all amazed at my cautious attitude toward the wardens, preferring to consider the outwards aspects of the situation rather than the essence. Their own ignorance aside, they had little time to listen to what had happened to me. Even if a few of them were willing to hear snippets of what I had to say—and how on earth did I manage to do that?!—they would soon move away, twirling their fingers against their temples as a sign of total disbelief.

I decided to avoid any undesirable communication with people and worshippers by staying at home for several days, preparing my own food and blackening page after page with accounts of my years in prison. One day, after I had performed the evening prayer, I fell sound asleep. In a dream, I saw myself going out on the night coinciding with the celebration of the Prophet's birthday. I left the house without changing my precautionary garb. By the gateway of the main mosque two men in civilian clothes stopped me, led me into an empty alleyway close by, and probed me from head to toe, firstly with an electronic device, then by hand. Taking off my helmet and coat, they handcuffed me and took me to the police station by the Sidi 'Abd al-Wahhab Gate (where the heads of executed people used to be hung in the old days). While I waited for the arrival of the police officer and his recorder, I was forced to spend the rest of the night on a bench outside his office. Curling myself up into a ball, I fell asleep, oblivious to my surroundings. At that point I woke up with a start. After checking everything carefully, I found myself still lying in my own bed.

On this new day there's a light tap on the door. No one ever comes to see me, so I leap up to see who is knocking. There is a devout shaykh whose general appearance and demeanor remind me of the imam at a small mosque downtown. Rumor has it that he was fired from his position for unknown reasons. Once I had greeted him and invited him inside to share my breakfast, he confirmed my impression, then proceeded to give me a few terse details about himself. He told me that he was now working in Noah's profession and owned a thriving carpenter's workshop. He had lots of customers because he was willing to make do with reasonable charges and refused to cheat people. He then launched into an amazing story, some of which was so disturbing that it left me with my mouth agape and my tongue paralyzed:

"Listen, my boy," he said. "I'm going to tell you some really serious things. Once you've taken them all in and thought about it, you'll want to consider the situation you're in now and protect yourself from all kinds of nasty outcomes. I have to begin with two pieces of bad news, in fact two deaths. Your mother—God have mercy on her soul!—died in a series of floods caused by torrential downpours of rain, leading to several landslides and the collapse of a number of houses. Her resting-place in Ouad-Zem is in a communal grave for those people who were swallowed up by the earth; the sheer quantity of mud and debris made it impossible to locate anyone. The second death involves your cousin, al-Husayn al-Masmudi. He had been fighting the jihad in Afghanistan and Iraq, then came back to the Awras Mountains two years ago. He joined some fighting groups there, but was killed in the region near Bumirdas. Your mother was convinced that you had perished in the sea along with all the other people who risk their lives trying to get to Europe; that's what happened to some of her neighbors' children. However, your late cousin, al-Husayn, who used to visit me regularly under cover, assured me that you had been rushed away somewhere, and he had no idea where. He made me promise to look after you if you ever came back, and I promised to do so."

As I listened to Shaykh Hamdan al-Mizati's shattering news, I shed a few dry tears and was struck dumb.

"So I can help you, my boy," he went on, "you're going to have to reassure me that the terrible years you've spent in prison which have so damaged your body and general health have not affected your mind or faculties. The first thing you need to do in order to reassure me is to take off immediately that helmet and the bulging jacket that some people assume is booby-trapped. This paranoia you have, that someone is spying on you all the time, is simply a devilish illusion on your part. The belt you're wearing is another piece of fantasy, child's play in fact. These little foibles of yours keep bothering the police; they smell a rat. Will you promise me to get rid of them?"

I handed them over on the spot and gave him a crowbar so he could break the belt.

"Take them by all means," I told him, doing my best to control my emotions. "Bury them wherever you like."

"Fine!" he replied, putting everything into a bag. "You've convinced me that your mind's still working. Now tell me what you'd like me to do, God willing."

"My dearest wish, Sir," I replied, "is to make a record of a truly horrendous period of imprisonment, one that lasted more than six years. If I were to tell part of it out loud, the people listening would laugh in my face; they'd be convinced that I was a raving paranoiac,

completely insane. I urgently need some medical tests, but I'm postponing them in case they provide me with disturbing information
that may depress me and thus prevent me from writing down my
story. Once I've finished my work, then let happen whatever fate
decrees. I want my testimony to be in written form, so that, once
I'm dead, some cognizant reader who is both aware and sympathetic
may get hold of it. So that's my dearest wish, but I can't possibly
achieve it in this cramped space where I'm losing all hope and my
spirit is almost completely crushed. It feels just as bad as those long
and bitterly destructive days I spent in prison."

The shaykh thought for a while, then suggested something that
offered me a blessed release.

"Between today's prayer times collect everything you need. The
late al-Husayn has assigned ownership of this place to you by way
of a contract. Tomorrow just after dawn you'll accompany me in my
truck to a farm that I own south of Oujda on the Angad Plain. God
willing, you'll be able to settle down there and complete your project.
The shepherdess who runs the farm and her daughter will take care
of you. So we've agreed then."

With that the shaykh stood up and grabbed the bag of stuff. I
escorted him to the door, kissed his shoulder, and offered him my
profuse thanks.

And that is exactly what happened. That devout believer kept
his promise. I spent the entire night in prayer, thinking all the while
about what the shaykh had told me, beginning with the two deaths,
then offering advice, and finally providing me with a truly blessed
means of escape.

Once we reached the farm, my benefactor introduced me to the
shepherdess, an energetic and strongly built widow and her middle-
aged daughter whose Bedouin garb was quite incapable of concealing
her wonderful buxom figure and radiant face.

We had a rich and filling breakfast together, and then the shaykh
informed the two women that I needed privacy and quiet. He asked
them both to look after me. He then embraced me, wished me luck

and success in my project, and said farewell. He promised to come back for a visit when time allowed and to serve as my very first reader.

Now I was left on my own in this large house which opened up on to fields, trees, crops and animals. I began to prepare myself for the project I had been contemplating. I was fully aware, needless to say, that the things I was going to record were merely the tip of an iceberg; I would have to allow for lapses of fact or memory and acknowledge that it would be utterly impossible to cover everything. I now started spending the whole day writing, although for part of the time I would go for walks and contemplate or else have brief, innocuous conversations with the widow. I intentionally kept my relationship with her daughter chaste and proper so that I could retain the respect of her mother and the shaykh as well.

My Torturess

1

The Shock and Terror Cellar

I have no real memory of what happened or how I came to find myself in this detention center where I have been squeezed into a solitary cell for three whole years. All I can recall is that three masked men who said they were from the secret police dragged me out of my bookstore—where I lived, put a lock on it, and then led me to a grimy car with dirty number-plates. Shoving me inside, they blindfolded me, then gave me an injection of some kind that made me lose consciousness very quickly. When I came round, I could sense that there were other people around me along with a loud noise that may well have been the sound of a helicopter.

Through my drugged haze I could make out a man, but not well enough to recognize him. He hurriedly gave me another injection, and the next thing I remember is having photographs taken of me naked from every angle. I was then given a blue prisoner's uniform and put it on when told to do so by an orderly. In the reception hall I had to hand over to him my suit, shirt, watch, wallet, card, and leather shoes, all of which were duly recorded in a register that I had to sign. He asked me to tell him what one plus one equaled.

"Two," I replied.

"One divided by one?" he asked.

"One," I replied.

Addition or division, he seemed to be giving me a choice.

"From now on," he said, almost as though he were naming a child, "your identity is going to be Cell Number 112."

Handing me a pair of rubber shoes that I put on, he told me to follow him. We were accompanied by two guards and went to an

1

interior room close by, with a sign on the door saying "Leftover lies." The warden sat me down in front of a flickering screen with lines and dots. Placing my right hand on the Qur'an, he told me to swear to tell the truth and nothing but the truth.

At this point I started to panic, especially when the orderly turned the light off. I heard a mechanical voice of some unseen speaker asking me questions: my name, date and place of birth, names of my parents, job. I gave them all the information I knew. When he asked me about my membership of a secret political party or a jihadist cell, whether active or sleeping, I said nothing in an automatic gesture of resistance. However, as soon as I felt a sharp razor touching my neck, I felt compelled to say something. What I said was that for a limited time I had belonged to a Sufi group. When they asked me what it was called, I replied the Yaqtin group. Asked about the shaykh who led it and his disciples, I paused for a moment and then told them that I could not remember.

The screen now went blank as though it had broken down. The orderly behind me turned on the light again and ordered the two guards who were yawning sleepily to take me to cell number 13 until the problem with the computer could be fixed.

That cell—how can I ever forget it?!—consisted of a flat storage space, parts of it illuminated by bright neon lights. Individual iron cages were strung along the walls facing each other; all prisoners inside them could do was either sit down or stretch out. No sooner had the orderly pushed me into one of the cages than my companion in the next cage greeted me with a blessing on the advent of the holy month of Ramadan the next day, and welcomed me to the shock and terror cellar—to give it its official name. The other people in cages greeted me in the same fashion. Some of them assumed that I was either a long-term prisoner on whose cooperation they had given up hope, or else a new arrival who was in the cellar either because of a mistake or else so as to make abundantly and powerfully clear to me that I was not in this detention center for some kind of outing or in order to consort with guards and managers who were playing jokes and having a bit of fun.

The cellar was just like an oven, and the people incarcerated inside had no way of knowing if it were night or day or hot or cold. That is what my neighbor told me, and he went on to explain that people who did not get sick usually passed the time either describing the reasons why they were at the prison, telling whatever stories and jokes they happened to remember, or playing cards or chess. All that was in addition to whatever time was spent praying by those who wished to do so and reciting the Qur'an and other liturgies. Sick and elderly people, some of whom had been there for more than a decade, had simply surrendered the keys to their life to their Maker. Some of them had been there for so long that their skin had swollen and festered so much that they could hardly move; others were doing their best to hasten their end by fasting all the time or refusing to eat.

On the evening of the first day of the holy month of Ramadan, people came to distribute the fast-breaking food; like the guards, they were wearing medical masks. As they made their rounds, we all put out our plastic bowls, and they poured a lentil broth into them, along with pieces of bread. Even though the light was very dim, I managed to make out two parts of an insect in my bowl. When I inserted my finger into the liquid, I came out with a dead cockroach. When I rushed over to show it to my neighbor, he congratulated me on my sharp eyesight. By way of information he told me that the majority of prisoners who were not fasting never looked at what they were eating. That led me to express my utter disgust at the inhumane conditions involved in this imprisonment, which were not only contrary to religion and morality but also against all known legal requirements. I accused the perpetrators of criminal behavior and swore that they would incur God's wrath and punishment. My companion advised me to shut up and say nothing, all in anticipation of heaven's verdict falling on the wrongdoers, something from which there was no escape. He went on to tell me that of all insects cockroaches were the least harmful; not only that, but they are useful for prisoners because they eat the bedbugs, lice, and daddy longlegs that crawl all over bodies day and night. He absolutely forbade me to flick them away if I ever felt them on my bodily extremities.

That made me feel even more disgusted; I almost threw up into my bowl, so I put it all aside. I now told my companion that I needed to relieve myself. He frowned and paused for a moment. When I asked him again, he replied that, if it was my bladder I needed to empty, that could be easily arranged with the orderly; but if it involved excretion, then that involved particular procedures that the orderly and his myrmidons could explain. Without further ado, I yelled for the duty orderly and told him my needs. Night had not yet fallen when he took me out of my cage; after obtaining the chief warder's permission, he took me to a platform with upright tin sheets. He showed me the way prisoners were taking turns walking across it. Every time it opened, they would spread their legs a little and excrete standing up. I watched as one of them lost his balance and fell headlong into the bottomless cesspool.

"So have you made up your mind?" the orderly asked me gruffly.

I had no choice but to take the risk and test my gymnastic talents. He inquired of me as to whether I wished to avoid exposing myself to danger or even death, and, without even waiting to hear my reply, advised me to avoid looking at what lay below and ignore the soldiers and foreign female troops who were taking pictures of people excreting from a nearby building. After succeeding in this utterly humiliating and foul test, I made my way back to my cage, frowning and downcast. My immediate companions congratulated me on my survival; it was as if I had traversed some difficult causeway or scored some colossal success in the Olympics. When I asked them what happened to people who failed this dreadful exercise, one of them replied that in most cases they would fall into a deep sandpit, particularly if the person wanted to put an end to his life. One of the others gave an answer to a question that I was on the point of asking: people who were either too weak, sick, or impaired to perform this exercise would be hosed down and cleaned by volunteer colleagues, whose reward would be in God's hands. When I said that I wanted to be one of those volunteers, they readily accepted my offer, but only on condition that the warden agreed. Accompanied by a guard, I went to see the warden. When I discussed the matter with him, his reply came from behind his face-mask, which reeked of wine.

"So who's stopping you?!" he yelled in a gruff tone, which said everything there was to say about his mean, sloppy demeanor. "Take the bucket, mop, and sackcloth, and make sure you don't use too much water. Now get out!"

I now set about my hard and dismal task, cleaning the cages I was assigned. You might have thought that the people in them were alive, but in fact they were not. Every feeling had been ruthlessly rubbed out; some of them seemed to be in a kind of perpetual stupor; others would smile at you as you were cleaning things out and mutter words of gratitude. By the time I had finished, I felt like vomiting. Had I not concentrated my entire attention on reciting a prayer to God and calling down curses on the evil and murderous tyrants who were perpetrating such things, I would have burst into tears. I went to the warder and informed him that the majority of inmates in the prison needed to be transferred to hospital.

He proceeded to lambast me. "Are you telling me my job, you son of a bitch?!" he yelled nervously, his face turning red. "Get back to your cage."

When I returned to my cage, I felt crushed. I lay down with my eyes closed, trying as best I could to digest everything I had seen and heard in the shock and terror cellar. I kept assessing the sheer horror involved in the context of instances of the most extreme iniquity, barbaric violence, and agonizing torture that some people seemed capable of inflicting on helpless prisoners who were their fellow human beings.

I told myself that, if I had not inured myself ever since childhood to a confrontation with emptiness and the vertigo it can bring on, I would by now have certainly succumbed to this dreadful experience. But getting through it once was no guarantee that I would be able to make it through other phases that were bound to follow. Would I be able, I wondered, to keep my health and sanity through the tests that were now awaiting me: eating dirty food, serving withdrawn hermits, staying in the same cage for hours on end, and so on?

The criminals and directors of this collective have one aim, to convert the human beings who are prisoners into mute animals, with clipped toenails, rotten teeth, shattered limbs, and bodily and spiritual power completely smashed. All such a prisoner can do is to give up and submit. He can rant and rave all he wants, provided that it all happens inside his mouth and his internal space. The people interred in this place have by now reached the very limits of their endurance; they can take no more of it. They have come to see death as a cheap alternative and to regard it as preferable to the utter humiliation they are suffering. They use all the limited amounts of energy and initiative that they possess to take turns during this blessed month reciting Qur'anic verses and selected passages from Prophetic eulogies and other prayers. For my part, I did my best to endure everything as well as I could. Once in a while the guards would shut us up, using clubs and rubber hoses to threaten us because of what they called our rants.

I spent almost an entire month or so like this, enduring the treatment they were meting out. I found myself forced, albeit unwillingly, to do certain things, such as going to the toilet in the way I have described and making do for breakfast with the basic minimum, after removing the foul insects that the food distributors consistently told us must have fallen into the vats by chance; if anyone did not like it, they would say, "Then give him some more gravy." Something else was to let the cockroaches roam all over your body, searching out the lice that were their favorite food. Things like that.

A few hours before the Night of Power, the collapse in my health just happened to coincide with the arrival of two guards. They took me from my cage and, with no warning, transferred me back to my previous cell. I had no time to say farewell to the people I had come to know in the shock and terror cellar; I just managed a brief farewell wave. They in turn promised to utter a prayer on my behalf as soon as this blessed day dawned and the heavens were open for prayers that would merit a response.

2

Spending Time in My Cell

My very own cell, no. 112!

It is very narrow, five and a half square feet in all, with two blankets and a toilet—the hole covered with a brick to stop rats coming out. It is obviously situated low in a basement where the stench is foul and the sun never reaches. To keep hunger at bay, I get two meager meals a day. A guard pushes them through an aperture in the steel door; all I ever see is his hand, never his head.

So here I am, a prisoner, stuck here for months on end (as far as I can remember). I adjust my life as best I can, devising a program in the hope, even if it is illusory, of making things a bit more bearable. So every day, as soon as I wake up, I spend some time—it may be long or short, it depends—staring at the cracks in the wall, their spiral configurations marked by areas of dampness. Sometimes I amuse myself by reading them as designs with suggestive images and various interconnected dimensions. But once I become aware again and chide myself, I spend the rest of the time on an activity that I much prefer to the periods when I'm allowed outside to walk or meet other prisoners. It is a blanket-based activity, and involves lying on my back, scrunching myself up in a heap, and withdrawing into myself. I bend, make myself into a ball, roll over, put my head between my knees, coil myself up, and then turn over on my side. I come up with some other activities too, things that may well challenge the vast lexicon of Arabic itself: I act the tortoise and hedgehog, I coil up into a spiral, I emparcel myself, I turn into a corpse, staying still and holding my breath for as long as I can before becoming corporeal once again. Even so, these various postures do not exclude still others:

7

stretching, sitting cross-legged, craning my neck, and being generally
fussy. I may play the hero, punching away at an illusory foe, then
laughing at him and letting out a belch. I imitate the roar of wild animals, then run away from them, making all kinds of chirping noises
in the hope of attracting birds to the small cans of water and other
things that I leave for them on the tiny upper window. I make other
gestures and noises as well, whether I'm stretched out on the bed or
sitting up, standing still, or walking around.

As another part of my daily routine I repeat segments of the Holy
Qur'an, something I am afraid of forgetting while I am in this horrendous prison. I start with the Sura of Yasin and then move on to the
Prophets in which Job, the exemplar of endurance and steadfastness,
is mentioned. I recite some Prophetic traditions as well, along with
literary texts by authors ancient and modern. A significant part of
the day is devoted to something that has gradually become the most
important thing of all: prayer, even though it involves using minimal
amounts of water or sand to cleanse myself when needed. Above and
beyond all this, there are other irregular activities that the guards
impose upon me. The prelude to such activities is always: "This isn't
a charity prison or a rest home for invalids. Tasks and services performed by prisoners are the means to pay for the food, showers, exercise, and housing that they all enjoy while they are here. Such duties
include emptying the garbage cans into the principal dump about
half a mile outside the main buildings; cleaning the kitchen, dining
room, hallways, corridors, and special cells; and other things."

Every time I was told to leave my cell to work, I would do my best
to restrict my conversation with other prisoners to a simple greeting
and an ever more polite response to theirs, so much so that my neighbors took to calling me "the dervish" or "the introvert."

With the arrival of nighttime, darkness falls and the light fades.
All movement now falls to its lowest level. Sometimes the evening
meal arrives, other times it does not. There is nothing to read, no
radio or television, no news about the world outside. Inmates have
trouble falling asleep; if they do manage to do so, there is nothing to

guarantee that they will not have nightmares or that various flying or spotted insects will not start plaguing them.

As I myself flirt with Morpheus, the god of slumber, and toss and turn on my bed, I find myself listening to my stomach churning and my limbs grinding. As I graduate from one nap to another, I have visions of the wonders of paradise, gorgeous women, wine, banquet tables that stretch into the distance for miles on end. That only happens if my sleep is not disrupted by some prisoner or other screaming and calling out for help. That, of course, wakes up all the prisoners in the block, who then proceed to curse and rage. That is exactly what happened for the nth time the day before yesterday when one of the prisoners started yelling and screaming because he was hanging from the ceiling vent so as to get away from the scorpions and snakes that were crawling around his cell. He claimed that surveillance cameras had been installed in his quarters. As an act of sheer defiance he used to curse, spit, and even masturbate. On another night it was the turn of another prisoner to raise a hue and cry about his nightmares and the evil genies preying on him. The night guards never moved or interfered, almost as though their ears were stuffed with wax or their hearts had been chained shut.

After I had spent an incalculable amount of time in my cell, I had the opportunity to leave it for a few hours. The purpose was not to let me get some fresh air or exercise, but rather to undergo a medical exam because I had come down with a fierce cough, accompanied by a shortage of breath resulting from my previous sojourn in the shock and terror cellar. Following complaints from my nightly neighbors or perhaps due to other considerations, I was rushed to the clinic. The nurse there gave me some tranquilizers till the doctor arrived at mid-morning. My cough lessened, and I began to feel sleepy, so much so that I had the kind of sleep the like of which I had not enjoyed since being brought against my will to this detention center, the purpose, name, and place of which remained unknown to me.

It was some time in the morning while I was still drowsy that I caught a snippet of conversation between two men:

First one: "We haven't interrogated this one yet. We need his information, so make him better so he doesn't die before we can question him."

Second: "I'll do the necessary examination. He may be able to stand on his feet today provided it's not tuberculosis. That's what we found on three prisoners yesterday, but they've been removed."

The examination they conducted showed that, at least up to this point, I had not contracted that disease—thank God! The problem was that my sensitivity to the dampness in my cell had provoked my cough and constricted breathing. The doctor gave me some pills and a spray and had me transferred to a cell in another wing; it was smaller than the previous one but was on the first floor in a building that got some drier air and sunshine.

3

Before the Investigating Judge

My health improves in my new cell, the number of which has followed me. Every time I feel the need for some fresh air, I stand on a chair and poke my nose through a window, which is open to the sky. Using all five senses I come to the conclusion that the place where I am imprisoned is either in the desert or else very close to it, far removed from any view of mountains or sea. However, the name and address of the location is known only to the people who run this detention center and their luminaries.

As I took some of my pills along with the first meal that I got through the aperture in the door of my new cell, the thought occurred to me that, when it came to my recent promotion and maybe even my release, this cough of mine could give me a stratagem, as long as I perfected its impact and timing. While I was ruminating on this idea (and other even weirder ones) and spraying my mouth, a guard came into my cell, tied my hands behind my back, and led me across a paved square and along numerous corridors to a distinctive building with offices and modern conveniences. The guard knocked on a door on the first floor, and I followed him into a large hall. Behind a table a fat woman was sitting, surrounded by files and a computer. Hurrying over, she proceeded to conduct a security check, using an electronic device to scan my bodily extremities. Once the exam was over and I had been overwhelmed by a veritable flood of perfume, she accompanied me to the interior office, bowing in greeting as she did so to someone whom she called "his excellency the judge." She pointed out that I had not offered my own greetings to his excellency, so I did so.

So, after a period of several months in prison, here I was finally in the presence of the investigating judge whom, as I have explained earlier, is the one to investigate the files of the accused and determine their fate. After taking a look in my direction, he told me to await my turn in a dark corner. In the meantime he was completing his session with a young man, the only part of whom that I could see was his back. In the corner, I scrunched up on the seat as best I could and started looking at the judge and listening to what he was saying to the suspect.

Viewed in all three dimensions the man I was looking at reminded me of the heaviest conceivable Japanese sumo wrestler. What caught my eye was his absolutely excessive obesity and his bald pate fringed with white. Then there were his enormous ears that stuck out like two hearing horns and his chin, which protruded from a bulging neck. I was struck by his sunken eyes nestling behind thick, shaded spectacles and his mouth (just like a chicken's anus), which was topped by a blond, Hitler-like moustache. All praise to the mighty Creator! Whenever he stood up to look for something or to exert some bodily sway over his interviewee, he would look like a wild beast hovering over its prey. His gigantic bulging presence made him seem like a huge elephant; the only thing missing was the trunk.

"So," he told the prisoner in a nasal twang, as he rubbed his neck, "you're no longer denying the accusations leveled against you; in fact, you're confirming them. Sheltering *takfiri** radicals who are now on the run; providing support for the families of the ones who are married; and failing to disclose their names and addresses. The only point of disagreement between us is that you're refusing to ratify your charge-document by taking the canonical oath. Instead, you're arrogating to yourself the right to take a different oath, one that sometimes involves swearing by the dawn and ten nights [Qur'an, Sura 89, v. 1], at others by the fig, the olive, and Mount Sinai [Qur'an, Sura 95, v. 1], and at still others by the afternoon [Qur'an, Sura 103, v. 1]. You justify this utter heresy on your part by claiming that you need to avoid any mention of God and His beautiful names in foul and disgusting places, dark and cruel, that being the way you choose to describe the places where we currently are. Is that right?"

"That represents the decision that I have come to," the young man replied in a firm, steady voice, "aided by God's help."

That remark made the investigating judge froth at the mouth in fury. "So, you total phony," he yelled, "who gave you the authority to make your own decisions?"

"Here you are, Judge" the young man replied, "calling me an unbeliever, when I'm a graduate of the Zaytuna University in Tunis. I only make such a decision when there is no textual authority . . ."

"Guards," the judge interrupted, "take this wretch and hand him over to the woman who knows how to deal with unbelievers and cure them of their sickness. She'll straighten you out and put your warped brain back on the right track."

I managed to catch a glimpse of the young man as he was led away by two guards. Walking with a steady gait and defiant expression, he raised two fingers in a victory gesture.

"By the heavens and the night-star," he said. "I have no fear of this female ghoul or her cronies. Umm Qash'am* is where you're all going, and, as they say, 'evil is the resort.'"

The judge now collapsed into his chair. Sweat was pouring off him, and he was panting hard. He pressed a button, and a young woman wearing a headdress appeared and handed him a pill and a glass of water. That helped calm his nerves, although it took a while. He asked her who Umm Qash'am might be, and she stuttered that she did not know. He told her to go and look her up in the dictionary so that the woman in question could be brought to see him. Acknowledging the order, she rushed out looking flustered.

At this point the atmosphere in the room felt like lead or even heavier. The judge fidgeted a bit, then cleared his throat. He told me to take the seat that the young man had occupied, and I did so, muttering a greeting to which he responded. Wiping the sweat off his forehead, he took off his spectacles and pored over my file. He was still cursing and swearing at the young man who had been taken out, calling him all sorts of names like "heretic" and "son of a bitch." Once he had finished reading, he put his spectacles back on. Surprising me with a very ambiguous expression, he asked me if I knew the son of a bitch who had been sitting in the place which I now occupied. I replied that I did not.

"That stubborn prisoner," he said, gritting his teeth, "is a warrior living in the past, an era long over, the kind of bully who relishes pain and desires nothing more than death and martyrdom. But our very own torturess, our female ghoul, will get to work on him and chop off his illusory sense of victory limb by limb . . ."

He stared in my direction, a scary smile on his face. "Hamuda," he asked me, "don't you agree with me that this brilliant expression, 'relishing pain,' with all its semantic and morphological contradictions, is absolutely marvelous?"

I frowned, not wishing to respond to something that in view of the circumstances seemed utterly inappropriate.

"Never mind!" he went on, clearing his throat. "Forget the question, and let's go back to you. From your file, Hamuda from Oujda, I deduce that you're a compliant kind of person, someone who likes company. There are a few small details, some obscure matters, that I'm sure we can clear up with God's help, relying of course on your total cooperation and a much needed veracity that you'll freely offer us. As we all know, lies and deceit are anathema; double-crossing and obfuscation are abominations. Confusing reality and fancy simply creates discord. By my very life, foul deeds such as these are the kinds of things that groups of vagrant poets and their camp-followers—fornicators, layabouts, and debauchees all—commit all the time. May God Almighty protect us against them, keep us far removed from their circles and squabbles, and guide us by His light to the clear, unvarnished truth!"

The only thing that brought this outpouring of rhymed discourse and dissimulation to an end was a light tap on the door. The young woman offered her bashful apologies, and he told her to come in.

"What do you want, young lady?" he asked gently, clearing his throat as he did so.

"I've looked for her, Sir," she replied, but I can't find her anywhere."

"Who?"

"Umm Qash'am, Sir."

"That's very disturbing," he replied without changing his tone. "Take a look in the biographical dictionaries and in Ibn Manzur's dictionary as well.* If you don't bring her to me, I'm going to deduct a third of your salary."

At this point I asked permission to speak.

"In Arabic, Judge," I told him, "Umm Qash'am is a phrase that was used by people in pre-Islamic times as a synonym for Hell. God alone knows best."

"Good for you, Hamuda" he replied, "and may God preserve you! As for you, young woman, kiss the head of this man who's provided you with a little light and taught you something you didn't know. Just one kiss will do."

Without moving from my seat I was given a warm kiss on the head by this unfortunate young woman. She asked permission to leave and stumbled her way red-faced toward the door.

The judge stared at me in amazement. "I notice that, when the secretary is here, you keep your eyes lowered and don't look straight at her!"

"I behave that way," I replied, "in obedience to the injunctions of our Prophet: 'He who looks at the beauty of a woman and turns away the first time, God will create a devotion for him, the sweetness of which he will find in his own heart.'"

"Good heavens, Hamuda!" the judge yelled in delight, "you're genuinely learned and your memory is a priceless gift!"

"Forgive me, Sir," I replied, "but my attainments are only modest."

"True enough, modesty is a known trait of the genuinely learned. Come over here, Nahid, and stand in front of me. Take off your headdress and shake your hair to left and right. Isn't that beautiful?! One female delight on top of another. Look at me, Hamuda. Am I supposed to be able to look away from this woman? I try; oh yes, I keep trying. I cover my eyes with my hands, but I keep seeing her as naked as Eve, and I want to have her even more. By the truth of God who created her and made her so lovely, it's all over. It reminds me of the chap who once said: 'Look away, even from female sheep.' That's what it reminds me of . . ."

"I think it was Abu Yazid al-Bistami* who said that."

"He must have been really frustrated! Looking away from female animals is one thing, but human females? No way, a thousand times no! What Ibn Sa'd* has to say in his *Tabaqat*, based on the Prophet's own dicta, makes more sense: 'In your lower world, he has led me to like perfume and women . . . ' Nahid, put your headdress back on and get out of my sight. Leave now!"

"Now, Hamuda," the judge went on, nervously wiping his face and bald pate with a handkerchief, "let's go back to what we were talking about . . ."

He started ranting and raving, as though talking to himself. "So that son of a bitch has insulted every single member of our august center here, even me! His file is already thick enough, but now he's gone too far. Mama Ghula will know how to make him suffer. Then the nasty heretic will soon realize what the endgame really is and who it is that deserves to feel the flames of hell licking around them in this world rather than the next, to be flayed by her whips and tied up in chains. You heard for yourself, Hamuda, the way he talked about Umm Qash'am in referring to all kinds of perfectly decent and upright people. When he's brought to trial and a verdict is required, you'll certainly be able to provide your own testimony, once I've given you, of course, all the necessary details about the heretic's case from its very beginnings and the way things have proceeded to their current state."

It occurred to me at this point that I should decline to testify in any case where the truth could never be known for sure, but I decided not to do so. It also occurred to me that I should congratulate him on the eloquence and clarity of his discourse, making sure that I made no mention of the occasional pedantry and affectation, but there again I decided against it.

The judge took off his spectacles slowly and gestured to me to come closer.

"Hamuda," he confided to me with his nasal twang to which he added a patina of affection, "the thing that's made me sympathize with you and not forward your file to a really nasty interviewer is that we share one particular trait in common. Do you know what it is?"

I replied that I did not.

"Both of us, Hamuda," he went on, "are graduates of colleges from other Arab countries. You have a degree is Islamic law, and so do I; you also have one in literature, as do I. But then the fates have sent us down separate paths, so let's thank God for giving us this opportunity to cooperate in disclosing the truth and dispelling all falsehood and deceit. All I need to do is to use my eyes to look at people's faces; I can tell what is in their hearts and the messages conveyed by their eyes. It's a gift I've had ever since my childhood. With the passage of time it has only grown and developed. God has used it to bestow on me examples to be gleaned from life's hard experiences and the tough, yet revelatory lessons that they can offer. Even so I've never believed that this perspicacity of mine is a match for Zarqa' al-Yamama*—all thanks to God for what he has bestowed on me."

He stopped suddenly and gave me a quizzical look, but I did not show any sign of wanting to respond or agree with him.

"At my circumcision ceremony," he went on, "my late father sacrificed a sheep and named me Hassan. He was inspired to do so by Hassan ibn Thabit, who, as you know, was the Prophet Muhammad's own poet (Peace be upon him!), someone who accepted the Prophet's eternal message and became a Muslim, thus saving himself from the proverbial valleys in which poets would lose themselves.* That is why, from my childhood days up till now, you'll find me every morning reciting as many of the beautiful names of God as I can remember. My entire aspirations are focused exclusively on what is good. I married a woman who had the feminine form of my own name, Hasna'. I always treated her kindly. When we did not have any children, she wanted to get divorced, and I let her go with all due charity. I still adhere to the same principles and beliefs. I particularly abhor all thought of the use of violence; in my attitude toward everything, I always make judgment calls and advocate what is the most acceptable. My constantly repeated slogan is: yes to the good and beautiful; no, and no again, to violence. If you believe someone, you'll get the truth. I have never beaten a prisoner, even though he may be a hardened reprobate. I've never tortured anyone, or even spat in anyone's face, be they male or female. That's the way I was born and brought up. Never in my life have I sacrificed an animal, even a lowly chicken, so how on earth could I do it to a human being? When it comes to things like hangings and executions, whether in Islamic domains or in the history of every kind of political and religious system, my entire body recoils and my soul shudders in horror. I'll admit that, once in a while, my imagination—but it is only that—leads me to feel like flaying the hides of certain nasty individuals, too big for their own boots; I have the urge to tear them limb from limb and throw them to the famished hyenas and lions. But now, tell me about your own violence."

My jaw dropped in amazement when I heard his request.

"Yes, I'm talking about your violence! Quite apart from the charge that you killed your mother's husband—something we'll be looking into shortly, there's the matter of the assault on a man whom you subjected to a severe beating, leaving him injured. You claimed that he had insulted your father by cursing him and spitting in his face. But your reaction clearly went way beyond the bounds of revenge and retaliation; not only that, but you also contravened God's own words in the Qur'an: "*If someone assaults you, reciprocate against him to the same degree*" [Surat al-Baqara 2, The Cow, v. 194], and His command: "*A soul for a soul, an eye for an eye, a nose for a nose, an ear for an ear, and a tooth for a tooth*" [Surat al-Ma'ida 5, The Table, v. 45]. In your case then, you should have been applying the just dictates of Shari'a law: a curse with a curse, one spitting with another—albeit with a bit more phlegm. But giving your adversary a nosebleed and kicking him in the face, which required that he go to the hospital, that's wrong. No, and again no!"

Here was this judge pronouncing God's own words in a tone of voice even more repulsive than that of a donkey—good grief, God protect us all!

"But Judge," I said, trying to lessen the burden of guilt and put things in perspective, "all that happened a long time ago when I was an impetuous youth! In any case, it's all been smoothed over."

"Youth and impetuosity, you tell me! Whatever the case may be, it's a page in your life that clearly shows a violent streak in your nature, a distinctly unsavory page that can't be erased with the passage of time, even though you may claim that it does. Traces of violence, just like fire under straw, are liable to burst into flame at any moment. And, if there's one thing they make clear, it's that you weren't praying at that time. Is that right?"

I maintained a stony silence.

"Fanaticism and violence are both repulsive," he went on. "As it says in our Holy Book: *Prayer forbids abomination and dishonor*" [Surat al-'Ankabut 29, The Spider, v. 45], and in our true religion . . . But no matter. While you are here and under guard, do you see yourself performing the five daily prayers?"

"That's between me and my Creator," I replied.

"No," he interrupted, "it's something that is significant to the investigation and interests me specifically. Otherwise how can I befriend you and trust you when I call on you to take the oath? I assume that you've either stopped praying as a subterfuge or to dispel certain misgivings you may have; either that, or you're being extra-cautious and praying in secret, just like someone praying the fear prayer. Which of the two possibilities is correct?"

"In the past I've prayed intermittently," I replied. "But now, while I'm your guest here, I've come back to it, ailing, scared, and sick. I can only perform virtual ablutions, turning towards Mecca in mind, not in actuality, reducing the number of prostrations and occasionally lying on my right side or else simply making gestures."

I noticed him shudder and his neck muscles tighten.

"In the past," he told me, "some prisoners managed to get hold of some pieces of stone to rub themselves clean, but then they started using them as weapons. I had to take them away and stop them using them in order to avoid chaos and preserve some semblance of order. As an exceptional gesture of sympathy I'll do my best to get you some smooth materials to use to cleanse yourself. My only request is that you do not replicate the behavior of a former prisoner here whose file I had to deal with (I think he's dead now). He confessed to me that he had spent his entire life right up to the time of his imprisonment only performing the prayer of fear, keeping the whole thing short and truncated and still wearing his shoes, with his finger poised over a trigger, whether real or illusory. He explained to me that the reason was that he was perpetually afraid of people and even of his own soul which was the advocate of evil. . . . But now let's get back to more important matters."

The judge now paused for a while, blowing pipe smoke either into the air or in my face. He addressed me once again in a gentle tone of voice.

"As I look at you from close up," he continued, looking straight at me, "I can see strands of good in a fierce battle with the vicious claws of evil; God the Merciful's armies are fighting the jinn of Satan himself. So choose which side you're on, and God grant you victory. Place your bets on the horses and see who will turn out the winner! Up till now you've been following a policy involving wise silence and tacit wisdom. That's been a good idea, in that in what follows your words will emerge decorated with pearls of truth and the clarity of accurate testimony. From the state of your cleanliness that I can smell and your general condition as I observe it, I can tell that your situation is not satisfactory. I'm going to issue instructions that you're to be given a lengthy shower with genuine local soap and to be fed properly so that your body and soul will be suitably refreshed. Once you've recovered your proper state of health and are back on your feet, you'll be spending an evening with some colored pencils. On some smooth paper you're going to compose a brief account of the murder of your mother's husband. There'll be a second report as well, this one in much more detail—the central core of the whole business—about yourself, your cousin, and the group of friends you both had; this one will have to be crystal clear, fresh water for the thirsty soul. By my very life, this is obviously the right thing to do at this point; it'll save valuable time and move things along. By reliev-ing distress, we might say, we'll help the nation progress. Let me also underline the advice I'm giving you: make sure that everything is expressed in the very clearest syntactic style, using only the most immaculate language in order to serve as a lamp that will illuminate the course of the thread and the excellence of what is said. All this will be a confirmation of the what the great polymath, Abu 'Uth-man Bahr al-Jahiz,* said many centuries ago, he being, as you are well aware, one of the great champions of Arabic rhetoric, of ornate discourse, and the heritage of Arabic learning. Remind me again of what it was that he said—and may God grant you a good testimonial when your final moments come!

This nonstop swirl of verbiage and utter nonsense made my head spin.

"If I remember correctly," I replied, "Al-Jahiz said something like this: 'All meaning is potentially out there in the public domain. What has an impact is the way in which phrases are balanced, the right words are selected, the phonetics are appropriate, and the water flows freely. The whole thing has to be properly presented and well crafted.'"

"That's right," he said. "You've reminded me. Our renowned scholar says in his *Book of Misers* . . ."

"No, actually it's in his *Book on Clarity and Clarification* and *The Book of Animals*. When he uses the phrase 'the water flows freely,' he means the water of truth."

"I'll check the source. If you're right, what would you like me to give you? Swiss or Dutch chocolate? Do you like such things? Who doesn't like chocolate?!"

The judge now leapt to his feet, held me gently by the shoulder and, with a superficial grin on his face, took me over to the door.

"Takes these pens and paper with you," he said, his eyes blinking behind his spectacles. "They're a gift from me. Get moving on your project, my fine and conscientious littérateur! I have this sense that it won't be long before we'll be seeing eye to eye on matters of mind and vision; through intuition and sheer good taste we'll coalesce. As for now, I'm entrusting you to God's care, so you can go back to your refuge safe and sound. Farewell!"

He stretched his hands towards me, still holding the paper and pencils, but then he realized that they were tied behind my back. He summoned his other secretary, the one who had brought me in, and she appeared immediately.

"He's leaving," he told her. "This chap's got two degrees, so his hands should not be tied like this."

He gave a signal, and she put the paper and pencils in one of my pockets, then accompanied me to her office. Once there, she informed the guard of the instructions that the judge had given.

A Wounded Man on My Bedcover

My refuge, safe and sound!

So here I am once again, back in my cell, with the rhyming phrases of the judge and his cryptic and ambiguous intentions still spinning inside my head. By now it is nighttime, and, as usual, I have surrendered both my hunger and worries to the opiate of a troubled, yet compulsory sleep. I have no idea how long it lasted, except that I was awakened by a gushing shower of water being directed straight at me by a man holding a hose by the door of my cell. I rushed over to another corner, assuming that the man must be from the fire-brigade who had been called in to put out a fire either in my cell or close by that was about to flare up. But the thought soon disappeared when the man threw me a towel and yelled at me that, by order of the investigating judge, I was to be bathed and soaped in the hope of recovering my health and energy. The water was suddenly turned off, and the man vanished. I took off my soaked clothing, rubbed myself down with a cloth that had stayed dry, then threw myself shivering on the bedcover to wait and see what would happen next.

I did not have long to wait. The door was flung upon, and a gigantic black man came in carrying a young man whose head and body were completely covered in bandages. He threw him down on the bed opposite mine and left without saying a single word. I went over, intending to introduce myself, and immediately noticed his crossed eyes and stub nose. From that I assumed that he had to be the young man whom the judge had been interviewing yesterday before me. I felt his pulse and jugular vein and determined that he was still just about alive. It seemed to me that he had been subjected to some horrific torture, akin to a surgical operation with no anesthesia. Hurrying over to the iron door of the cell, I started banging on it with both hands. "Have some mercy!" I yelled. "This man's dying." I kept on yelling till I was exhausted; my voice gave out and I choked up.

I went back to check on the young man; he was saying a few obscure phrases with his finger raised. Was he trying to conceal his wounds and bruises or struggling with an imminent death? What's to be done, I asked my impotent, grieving soul. I started yelling again, this time using a metal plate to bang on the door, but I had to stop when my neighbors started complaining and I was threatened with "solitary." According to those who had experienced it—and we seek God's protection against it!—this "solitary" involved being put into a dark cell on your own. People were lost when they went in, everyone said, and a different person when and if they came out, depending on the length of time inside and the conditions once there—the lack of food, drink, and air. For that reason I decided to give up and comply, since I had no desire to complicate my situation and make things even worse than they already were.

I sat down beside my severely wounded cellmate and spent quite a while in a complete panic. I heard him ask for some water, with his tongue hanging out, and gave him as much as I had left. He asked for more, so I squeezed some drops into his mouth from the cloth that had been dampened by the shower that had woken me up that morning. He muttered something, and, when I put my ear close to his mouth, I gathered that he was thanking me and asking if I was the one whom he had spotted in the judge's office the day before. I told him that I was, and expressed my relief that he was showing signs of regaining consciousness. I begged him not to talk too much so he could recover his strength and well being, but he insisted on talking, albeit in clipped utterances. Even though his voice was still very unsteady, his statements became gradually clearer and were more and more comprehensible. In that way I told him briefly who I was, how I had come to be arrested, and what the charges were against me. I was anxious not to get him too worked up, so I did not ask him the same things, but even so he started muttering to the effect that his name was Ilyas Bu Shama. He had both suffered the same fate and been subjected to the same trials and tribulations, the only difference being our places of origin. He was from Tizi Ouzou in Algeria, and I was from Oujda in Morocco. All of a sudden he started breathing so heavily that he could not speak, so I asked him to stop talking till he had recovered. He did so, and that allowed me time to wipe his sweating brow and clear my clogged ears. Looking at the meager amount of food I had left on my table, I urged him to eat it, but he refused. From his gestures he made it clear that by now his stomach was inured to hunger; food was the very last thing he wanted to bother about.

Now there was a ringing silence filled with misgivings and paranoia. The person lying on the bed was clinging to life, obviously gravely wounded both outside and inside, palpably fragile and sick. His breathing was weak, as light as a hair or a feather, and the body involved was within an inch or less of turning into a corpse ready to be buried and forgotten. And now, here I was, totally unable to help him, even if it only meant using my voice to reverberate through the corridors. I am not one for crying, but I could feel tears of frustration in my eyes, which kept dropping on to my cheeks. The only thing that stopped them was the voice of the guard telling me to take my food as he passed it through the aperture in the door. He made it clear that the food was only intended for me; my cell companion was to be denied food for three consecutive days. I took the bowl and saw that the contents consisted of a broth mixed with pieces of bread, onion, and potato. I put it down next to my colleague.

"What's happened?" he muttered as his eyes opened slightly.

"My friend," I told him, "what really needs to happen is for you to give up your hunger strike and eat some food . . ."

He pulled my ear close to his mouth. "I've been through so much," he told me, "that my breathing makes it hard to talk. What's more, if I eat anything, I'm afraid I'm going to throw up or foul myself in my bedcovers. No way!"

I did my best to reassure him. "If that happens," I said, "I'll carry you on my back to the pit over there in the corner. Everything will be fine."

The young man gestured his agreement and even gratitude, so I propped his head up on my cushion as best I could and started using my wooden spoon to feed him what was in the bowl. I kept encouraging him to keep eating, and eventually he managed to consume it all. I congratulated him and then listened carefully as he thanked me profusely. Now I was feeling even happier: he had eaten something, and there was a real hope of saving him. God be blessed!

He now asked me to let him lie back, so I cleaned his mouth, wiped the sweat off his brow, and put a cover over him so he could relax and get some sleep. I promised to stay close by, ready to help him, and not to doze off. He pulled my head towards him and kissed it.

"Did the judge ask you the same thing as me?" he whispered in my ear. "I've refused to compose any statements about you."

"Yes," I replied, "he gave me pencil and paper. I don't know where I've put them. In any case, I'm not going to do it."

"My dear friend," he said, "you should do it. I would advise you, in fact, I would beg you, to carry out his instructions immediately. Otherwise you're going to suffer the same fate as me or even worse. They'll hand you over to the professional torturess, who's an expert in all kinds of degradation. The worst of them she's learned in specialized foreign centers, but she's also invented others of her own that she delights in testing on imprisoned suspects like you and me. Compared with the torture she inflicts, the torments of the grave are a joke, child's play. I don't want you to fall prey to the woman they call Mama Ghula—and may God protect you from her barbaric madness! I'm begging you from the very bottom of my heart to do what the investigating judge says so you won't make him angry. That way you'll be able to avoid his revenge just as you would avoid AIDS and other contagious deadly diseases. Beware, I tell you! As the proverb has it, 'He who warns is thereby excused' . . ."

He was so insistent in offering me counsel that he collapsed; I was worried that he might have had a sudden heart attack or a life-threatening brain hemorrhage.

"I fully sympathize, my friend," I told him. "But think of yourself and of me, and stop talking. Tomorrow morning we can talk some more about this topic and others as well."

"I need to piss, damn it!" he said. "Help me up."

I carried him over to the corner, helped him relieve himself, then carried him back to his bed.

"My friend," he said, "let what I've been through have some benefit for you. Mama Ghula was not satisfied simply to put me through all kinds of torture. She handed me over to that enormous black man. He took away my honor and subjected me to anal buggery of the worst kind, all because of my stubborn resistance. Promise me you'll write those statements for the investigating judge and lay out things with crystalline clarity. That way you'll save yourself from unbelievable torture and all kinds of degradation."

I gulped in sheer panic and horror when I heard what he told me about the buggery.

"May God fight them all," I managed to say, "and place them in hellfire for evermore! And I'll do my best, my friend, particularly since I've nothing to hide."

He gestured his approval.

"I may not make it through the night," he managed to get out. "O God, I hereby testify that I have passed on the information to this poor servant and have offered advice . . ."

He pulled me head close and kissed my forehead with tears in his eyes. I in turn kissed his bandaged head and wished him a restful night. I lay down on my own bedcover; as I tried to get some rest, I was thinking about what my companion had told me.

5

How Can I Write My Report about Myself?

I slept very badly and woke up abruptly to the sound of the guard yelling at me to get up because, as he put it, exercise is better than sleep. I got up at once and looked for my companion under his bedcover, but there was no sign of him. I asked the intruder into the cell, but he refused to say anything. My mind in a whirl, I had no choice but to stumble my way behind him. He brought me to a courtyard enclosed by high walls on the top of which were watchtowers. The guard told me to start walking in a circle along with all the others and not to talk; he warned me that his eyes and those of the other guards would be on me all the time. I obeyed his instructions, but, whenever I could, I asked the people near me if they knew where we were being held and if they had any information about a prisoner called Ilyas Bu Shama. The only reactions I got back from my fellow sufferers in this prison were reluctance and denial. Once this "exercise is better than sleep" period was over, everyone went back to his cell; I found myself yet again facing the guard who locked the door and went away. I decided to keep exercising and started pacing around the cell, although my mind was preoccupied with questions and doubts and I continued to be deeply worried by my situation.

My routine inside the cell now continued unchanged. The time I had spent with the prisoner named Ilyas Bu Shama had left a whole series of questions that I was anxious to clear up and finally resolve— the time had gone by so quickly and with such bitter consequences. Maybe there was nothing to it, but I was eager to know how those crafty monsters had managed to come in and take the sick man out without his yelling and protesting or my hearing a thing. Had they drugged him or put something over his mouth?

And now was I supposed to respond to my companion's insistent pleas to write reports about myself and my contacts, all in order to accede to the investigating judge's demands? Yes indeed, I had to do it, if only to avoid adding recalcitrance to the list of crimes in my file or, at the very least, to find something to pass the time and relieve the endless pressure on my nerves.

My stomach may have been empty and my mind distracted, but even so I took the pen and pencils out from under my pillow. First I did some breathing exercises and set my mind to concentrate, then I sat down to write. I composed the paragraphs that now follow as requested. After some editing and finishing, this is how they came out:

I, the undersigned, currently under provisional incarceration in an unknown location, hereby testify that I am innocent of the array of charges laid against me. I deny them completely and in detail and without the slightest reserve or hesitation. Here is my account:

I was born in the desert region outside the small city of Ouad-Zem, a few kilometers from Khouribga, center of the Moroccan phosphate region. The land around there is low level and open all the way round. But, however open and welcoming it may have seemed, I found it confining; to me it felt like a spacious prison with no bars, an endless marsh with stagnant pools.

Even now, I can still see myself sitting in various parts of the plot of land (less than a hectare) where my father worked as a share-cropper. As I watched my father, whose wrinkled face reflected the hard work he had to do and the ongoing worries about seasons of drought, my facial expression became permanently depressed. When the sun went down each day, we used to sit around a table with some bread, lard, and tea prepared by my ever patient mother for us to eat. Once in a while we would look at a cow, the chickens, or the walls of our tiny house; at other times we would stare at the poor, dun-colored soil or the insouciant distant mountains. Many, many times I watched as my father would do his best to control his temper as he shuddered, removed his turban, and offered up a prayer to the ever observant heavens which were always cloud-less and tediously blue. "I'm the one who's worked it!" he used to yell over and over again. "I cleared it, ploughed it, and sowed it. For heaven's sake, have pity on us, set us free!" He would fin-ish by muttering angrily: "We've defied the heavens so much that now they're treating us so cruelly. Hamuda, get up and fetch some water, and tell your mother to heat up yesterday's harira."

In the area where we lived well water had dried up and seeped away. The only source for filling ewers carried on donkeys was a waterwheel some two kilometers away. When I had finished that particular chore, I used to poke at the dirt under my feet, kick-ing up stones and soil, as though somehow I could take on the overpowering drought, transform the straits our family was in, or question what fate had in store—and all in quest of an escape from my misery and frustration.

Drought!

Agricultural science and those in the know about such things tell us that farmland cracks up and languishes whenever water becomes scarce and vanishes. Anyone looking at Ouad-Zem and the region around it should never feel any satisfaction!

In 1994 it was plowing and planting season, all in anticipa-tion of rain. But weather bulletins and climate forecasts had other things to tell the farmers in their particular form of language: don't expect your region or the country as a whole to see winter winds blowing or copious pouring rain accompanied by thunder and lightning, bringing with them the kind of downpours that people in the know refer to as "rains of charity and mercy"!

Fat chance of that ever happening . . . unless, of course, the mir-acle of miracles were to happen, the Merciful God were to take pity on his human servants and animals and revive His moribund earth!

So in anticipation of what might or might not happen, the observant eye can spend time measuring the sheer impotence of mankind through clouds of a different kind, the ones that sneak their way into your gut feelings.

The same observant eye can also lean over an individual plot of land and observe the relentless march of drought, the way the dust begins to pile up and the color turns ashen because it is so parched. All kinds of opportunistic plants and nasty insects start to emerge through the cracks.

That same eye can give the ear information about the cracks and crevices in the soil as it disintegrates and the cancer spreads. It can also let all the senses know how the soil's creviced tongues dangle downwards, driven by thirst and heat in a desperate quest for water and moisture.

That same eye can move toward the trees scattered across the landscape, they being of a particularly stolid and tolerant species. The leaden weight of the heat will show itself in the pale leaves and scanty fruit they produce. The only birds that will perch on them will be ones that can make do with a minimum of pecking and find it hard to hover and fly away.

I used to take pity on that wretched species of bird and gaze at them with my own sad expression. My own stomach was often deprived of meat, and so I started targeting them with the catapult I'd been given as a child; by now I had become quite a good shot. However I had my own rule, indeed my special restriction: I had to be very sparing and stingy with myself. No putting sticky stuff on the branches, and no more hunting than was needed to keep hunger at bay. That kindly and environmentally friendly limit was to avoid giving the birds taking refuge in the trees any notion that they were being subjected to a kind of universal assault, expulsion or extermination. In fact I was so anxious—and God is my witness—to keep the situation the way it was and the possibility of their returning to their nests after flying away that I put some seeds and various kinds of food in cracks in the trees and even moistened them with some drinking water. So God Almighty can testify to the fact that my very parsimonious and stingy hunting escapades were conditional on the birds reproducing themselves in sufficient numbers. If that did not happen, you would see me amusing myself by aiming my catapult at stray rabbits. I could usually hit the young ones or others that were not fast or crafty enough.

A persistent feeling of misery and impotence began to take hold of me about four years ago. It happened immediately after my father dropped dead over his plough in the field where he used to work, the place where he had struggled and sweated his life away. He was a simple, crude famer who had married twice before without having any children, so he had simply divorced the women. My feelings had only intensified when my mother remarried, that farmer who had housed her in his humble home with its cursed plot of land attached. It so happened that this new husband of hers brought an end to my studies when I was seventeen and made a habit of forcing me to undertake really hard tasks and insulting me in the process; it was just as if I were a pack-animal ready for work in field and house, all in return for a meager bite to eat and a bed of straw and alfalfa.

I'm someone with big ideas but little power to implement them. I have to admit that words are incapable of describing the kind of oppression and misery I feel in a land where, every time the plowing and sowing season comes round, all we get is drought, occasional drizzle, but no real rain. Whenever that happened, my mother's boor of a husband used to get even crazier than ever. He would yell in my face that I had to take care of myself and find something else to do far away. He explained the tensions caused by the drought as being God's punishment on people like me who were recalcitrant and thus merited His anger.

The entire scenario was one of oppression and misery: no sustenance from the land, and a mother's husband who would never stop threatening and cursing me.

My poor mother in her fifties!

If it were not for her, at the very first sign of violence from her husband, I would have severed all bonds of obedience and sought my own path somewhere else. However, it was my mother who served as the invisible thread tying me to this wasteland, the shackling bond that, growing ever more feeble, could never envisage the possibility of leaving her desert landscape even in her own dreams. This then is a portion of my autobiography. Anything in it that may seem expansive or overblown represents the excess of a stupid mind . . .

At this point I added a few paragraphs, exculpating myself with regard to the death of my mother's husband and explaining my forced departure from Ouad-Zem for Oujda.

The hall was abuzz with voices taking turns to recount the list of charges that had led to their imprisonment in some completely unknown location; all of them were challenging the legality of their arrest. It was difficult to hear, and there were constant interruptions, so I could not make out a lot of what they were saying. Not only that, but I was still distracted by the need to write everything down; I wanted to get the weight of the judge's demand off my shoulders as soon as I could. All of a sudden, the prisoner closest to my cell asked me to recount my own charges and to raise my voice as much as possible. Thanking them for their concern, I made do with reciting the contents of what I had written as a response to their questions.

"I'm accused," I told them "of killing my mother's husband with a deadly catapult shot, an accusation that I totally deny and reject. I am completely innocent. That said, however, I don't deny that I occasionally dreamed of killing that oafish farmer, especially when he set about beating and cursing my mother. Whenever I took refuge in a cave, I used to have that very same dream. I used to read there and memorize passages till sleep overtook me; sometimes I would grill a bird or the occasional rabbit along with some bread, cumin seeds and salt. However, as everyone knows, there's always a large gap between dreams and actual implementation. Then there's the fact that a catapult shot may hit a bird or rabbit, but often won't necessarily kill it. So how is someone firing a catapult from a distance supposed to be able to kill a human being who is larger in every dimension? The worse that a catapult can inflict is a bruise or a surface wound of some kind. How can that possibly compare with a shot from a silenced revolver or a Kalashnikov?

"I came to call that cave 'my cave' because I claimed ownership to it; no vagrants or wayfarers ever came by. It was there, deep inside and in complete silence, that I was able to pose my frustrated, wounded soul the question of all questions, the answer to which potentially opened up all other answers: 'Is this really a life I'm living, or simply a dreadful nightmare?' After innumerable periods of contemplation, I came to the conclusion that my only solution and escape lay in leaving this miserable desert region and looking for a more hospitable environment in a city.

"As night was falling, I got up and went to the house. I found my mother sitting in the dim light of a gas-burner; she had her head in her hands and looked sad and distracted. I sat down by her side to offer her some comfort and consolation. As usual, I listened as she said nice things about me, how she prayed that God would grant me success and that what would be would be. I did not interrupt this flow of prayers except to mutter an occasional 'O Lord!' or 'From your lips to God's ears, dear mother!'

"I thought this was the appropriate moment, so I launched into a speech in which I tried to convince her that I was leaving but would still be in Morocco, not in some Christian country or some vacant region in the world. I wanted to make sure she realized that I would always be at her side in times of trouble and hardship or whenever her husband turned unruly and violent.

"It was a dawn in fall when I left; it felt exactly like summer. Both my mother and myself were totally grief-stricken. She wept uncontrollably and kept praying that I would be successful and my path would remain free of evils and the temptations of prostitutes and other anathemas. Before leaving for the bus station with my only suitcase, I told her husband that, if he did not behave in a God-fearing manner towards my mother, I would cut off his nose and break his bones. 'You can go to hell,' I heard him brag. 'The devil take you!'"

At this point I sensed that my neighbors, even those right next door, were quiet; I could even hear some snoring. I waited for a while to see whether they wanted to hear any more, but everyone was tired, it seems, and there were no requests. With that in mind, I went on recording my report:

My new residence was in Oujda, capital of Eastern Morocco, close to the border with Algeria. It is where mountains, plains, and river valleys come together. It was the entry point used by the French colonial forces to arrive in Morocco. In older times it was often known as "the city of bewilderment." I did not head there because I had a particular preference for it or was trying to glean some good luck from the fact that my ancestors had lived there. All I wanted was somewhere safe where I could find a job.

I was hoping that my only cousin on my mother's side who lived there might offer me some help. Through his good offices, that is the way it turned out. He was an astute, proud, and generous man, mild-tempered, good company, and multi-talented. In his forties, he had already lost both his parents and was a self-made man. He may have been married before but had no children. He was forever concerned about the poor and indigent and offered them as much help as he could. He was always restless and traveled a lot.

When I arrived in town empty-handed, doing my best to keep my anxieties and sense of loss to myself, he gave me the warmest of welcomes. He provided me with a sense of security by installing me in his bookstore, which he had been on the point of shutting because of the failing economy and the small number of readers. He put me in charge and gave me a regular monthly salary.

I spent four years in Oujda, during which I enrolled at school and obtained my high school diploma; at university I obtained a BA in literature and another in Islamic studies. The reason for these successes of mine clearly goes back to my almost continuous obsession with reading and study, much aided by the amount of spare time I had in the bookstore with its supply of valuable sources and other texts I brought there either through purchase or exchange. Once my commerce in books began to be successful, I set up specific opening and closing times. That way I was able to devote my attention to serious customers, and then set about reading the books for myself. I often used to spend a good third of the night concentrating on my reading; the only thing to interrupt the process would be moments for reflection or the need to reset the traps for the rats, who chewed on the paper or were merely scavenging.

Whenever possible, I used to visit my mother in the desert near Ouad-Zem and see how things were going for her. She would always reassure me and try to avoid mentioning her husband, whose health was rapidly declining. He used his illness as an excuse to lie on his side all the time and cling to her for all he

*was worth. At the end of every visit she used to load me down
with food, accompanied by copious prayers and kisses. That's the
way things stayed until I recently received news of his death after
the funeral and burial. When I visited her before I was arrested, I
found her restored to her old self, as though she had at last managed to relieve herself of a painfully heavy burden. She was man-
aging the plot of land that she had inherited, and had no need
either to sell or abandon it. After that we lost contact with each
other since, entirely against my will, I have found myself as a guest
in your midst, a prisoner with no trial or fixed charge against me
duly backed up by factual evidence and motive.*

*This and only this is what comes to my mind. Anything else
may belong to that region where the devil of human kind may
wish to recall whatever it is. Farewell.*

Folding up the sheets of paper, I hid them where the anticipated
shower from the water hose could not get them wet. All that was in
the expectation that the investigating judge—may God not show his
face again!—would be asking for them. That done, I lay down and
surrendered to a restless sleep, one without color or taste, one for
whose visions and flashes I had no explanation—apart, that is, for
the last one of all, in which my mother appeared to scold me for staying away for so long and losing touch with her.

"I haven't had a single card from you," was exactly what she
said, "even though you may be in some remote corner of the globe.
Just let me know for sure that the sea hasn't swallowed you up, as it
seems to be doing with lots of young men these days."

"Actually, Mother," I responded sheepishly when I had woken
up, "I have been swallowed up, but by a vast desert. I'm in a terrible,
ghastly prison in some totally unknown location; the weather here
is either hellish hot or freezing cold. No letters come in, and none
go out. All you can do, Mother, is to abide in patience and pray for
me—God alone has the power and might!"

6

In the Clutches of the
Investigating Judge's Secretary

I was woken up at heaven knows what hour by a gruff voice proclaiming that exercise was better than sleep. Before that, I had been
involved in a dream set somewhere between Ouad-Zem and Oujda.
The hero was my cousin, who kept asking for me and seemed really
sad and worried by my extended absence. When I woke up, one of
the guards was telling me to do some warm-up exercises in my cell—
jumping jacks, hopping on one foot, push-ups, and shadow boxing.
I was deeply involved in the last activity when the guard told me to
stop, but I refused on the grounds that I had not yet administered the
knock-out punch to my adversary; in my imagination that person
was the investigating judge and no one else. The guard rushed over
and frog-marched me to the prison courtyard, where group exercises
were being conducted under the general slogan *"mens sana in corpore sano."*

Once in the prison courtyard, most of the inmates doing exercise were simply walking around the perimeter one behind the other.
Each person had to be two or more meters apart from others; all talk
was forbidden, even the vaguest whispers or gestures. It was only a
very small minority who decided to run; they may have been either
newcomers or else those who had yet to be subjected to torture.

Just before the exercise period came to an end, I spotted my former cell mate, the one called Ilyas Bu Shama, in the distance. Quite
spontaneously, I went over to ask him how he was and to check on
his health. One of the guards stood in my way and threatened me

with the dungeon if I did such a thing again. I went back to my place, hoping that there would be no repercussions.

The milk that they brought for breakfast smelled like camel's piss. I avoided it altogether and made do with a few pieces of bread that I moistened with water. I could recall some of the statements made by Sufi ascetics, which managed to provide me with the proverbial "milk and honey" that I needed. From a bodily point of view, it suggested avoiding the expenditure of too much energy during exercise time, both because it was easier and because the temperature was really cold early in the morning; from a more psychological point of view, the only path I discovered for reassuring myself and fending off depression was a thread that descended from on high, offering illumination and support, thus releasing me from the state of mind that I was in, even though it may have been pulling me toward some other level of spiritual existence. While I was indulging in conjecture and trying to work out how to fill my day with useful activities, the above-mentioned enormous black guard came in and gestured at me, the import of which was that the judge's secretary was ordering me to appear before her with my report. As soon as I had retrieved the papers from their hiding place, he grabbed me by the wrist, and I left the cell alongside him. I either stared at the ground in silence or else sneaked glances at the passersby in civilian clothes, whose faces showed them to be foreigners. The black guard handed me over to another guard by the door of the judge's office. The latter proceeded to search me, then tied my hands behind my back before informing the secretary that I had arrived, whereupon she instructed him to remove the bands from my wrists.

Once in the secretary's presence, I was stunned by the difference between the veiled, *jallaba*-clad woman of yesterday and the modern, brazen, and attractive female I saw in front of me now-honey-colored eyes, heavily kohled eyelids, a beautiful, heavily made-up face, and blonde hair skillfully coiffed. I looked at the floor so as to lessen the effect she was having on me and then accepted her invitation to sit down and hand her my report.

"Oh yes," I heard her tell me in a coquettish tone, "I'm the one you saw the last time you were in this office. Every Friday and religious holiday I wear the veil—or, rather, I wear traditional clothing. Apart from that, I'm thoroughly modern, as you can see. There's religion, and then there's the world, as the investigating judge is fond of saying. So what have you had to say?"

"You, the phony judge, and everyone else here," I thought to myself, "can all go to Hell. By God, you have no share of either God or of this world!"

"What did you have to say?" she repeated her question.

"In my report," I told her, "I've said what I've said, and that's it."

"You've just reminded me," she went on. "The judge is busy, so he's asked me to make a typed copy of what you've said so he can read it. I have to prepare a summary of it in French for Mama Ghula. So what did you say?"

"OK," I said.

I paused for a few moments to collect my thoughts, then started reading out my report, in a loud voice at times and muttering at others. I noticed that she kept skipping entire paragraphs, then using the gold pen she was holding between her heavily lipsticked lips to underline particular words or whole lines. She would ask me to explain phrases she did not understand; for sure, I had failed to do any editing or had scribbled them too quickly in one of the fits of nervous depression that affected me sometimes. I asked her to give me the context again, and she moved in my direction, bringing her high heels, her half-exposed thighs, and her plunging neckline with her. Repeating the word "context" with a laugh, she leaned over me with her ample bosom in full view and spelled out each word for me with her gold pen. Under the spell of her peerless beauty and the attractive perfume she was wearing, I started tamping down my animal feelings and instinctive loathing. I kept sneaking looks at her legs as, given the context, I made the necessary changes and adjustments to my manuscript.

In this particular situation, it occurred to me that I might leap on top of this woman who was controlling me with her surging femininity and do to her what bulls do to cows. Once I had had my way, I would counter her accusation of sexual assault by accusing her in turn of sexual arousal. I was the one who was imprisoned and oppressed, and the difference was made that more obvious by her provocative dress, her suggestive movements, and her flirtatious chatter. My reasoning would certainly be persuasive: one evil deed promotes another, and the one who starts is the wrongdoer. However, I was aware of being in the same position as Joseph—may his remembrance be sanctified!—even though I was certainly not as handsome or devout as he was. For that very reason I decided against such an idea, cursing as I did so the evil temptations of the devil, not to mention the many salacious women of this morally corrupt era of ours.

The secretary herself may have become aware of the turmoil going on inside me, because she returned to her chair and gave me a series of ambiguous looks. Taking a mirror out of her handbag, she freshened the makeup on her cheeks, eyes, and lips, as though she had just emerged unscathed from a passionate conflict of some kind.

She now adopted a warmer, softer tone. "Words of wisdom now decree," she said, "that you remove all the padding from your statement, and there's a lot of it. Instead only include things that will help the investigation. Yet more wisdom: concentrate on eradicating any statement that smacks of a question. In the center's constitution, Article Seven of the section on interdictions stipulates that the suspect is not permitted to ask questions, even though it be in a surreptitious or indirect fashion; on the other hand, the suspect is completely obliged to respond to the all investigating judge's questions. So what did you say?"

"Madam," I replied, "I have . . ."

"Miss," she corrected me.

"So, Mademoiselle," I replied defiantly, "I have nothing to add or delete. Either the whole report is accepted, or it's all deleted."

Leaping to her feet she came over and started chastising me.

"The judge will remove exactly what he wishes from your report and will compel you to tell the truth about yourself. Should you refuse or behave defiantly, Mama Ghula will be able to remove you from existence with one flick of a knife. Are you belittling me because I'm a woman? Just take a look at my hand: it may have silk gloves on, but it's made of steel."

With that she slapped my face so hard that I almost fainted.

"And that's just a sample," she yelled angrily, her eyes red with fury. "Now get up and get out!"

Once outside the door, the black guard who had escorted me to the toilet started describing the woman and the restrictions I was under. I understood that what he was doing was letting me purge myself of illicit thoughts, something he undoubtedly had to do with every man who found himself sitting with and talking to this temptress of a woman and possessed even the slightest degree of masculinity and chance.

7

Yet Another Wounded Man on My Bed

Back in my cell, I noticed that my bedcover was sticking up as though it had been stuffed with straw, alfalfa, or something like that. I lifted the bottom part, only to discover two human feet. I thought it was Ilyas Bu Shama, so I yelled his name as I lifted the top part. I found a head completely wrapped in bandages; all that was visible was a pair of closed eyes and a thin moustache that made it clear that it was not Ilyas, unless he had recently started a moustache. I lay down on the other bed, my mind going over all the images and scenes that I had witnessed in this strange, horrendous place whose exact location and the nature of whose functions and purposes were still a matter for conjecture and guesswork on my part. Just as I was dozing off, there was a knock on the door, and I was given some lunch through the aperture. I asked if my new cell mate was Ilyas Bu Shama, but the guard said that he knew no one of that name and then went away. I was now left with the question as to whether my particular cell had been designated as the favorite spot for major casualties, the prisoners who had been subjected to the very worst kinds of torture.

I sat there toying with pieces of bread that I dunked in a tasteless broth, if only to stave off a rampant hunger. Thoughts kept occurring to me, intended to clarify the situation in which I found myself and dispel some of my worst suspicions and anxieties.

Through the absolute silence of my contemplation there now broke an intermittent moaning from the person spread-eagled on the bed in front of me. I rushed over to say how glad I was that he had regained consciousness, but—amazingly enough—he started pushing me away with both hands and saying things that showed how frightened he was of me. There was nothing I could say by way of assurance and comfort that managed to calm his growing panic. I moved quickly back to my own corner and huddled there, all the while listening to him as he raved that I was a double agent charged by the administration with spying on him and providing details of his periods of movement and rest. I pronounced a solemn oath to him, saying that I was a prisoner with all the same concerns that he had; I was neither an informer nor a spy. He did not respond, but I think that my solemn oath penetrated his hearing. I did the same thing twice more, and at that point he signaled to me to come over. I sat down by his head, and he stared at me with tear-filled eyes. He now uncovered the lower half of his body.

"Look, my friend," he told me in a crushed tone. "See what those bastards have done to me! They've castrated my right testicle, and they've threatened to do the same with the other one if I don't do what they ask and cooperate."

I did my best to control my emotions and hold back tears.

"God fight them and destroy them in this world before the next!" I said. "But tell me, my friend, what kind of cooperation is it they want from you?"

"They're asking for the names of a jihadist cell that I don't even know. They want to know about a number of people they're looking for, some of whom I only know in passing—a connection as thin as a spider's web, others who are either friends or relations. Was I supposed to do evil to people who have been good to me or implicate them so as to avoid the kinds of dire punishment that this woman called Mama Ghula inflicts on people? I am a God-fearing person. If I did such a thing, I'm afraid I'd spend all eternity in hellfire—and 'evil is it as a resort.' My friend, do you agree with me on this?"

"Of course I do!" I agreed spontaneously. "In my view you're replicating the actions of our noble Prophet who possessed the very noblest character."

"When that fiendish torturess finally gave up on me," he said, "she brought in someone wearing a mask whom she described as the center's deputized surgeon. She ordered him to do what he did. Shall

I take off the bandage from my scrotum and show you the bloody scar?"

When I fervently indicated that I did not wish to see it, he acquiesced, albeit reluctantly. He now succumbed to a flood of violent tears, only interrupted by a question:

"If you were in my place, my friend," he asked, "what would you have done?"

I stared at him, panic-stricken and lost for words.

"I'm almost thirty," he went on, "and I hope to fulfill my religious obligations by getting married. The surgeon swore to me that even with a single testicle you can still get married and have children, just like someone who can see with only a single eye, or has only one lung with which to breathe, or one kidney to purify his blood. Now I'm faced with two choices, each one of which is a bitter pill to swallow: to continue with my resistance, in which case the result will be complete and terminal castration—and, once that is done, which woman would ever accept me into her bed? Either that, or else surrendering and losing all respect with people. I tell Mama Ghula and the investigating judge everything I know about the people they are looking for. I'll be cooperating with a gang of spies and undercover agents in getting them arrested. So answer me, friend: if you were in my place, what would you do?"

I frowned, not only because the question itself totally dismayed me but also because I was being forced to make a choice.

"For the time being you can remain neutral and say nothing," he went on. "but don't be surprised if one day during your time in prison you find yourself having to answer the very same question. But for now, give me something to eat and drink, then let me rest. I've already talked too much."

I swiftly responded to his request. Before he fell asleep, I asked him his name.

"'Umar ar-Rami," he replied.

When I asked him where this prison was located, he signaled that he had no idea.

As I wrapped myself in my bedcover, I could not help thinking about this helpless man, now threatened with the loss of his second testicle, and then about Ilyas, the man who had spent the night in my cell but was not there the next morning. My mind was churning with all sorts of questions and uncertainties, sending me into a bewildering vortex of fear that was only dispelled when a guard came tiptoeing into my cell and signaled to me to follow him.

"Exercise is better than worry," he whispered in my ear.

Quite the contrary, in fact. On this ultimately scary and vicious vessel, such emphasis on exercise was yet another problem. The people in charge had completely transformed its significance; the well-known proverb "*mens sana in corpore sano*" had been converted into a combination of a sick joke and a demeaning routine.

In the dismal paved courtyard the atmosphere and regulations were the same as before. What was new and different this time was a circle of prisoners with hands and feet shackled; they were some distance from our circle and were wearing dirty white clothing. They kept moving in a circular pattern between barbed-wire passageways and were being observed by heavily armed guards. I managed to ask the prisoner in front of me in a whisper who these other prisoners were, but he did not reply. I also asked him about someone called Ilyas Bu Shama, but he simply shrugged his shoulders. The same thing happened with the prisoner behind me.

I realized that there was no hope of sneaking a conversation with the prisoners in my group, so I simply started walking around in circles like everyone else without taking any risks or wandering off. I made do with building up a sense of resistance in the face of so much adversity and sniffing the fresh air outside the confines and aggravations of my cell.

With the blowing of a whistle the exercise period came to an end, and the prisoners in blue uniforms were taken away for their communal meal. Like everyone else, I joined a line, which passed in front of someone who distributed the food, then sat at a wide table designated for my use along with four others. Everyone had a bowl of broth, along with some lentils and pieces of meat, a complete loaf of bread, a banana, and two pears. Was this supposed to be a festival meal I knew nothing about?

Complete silence prevailed, only broken by the clanking of spoons, swallowing noises, and ambiguous hand movements under the table. I am an inveterate meddler, so I asked what was the occasion for this feast. No one answered. At that point one of the people at the table got up and went to refill his bowl, whereupon my immediate neighbor took advantage of the other man's absence to tell me to stop talking; his reason was that spies were regularly planted among the prisoners. I asked him about the other group of fettered prisoners in white clothing, and he replied that they were people with life sentences. Whenever one of them died, he could simply be wrapped and buried in those dirty white garments. I then asked him if he knew either Ilyas Bu Shama or 'Umar ar-Rami, but he shrugged his shoulders. As soon as the other prisoner came back, he stopped talking. For my part I now focused on my bowl and finished what was in it. When I looked up, it was to see the man who had returned staring hard at me, his expression a tissue of hatred. So, I decided, that is how relationships work between inmates in this extraordinary and barbaric prison; a network of ambiguity as to roles and a predominant sense of suspicion and fear among individuals, all accompanied by a lively trade in information and rumor with its cryptic signals and codes.

When I returned to my cell, it was to find that my new cellmate, 'Umar ar-Rami, had vanished into thin air, without leaving any note or the slightest trace. I felt exhausted and lay down, watching as night fell. I prayed for heaven's mercy, begging for relief from my misery and help in comprehending what was happening to me and going on all around me every day.

8

My Session with Both the Investigating Judge and His Secretary, Nahid al-Busni

Next morning, I was shaken awake by a guard who escorted me to the administration wing and stopped me in front of a door.

"By order of his excellency, the investigating judge," he told me, "you are to enter this bathroom, wash yourself, shave your beard, clean your teeth, powder yourself, then put on a new shirt and blue suit along with a necktie. You'll find everything inside. I'll be back in twenty minutes."

He locked the door behind me and left. It took a moment for me to recover from my shock and surprise, but then I set about beating the time limit he had imposed. The hot water covered my entire body, and with the help of some soap and vigorous rubbing with a cloth, I got rid of most of the grime. Once I had finished washing, I dried myself with a big, soft towel, cleaned my teeth with a fresh toothbrush and toothpaste, trimmed my beard according to the correct Sunni practice, powdered myself, and then put on my new suit. They had forgotten just one thing: shoes to go along with the suit! Putting on a pair of rubber slippers, I sat on a chair. At this point I was scared, because the thought occurred to me that this cleansing routine might be the way prison officials used to deal with prisoners who were about to be executed—a sort of anticipatory wash of bodies that would soon be buried.

The only way I could find to keep my fear and confusion to myself was to concentrate even harder on cleaning my teeth and combing my hair back. When the guard suddenly came back into the room

47

I swallowed the toothpaste in my mouth, and then expressed my thanks. I told him I was ready. I asked if I could bring my old clothes and some of the washing items with me.

"That's all yours," he said. "Throw your old clothes in this bin, and put the tie on."

I had a hard time stuffing the washing materials in my pockets. He understood that I was no good at tying ties, so he helped me with that before escorting me to the investigating judge's office.

An energetic young woman welcomed me with a smile.

"Nahid al-Busni at your service," she told me softly as she offered me a chair. "His excellency is on the phone . . ."

No . . . the secretary with whom I had sat on the previous occasion was quite different from this polite and punctilious young woman. I began to assess how different the two of them were: this one was of medium stature while the earlier one had been exceptionally tall. Both of them were beautiful and neat, but their features were different. This new secretary's demeanor, unlike the previous one, was much more modest and staid, while the transparent muslin head scarf that they both wore was not intended to hide their carefully coiffed hair.

The intercom bell rang, and the secretary took me into the judge's office. He welcomed me with a smile and congratulated me on my freshened appearance. Asking Nahed to bring me something, he invited me to take a seat in front of him.

"Coffee or tea?" she asked.

"Bring him some semi-sweet coffee," the judge told her as he fidgeted in the leather chair behind his huge desk.

Once she had left, he gave me another smile and fiddled with his clipped moustache.

"I used to know another woman from Fez," he told me, "who used to pronounce the consonant 'qaf' as 'hamza'; she also turned the 'raa' into 'ghayn.' Even worse was an Iraqi woman in my service—God forgive her—who used to turn 'k' and 'j' into all sorts of weird sounds. So, whenever she wanted to express her condolences to the relatives of someone who had died, she would say to each one individually: 'May God increase your penis' (intending to say 'your reward,' as I'm sure you've already realized). To God alone belongs all that He has created! But when it comes to typewriting, the secretary always sticks to the written form of the letters and not the way they are pronounced. I've hired this particular orphan woman because she is devout and respects the Creator. She has memorized his Holy Book and uses its teachings in her treatment of people who come for interviews. Her male and female colleagues call her Benazir, because her conduct and actually her appearance and head-wear as well remind people of Benazir Bhutto—may God preserve her as a wonderful model in this world of ours in anticipation of the next! In fact, this secretary is a great admirer of Benazir Bhutto, even though she is not interested or involved in politics."

The young woman now brought me a cup of coffee and some pieces of chocolate.

"You're not interested in politics, are you, pretty lady?" he teased the young secretary. "Go on, say 'You're so right,'" he said gesturing at me. "'You're so right' is the only possible correct answer to this plague against our language. Only that way can you be sure of not committing some grave offence against the grammatical rules of the Arabic language. So tell us, 'You're so right.'"

"You're so right!" she replied dutifully.

He then asked her to recite the shortest sura in the Qur'an. She really wanted to leave, but nevertheless recited it bashfully:

Verily we have given you abundanf,
So pray to your Lorf and sacrifife,
Verily the one who loathes you is clippef.

As she turned to leave, she was singing: "The man who tells me he loves me, I'll serve him coffee with my own hands."

"You can leave now," the judge yelled with a smile. "May God forgive you that reading that I requested, just as he forgives the proponents of the seven readings of the Qur'an. But when it comes to Jumana, the previous secretary, who seems to have relied on her femininity alone, the Lord God will never forgive her the way she treated people with such violence and corrupted their piety with her flagrant sensuality. Weak-willed people and prisoners straying from their faith and practice were all proclaiming her name and falling in love with her. Tell me, did anything untoward happen to you while I was away?"

I stared at the floor and said nothing.

"That cursed woman," he screamed angrily, baring his teeth, "that tart! I told her to treat you properly, and she promised to do so. Did she hit you? And anything else . . . ? Damned woman! Her case reminds me of another woman, even worse in the pre-Islamic era. If a great poet of his generation and lineage had not fallen in love with her and immortalized her in his famous *mu'allaqa* poem,* she would have been unknown and forgotten for all time. Do you know who I'm referring to?"

I indicated that I did not. Clearing his throat, he sat up in his chair like someone about to convey some heavy news to me: "That pompous, flirtatious woman who strutted about like a peahen was the beloved of a poet who composed about her two lines of poetry that, by God Almighty, have no peers in the whole of secular Arabic literature. So remind me. It starts: 'As I recall thee, the spears quench their thirst . . . ' Finish the line for me, Hamuda!"

I reluctantly responded: " . . . on me, and the Indian swords drip with my blood."

"O my God, how wonderful!" and "I longed to kiss the swords because . . ." "Go ahead and finish it, Hamuda . . ."

"they gleam like the teeth in your smiling mouth."

"Even though the poet 'Antara* recited such glorious and eloquent lines, the cursed 'Abla was totally unaffected. Her heart never even fluttered. In fact, she rejected the black poet whose heart and mind were of purest white! Don't you agree with me that this woman, 'Abla, was cursed—not only that, but a prostitute and nasty racist at that?"

I chose to say nothing.

"There's a huge temporal gap between the defeated pre-Islamic poet and you, but there's an element of similarity as well. While he chose to express his love and frustration over 'Abla in the form of a magnificent poem that has lasted through the ages, your relationship with the former secretary, Jumana, is best described by the old proverb: 'there's many a trial that brings its own reward.' At least you've proved that your masculinity is still intact. God be praised, and to Him be all gratitude!"

He now lit his pipe and offered me either a cigarette or cigar. I refused both.

"In my own humble opinion," he said with uncharacteristic modesty, "there's no text that forbids tobacco (unlike the proscription on wine). In both cases I strive to maintain a moderate position. In your case I suspect that you avoid alcohol and use analogy to deny yourself tobacco and opium. Am I right?"

"Certainly," I replied. "Health is what matters for everyone. It's better to be cautious than to get sick and have to be treated."

"True enough, by God, true enough! And yet, these times of ours are full of tensions and annoyances. You need some form of tranquilizer to deal with them all."

He fidgeted in his chair, blowing smoke right in my face.

"I used to let suspects come in this office," he told me nervously, "with all their filth and stench. For the sake of truth and the need to discover it, not to mention pleasing God Almighty, I would put up with it all. But when I returned from responsibilities abroad, I issued instructions that from now on nobody would be allowed in until they had been properly cleaned and perfumed. You're the very first one to be treated this way. The thing that's made me take your side and stopped me forwarding you to a much nastier interviewer is that we share something in common. Do you know what it is?"

"You told me about it earlier, Your Honor," I replied in spite of myself. "We're both graduates of colleges in Arabic-speaking countries. You have a degree in law and so do I; you also have one in literature, and so do I."

"That's right," he replied, "and yet fate and careers have sent us in different directions. So all praise be to God who has so arranged things that we meet and can thus expose the truth and eradicate falsehood."

He paused for a moment, giving me a hard, inquisitive stare.

"But what truth and what falsehood, Sir?" I asked in dismay. "In what particular spot on earth am I currently located? What's the purpose of this arbitrary imprisonment and excessive torture that is sapping my health? Do you want me to burst into tears and beg you to take your collective hands off this poor body of mine that is starting to lose weight and deteriorate?"

The judge's face turned purple with rage, and he started thumping the desk.

"No questions are allowed," he yelled at the top of his voice. "Come in, Nahid, and read this stubborn idiot Article Ten of the section on non-permitted conduct . . ."

The young woman took down a tome from the shelf.

"The tenfth article from the section on internal regulafions states . . ."

At this point, the judge who was frothing at the mouth in anger, snatched the tome away from her and carried on reading.

"'Questions are the particular province and competence of the investigator alone. He alone is legally permitted and competent to formulate and pose questions. The accused person is not permitted to engage in questioning unless he is asked and permitted by the investigator to do so. However the investigator is in no way obliged to record the question or to answer it. End of article.'"

He continued smoking his pipe.

"So, Hamuda from Oujda," he went on, "do you have a joke for me, something to restore the sugar balance in my blood?"

I was so overcome and perplexed that I could think of nothing to say. The secretary slapped me to make me pay attention.

"The judge is asking you a question," she said.

"No violence, Nahid, no violence," he told her in a gentle tone intended to calm things down. "God is my witness that, even when

I've been cross-examining the very worst offenders, the kind of people who hate having to tell the truth, I've never tortured anyone, hit anyone, or spat on anyone. It's just the way I was made. Violence spoils my mood; more than that in fact, it ruins my religious devotions. This rogue sitting in front of me here is trying to provoke me and refusing even to tell me a joke. Okay, so I'll tell myself one, in the hope that it'll calm me down. As the proverb says, 'Nothing scratches you as badly as your own fingernails.' You can listen too, Nahid, before you leave us. 'Once upon a time there was among the Bani Khafajah a shaykh, who, when night fell, used to get a particular type of ache, the kind in which cocks with hens partake . . . But, what's more significant that all that, is that this shaykh of ours had an ongoing feud with his colleagues because they accused him of confusing the months of Sha'ban and Ramadan. He regarded this accusation as an obscenity and forcefully denied it. 'If you all think it's fair to accuse me of something,' he told them, 'then at least make it something that I really do; then I'll admit it.' When they asked him what that was, he replied that it was not confusing Sha'ban and Ramadan, that was his main point. It was actually two other months, Shawal and Dhu al-Qa'da! His colleagues spent a month and a half cackling over that one!"

As Nahid left in consternation, the judge sat there guffawing and rubbing his stomach.

"My good shaykh of old," he continued with a chuckle, "may you have been well rewarded, and you tribe of Banu Khafaja, I trust that you received God's blessings! You've improved my mood by giving me a good laugh—may God grant you to laugh on the Day of Gathering and afford you not one, but two paradises from His bounty! But now, Hamuda from Oujda, back to you, and let's get serious again. You've put me in mind of someone who's stopped talking for months as a kind of fast, and then decides to break the fast with an onion, or, worse yet, with shit. Your report's badly written; in fact, it's drivel. I'm an investigator, so why should I be bothered about land and drought, your love for your mother and hatred for her husband—that stuff, and all other kinds of irrelevant padding? Any more, and you'd be telling me about the day you were circumcised or the first time you fucked a woman or a cow. There's a disjuncture about your discourse, one that's far removed from that elegance and clarity that I requested of you. You neither accepted nor responded to my call. As a result you've lost a golden opportunity to get away from those pedestrian modes of expression that are now so current and to invoke more refined and tasteful concepts and phrases. There are countless possible examples I could cite: things like 'tomb,' 'grave,' 'fate,' 'perdition,' 'gloom,' 'darkness,' 'commitment of grievous sin,' 'to be bad,' 'to be scared,' 'to go crazy,' 'to become level,' . . . it's all a veritable catastrophe, a horrendous crime for us to abandon the contents of our glorious Arabic lexicon, allowing it to be ignored and forgotten, to be ravaged by the savage jaws of ignorance and contempt."

He paused for a moment to catch his breath.

"How is it possible," he went on in a blunt tone," that you got a degree in literature? Is it a fraud? Maybe you filched it or managed to purchase it in these corrupt times when standards have fallen so badly. You've been trying to show that you're innocent of the crime of murdering your mother's husband and to portray yourself as a peaceful and ethical person. But that's just one charge against you, and there's still another one that I'm aware of. In spite of all the suspicions hovering around you, I'm prepared to overlook it, but only on condition that you provide me with the fullest possible account of all the perverted activities of your cousin, al-Husayn al-Masmudi—all his secrets, his movements, and his dangerous secret contacts. Your life preserver rests in your own hands. I want to know everything about the person who uses the street name Abu al-Basha'ir. Forget all about the kindnesses he may have done you in the past. I know all about that already. That's what's led my agents to arrest you and place you under supervisory detention. Think things over carefully, then write me an eloquent and relevant report. That'll save your skin, allow us to be rid of you, and let you have some peace."

At this point the telephone rang.

"Eat the chocolate," he told me as he grabbed the phone.

"My respects, Colonel," he said. "Yes, Sir, the members of the terrorist cell you're mentioning have all confessed and provided us with extremely useful and detailed information. Yes, that's right . . . there are seven of them. Six of them have signed a document requesting a pardon and announcing their repentance. The seventh had a heart attack in Mama Ghula's cavern. Yes, she tells me that she tortured him after he'd tortured her by refusing to talk. That's right, Colonel, one evil deed deserves another; and the one who starts is the worst offender. Yes, Sir, I'm on to it . . . I hear and obey . . ."

He waved at me to leave, and I did so. As I passed by the secretary, Nahid, I decided to play the fool, so I gave her a knowing wink, my mouth full of chocolate. She shuddered, then rounded on me.

"You're a nafty man," she said, "not only that you're impolite and impiouf!"

"Thankf so much!" I replied, imitating her pronunciation and blowing her a kiss.

With that, I left in high spirits and encountered the guard waiting outside by the door. Two other guards had another prisoner with hands and feet tied who was waiting to appear before the investigating judge. He was undoubtedly one of those dangerous people I'd just heard about. I wondered if the time would come when I too would be one of those if I carried on refusing to cooperate by submitting to their will and serving as one of their agents.

On the way back to my cell I indulged in a sincere desire to get to know the guard better and open a line of communication. So I asked him how he was and what his professional and family situation was like.

"Fine," was his only response.

When I tried to expand on the conversation, he begged me not to expose him and his salary to any risks. So I said no more.

As he locked my cell door, he told me that tomorrow there was supposed to be a soccer match between two teams of prisoners. He suggested that I get ready and go to sleep early.

I checked my bed and all the corners of the cell to see if there was anyone else, whether alive or dead, in the cell with me. It emerged that this time I was on my own. I noticed that there was still some food left in my bowl. At this point I remembered the treasure trove that I'd stuffed into my pockets that morning, so I hid the bottles of perfume and soap under my pillow, and cleaned my teeth with the brush and toothpaste. I did some exercises to warm me up, all in preparation for falling asleep. However, I was so worked up that my churning brain would not let me sleep until very late; sometimes I would be thinking about Nahid al-Busni—at others, about the nasty and complex personality of the investigating judge. I kept coming up with things that motivated and terrified me in turn, the kind of talk that was intended to crush my ethical self and sense of purpose, whether the method involved hypocrisy or deceit—and all of it accompanied by a generous dose of decadent pseudo-erudition.

9

A Prisoners' Soccer Game

Our appointment for the soccer game happened next day in the searing midday heat. It took place on a sandy field behind the detention center's main buildings. According to the announcement made over a speaker hanging in one of the windows, there were to be two teams of prisoners. I noted that the team I was on, which was called the Black Beasts, was entirely barefoot or, like me, wearing rubber sandals. Most of them looked emaciated and weak. By contrast, the other team, called the Red Barbarians, was wearing professional soccer boots; they all looked like very fit rugby players. When I asked one of my teammates standing near me what this utter disparity meant, he looked around and then told me that I would soon understand. For the time being it was better to say nothing.

After we had done some warm-up exercises, a female referee dressed entirely in black summoned us with a whistle blast. It was clear from her appearance that this was indeed Mama Ghula of evil repute. She addressed us all in her beloved French, using the military tone of voice of one who brooks no argument regarding her orders.

"Soccer here," the translator told us, "is not the game you're used to seeing. Here, as in everything else, we do things differently and invent our own rules. The game will have only one time period; there'll be no second half, overtime, or rest period. One period, and that's it. The goals will be counted, but the victors will be those with the necessary staying power to keep resisting, without giving up or withdrawing. Now put your trust in God that victory will go to the stronger side."

After this weird introduction, she tossed the coin to start the match, and my team won. She then went and checked on the two goal nets and spoke to some of the guards who were standing on the sidelines with their guard dogs. The Red Barbarians team now proceeded to launch a verbal attack on us, using every conceivable kind of abuse and vile language, all accompanied by threatening gestures. Some of my teammates responded with abuse of a lesser kind, and there were exchanges of spitting and punches as well. This totally unsporting conduct only came to an end when the female referee came back and blew her whistle to start the game.

For something like half an hour, the ball never left the feet of my team—more's the surprise! We managed to score eleven goals, four of them by me. There were no serious attacks from their side and very little challenge or resistance. It reached the point that, every time our forwards were heading toward their goal, the goalkeeper would show his alarm by huddling up or run along the backline, yelling and screaming, while his colleagues simply laughed and guffawed.

But after we had scored the seventh goal, I got the impression that some kind of conspiracy was being launched against my team. I pointed this out to my teammates every time we scored another goal. However, most of them were overjoyed at the team effort and the success we were having; they accused me of being a pessimist and weakling. For them, the name of our team, the Black Beasts, was fully justified. But, when their bodies started to tire and it became much harder to get to the other team's goal, with shots going wide or missing altogether, they started to agree with me. From then on, it was a matter of dragging their legs around in their own half and never moving out of it; if anyone did move out, it was as though we were out for a stroll—like someone playing golf or walking in a public park.

Just a few minutes later, everything changed completely, and went from bad to worse. Our opponents had already had their share of fun at our expense, and now they turned serious. It was time for attack and revenge. Showing us their muscles and powerfully fit bodies, they proceeded to turn the soccer field into a savage war zone with a series of nonstop powerful attacks. They forced us into our own half, moved toward our defensive line, and set about viciously attacking any of us who had the ball or were even standing anywhere close. Gradually, our team started to collapse with bruises, fractures, and severe wounds; players who lost consciousness were transferred to the clinic. The rest of our team was left spread-eagled on the sand, bleeding and groaning. One of them happened to be the man whom I had asked about the extraordinary difference between the two teams. I leaned over to offer him some comfort.

"Now I think you understand," he told me between pants. "The team that resorted to such violence and aggression to win the match consists of prisoners who are acting as agents and others in preventive detention who joined our team as substitutes for our wounded . . . If you yourself haven't been hurt and evacuated beforehand, you'll find that they're all unhurt when the game is over."

And that is in fact exactly what I saw: those men, the majority of whom had paunches and never did so much as break into a run, walked and strutted about slowly, smoking and quaffing beer. If the ball happened to come near one of them or they happened to collide with it by mistake, they would either get rid of it or, as happened most of the time, pass it to one of the opposite team in a scandalously obvious way. Some of them even clustered near the other team's goal. Even if the ball had been presented to them on a golden platter, they would have simply toyed with it for a while, then got rid of it somewhere far from the goal itself. Meanwhile, a newspaper correspondent kept yelling into a megaphone, something that had been mostly inaudible up till now; he was spouting a lot of stuff that made no sense, but—by God!—it had not the slightest connection with the game.

With the sweat pouring off me from the heat and my own emotions, I rushed over to the referee—the bitch—who had moved over to the sideline and was lounging there smoking and showing off her stunning backside. She seemed to have forgotten what she was supposed to be doing and had either lost or swallowed her whistle. I told her about the way the other team had committed so many infractions and violent assaults on our players. She proceeded to twist the tie that I had forgotten to take off, slapped me on the head, and told me (as I understood from the French) that I was to get my stinking body out of her sight and take over from the goalkeeper who had fallen asleep in our goal. Failing that, she would issue a severe report against me, documenting my defiant attitude and contravention of the rules of the game.

I now headed straight for the goal, where I did my best to staunch the bleeding from the at least thirty wounds and cuts that the man in the goal had received. Once I had made sure that he was still alive, I took up position between the two goal posts, ready to fend off attacks. I saved two goals, but managed to lose my rubber sandals, which by now were in shreds. However, the third shot, kicked from very close range and with all the force of a rocket, hit me square in the face. I collapsed to the ground, feeling dizzy. Some of their players now rushed over and started poking fun at me because the ball had gone in. They kept on patting their backsides and stomachs in clownish gestures.

With a few deep breaths I managed to recover somewhat and once again stood in the goal, but without any shoes. I watched as those of my teammates who were still on their feet would receive a pass but be prevented from passing the ball on. Instead, they would be felled to the ground. This time, one of the other team got hold of the ball through sheer violence and moved in my direction. He stopped about a meter away from me.

"With this shot," he threatened, "I'm going to fuck you! Here's a finger to your mother's religion!"

I looked at his face.

"Ilyas," I yelled. "By God, you're Ilyas! How are you, my friend?"

"No, I'm 'Abbas ibn Firnas!" he replied.*

He now proceeded to do some clownish stunts, his hope being that, by kicking the ball between my legs, he could make me look stupid. But, to save face, I flung myself at the ball and managed to stop it going into the net. I stood up with the ball in my hands. He now hit me so hard that I fell to the ground, then shoved both me and the ball into the net. He started kicking me hard enough that I eventually lost consciousness.

10

My Worst Night of Torture

My sunny cell!

Here I lie, after being subjected to that slugfest yesterday that masqueraded as a soccer game. I'm stretched out under the bedcover, doing my best to keep my bruises and wounds to myself, and occasionally taking a bite from the meager portion of food on the table. I keep turning over my current situation in my mind and thinking about what might happen next. That is the way I stayed until my eyes eventually surrendered to a deep but restless sleep.

I was jolted awake by the sounds of loud footsteps and started to panic. The gigantic guard appeared, pointing the wavering beam of his flashlight in my direction. Forcing me to get up, he pushed me towards the door of my cell. I was eager to chat with him and so I asked where we were going, sharing with him my opinion that the weather was very nice. I had hardly opened my mouth before he showed me his semidetached tongue and pointed to his ears as a way of showing me that he was both deaf and dumb. When the air turned moist and foul-smelling, I assumed that we were now in some kind of cavern where foul and obscure purposes were being fulfilled. My intuition was confirmed when the guard made me sit in a corner alongside a row of other people. Now I was stunned to be confronted with a scene that beggars description. There was this female ghoul about whose barbaric cruelty I had heard so much, the woman I had seen close up at yesterday's soccer game. This time, she was semi-naked, pouring with sweat and devoting herself to torturing a man strung up by his feet. She was beating him savagely and hurling all sorts of foul abuse at him as he hung there upside down—disgusting expressions peppered with phlegm-encrusted spit. She kept raking his skin with a sharp brass instrument that tore away at his body and made it bleed profusely.

Behind her stood three armed guards who looked totally repulsed by the whole thing. She kept on repeating the same question over and over again.

"What I want is the names of the people in your sleeper cell."

One of the guards came up to her and whispered in her ear. At that she threw a fit.

"These cowards are all one and the same," she yelled in French. "Once you get serious with them, they all faint. Take this wreck back to his cell. Tomorrow, by all that's holy, he's going to talk."

She indicated to the gigantic guard to take him away and sank into her chair, panting and exhausted.

For a few leaden moments I found myself looking around in sheer panic, not least because I and the other man with me could hear the groans and screams emitted by prisoners in neighboring rooms, along with the barking of dogs. Once things had died down a bit and the woman had had a chance to recover, she yelled: "Next one!" (the French *"au suivant"* echoing the title of a Jacques Brel song in which a prostitute is calling in her customers who are waiting in the hallway). But in Mama Ghula's case the same phrase implied the next person to be tortured. A guard pointed his finger at me and thrust a bowl in my face; it was filled with lentils and butter paste, all mixed in with bits of sausage and bits of meat of indeterminate kind. A genuinely satanic brew—may God never inflict it on anyone! The guard cautioned me that I had to kneel down and consume the entire contents of the bowl immediately. He explained to me that his boss would never deal with me unless and until my stomach was completely full. I had no option but to do as he said, although, once I had finished it, I plucked up enough courage to ask him what kind of meat I had just swallowed.

"Pork," he told me with a dry laugh, "pig-meat. That's all pigs like you get to eat here, pig-meat mixed with salt sea-water. Next time you come, if you've been stubborn, it'll be mixed with the piss of his excellency the director and his wonderful assistant in whose presence you happen to be at this moment . . ."

"But my religion," I interrupted, "forbids me to eat pork."

"Your religion, you say?!" he replied. "God curse your mother's religion! If you belonged to a religion, we wouldn't be seeing your dirty face here. But enough nonsense. Get up, the boss is waiting for you!"

I thrust my fingers down my throat, hoping to make myself vomit, but I failed. With that I stood up and went over to the woman. I gave her a searing look, intending to save face.

"What you're doing here," I told her, "is evil."

She pulled me towards her with a laugh. She started squeezing me in her tattooed arms and her ample bosom, just like a mother with her suckling child. I felt completely helpless and stunned as I found myself forced to rub up against her vile body, confronting her lewd and distracted expression, and smelling her sweat and her cheap and nasty perfume. I had to listen as she used a tone of apologetic complaint to whisper things in my ear in a mixture of languages, covering my face with tears blackened by the kohl she was wearing on her eyelids. The gist of her remarks was that the man I had seen hanging upside down was an evil person, an uncouth egomaniac who had made up his mind to keep his particular game a secret from her and stick to his own brand of truth. However, what she needed was to have him open his heart to her and share his secrets. If he refused to do that, he would make her unemployed and ruin her life. With a phony lust and coquetry she then proceeded to carry on her chatter in French, but this time I made it clear that I could not understand her. She then started talking in Arabic to the extent that she could, albeit it with a foreign accent that was partially fabricated but mostly natural.

"Listen, Cheri," she told me, "this breast isn't just a piece of bandage. What do you think of it? Do you like it? Tell me the truth. It's yours; you're going to suckle from it and kiss it. But if you bite it, like that dog who came before you, then I'll castrate you with no mercy. You can still ejaculate, I trust . . ."

With one hand she thrust her breast into my mouth, and with the other she grabbed my penis as though it were a piece of dough. She started feeling and squeezing it as though to measure and weigh it. I started moaning, and that led to her to interpret things in her own debauched and perverted fashion.

"Not bad," she yelled, "not bad."

All of a sudden her tone became threatening and coarse. "But if you start playing fainting games on me," she went on, "I'm going to feed you your own shit. So which cell do you belong to, whether active or sleeper?"

"I don't belong to any cell," I replied in a panic.

"Oh really!" she said. "Then how come you confessed to the lie detector that you joined an active cell?"

"I never did. It's lying!"

"The lie detector's lying! Damn you!"

"Or maybe I told a lie because I was being threatened . . ."

"OK, but here you are now in my warm embrace. So tell me the whole unadorned truth. Whisper it in my ear if you like. What's your cell?"

"Oh yes! Now I remember. In the past I used to belong to a small group that called itself the Yaqzin group or something like that . . ."

"An awake cell!* Bravo, sweetheart! Tell me about its activities."

"A mystical ceremony, Madame . . ."

"A mystical ceremony?"

"A kind of ecstatic dance. Members of the group shake their bodies in an increasingly frenzied movement so as to achieve a state of exhaustion and oblivion aimed toward the transcendent."

"You're talking in riddles. Tell me what the members discuss."

"Nothing, Madame. They only recite a single word, no other . . ."

"What's that word?"

"God lives, God lives! It's a phrase that emerges from the very depths of the devotee's inner being and continues till he loses all consciousness and finds himself living in the realms of worshipped God . . ."

"God lives?" she asked impatiently. "Is that some kind of code? A secret password?"

"No, no, God forbid! It's an expression of the unity and mention of the One Creator. It demands that indifference and forgetfulness be banished in order for true thought to be aroused in the presence of the Merciful One."

At this point her face turned red in anger and her voice cracked.

"That's all gibberish," she yelled, "Who's the leader of the group?"

I came up with a name on the spur of the moment.

"Musa ibn Zulayqa, Madame," I told her, "if my memory serves me right. But he died a while ago."

She now started reciting a whole list of names to me, slowly and with obvious tension in her voice. When I responded with a whole series of "no's," sometimes softly, other times out loud, she rounded on me in fury.

"And what about Ilyas, your former cellmate?" she screamed at me. "That nasty little catamite!"

"Ilyas Bu Shama?" I asked her. "How is he? Where did he disappear to?"

"I'm the one asking the questions, bastard!"

"Oh no, I'm perfectly legitimate. You may not insult my mother!"

"So how many times did you sleep with Ilyas; I mean, fuck him?"

My entire body shuddered in horror.

"Never, never!" I yelled as loudly as I could.

"Never?" she replied with raised eyebrows. "Not even a caress or a kiss?"

"Never. My faith totally forbids homosexuality."

"So is that your final word?"

"Yes, my final word, Madame . . ."

"It's Miss, you ass!"

I wanted to placate my interviewer and lessen the tension

"Mademoiselle?" I said. "You mean, you're still unmarried?"

"What do you mean?"

"You're still beautiful and desirable. I would imagine that someone must have raped you at some point or got you into bed . . ."

"Listen! My personal life is sacred. Do you hear me, sacred?!"

"Cigarette!" she yelled to the guard.

The guard lit a cigarette and put it between her lips. Meanwhile, she kept clutching me without relaxing her grip at all. She started puffing away nervously at the cigarette and put the ash in my ear. As politely as I could, I suggested that my ear was not an ashtray, but that made her furious. She stubbed it out on my chest and threw it away, totally unconcerned about my cries of pain.

I tried to control my nerves as much as possible. It occurred to me that I could take advantage of the somewhat lightened atmosphere and at the same time earn her sympathy if I played the fool a bit. I would accept her invitation to solve our dispute by engaging in a boxing match with her, following the usual rules for the sport. I was surprised when she accepted the idea with a guffaw. When she told her assistants, they guffawed too, and, once the news spread to the other people who were waiting to be cross-examined and tortured, some of them let out a strangled sort of laugh as well.

I was well aware, of course, that the balance of strength was not in my favor. Mama Ghula was much heavier; I was something like a flyweight. Even so, I decided, at least mentally, to put my faith in my own innocence. Every wronged person, I told myself, was obliged to defend himself. In any case, I had always felt an inborn proclivity for the honorable life and was always keen to endorse the loftiest examples of human advancement. As I was doing some warm-up exercises, I started rehearsing some of those principles, including expressions like "Even gnats can make the lion's eye bleed," "There are things in rivers that you won't find in the sea," and similar expressions.

Mama Ghula yelled at me to stop talking nonsense. She selected a prisoner to act as referee and gave him a whistle. She then forced the small group of prisoners waiting there to testify that I was the one who had suggested this contest, no one else. The referee now brought the two of us together and reminded us both of rules forbidding either scratching, biting, or striking the head or the sexual organ. My hands were wrapped in strips of cotton (with the agreement of the boss-lady), then the whistle was blown to signal the start of the first round.

I decided to defend myself and protect my honor by extending my tied hands and giving my opponent threatening looks. I imitated the tactics of the Muslim American boxer, Muhammad 'Ali—May God cure his Parkinson's disease and grant him a long life!—by taking on the role of a bee, painful opportunistic stings involving a lot of feinting and rapid dancing movements, but avoiding any clinches or bodily contact. I was able to land some painful blows to her face, chest, and stomach, all to the accompaniment of a veritable shower of cheers from the guards, followed by the prisoners as well. However, no sooner did the first round drawn to a close than—wonder of wonders!—my opponent looked scared and ran over towards her assistants who were competing to see who could emit the most piercing laughter. Wanting to continue my display of defiance, I took several steady and courageous steps in her direction. I taunted her and told her to come away from her corner and show herself.

"If you're a woman of steel," I said, "come on out! Now to the final round when I'll beat you fair and square. It'll be a knockout."

The underlings carried their boss to the middle, albeit with the greatest difficulty, and stood her up on her two feet. With a blow of the whistle the referee indicated that the second round should begin. Mama Ghula was looking exhausted and shattered, so I took advantage of the situation to aim a merciful blow to her right temple that sent her crashing to the floor unconscious. The referee counted to ten in order to stop the fight, while the guards outdid each other in making fun of her. I made my way over to the group of spectators, who were all proclaiming victory, yelling, "The bee's the winner, three cheers for the bee!"

Flushed by my success, I hugged all the prisoners who were celebrating my victory one by one, including a female prisoner who was wearing a head scarf. I then went back to the defeated woman, who was still spread-eagled on the floor, and strutted around her like a peacock. I told the referee to count out another ten or more, but he refused.

"No, no!" he said, "The rules are the rules."

I was getting ready to move away victorious when, right out of the blue, the woman pounced on me from behind like a leopard and threw me to the ground with a gymnastic move that only a category-one professional wrestler could manage.

Now I realized why it was that throughout the fight her assistants had never stopped laughing. Mama Ghula had been simply toying with me, turning our fight into a farce. I had obviously been wrong to imagine that any boxing match with her would follow international rules. I was even more in error when I had imagined that in any bodily contest with a female opponent, whether involving Roman or Japanese rules, I could be the winner; at the very least it would be a draw. As it was, I now found myself collapsing under the weight of this barbaric female ghoul, groaning as she throttled me and completely unable to move or resist. At this point I had good reason to doubt my previous masculine calculations. Could I somehow comfort myself with the thought that "there's many a trial that brings its own reward"? Perhaps my idiotic behavior might convince her that there was something wrong with my head; she might show a little mercy and treat me with less violence.

My thanks to God were profuse when this harpy loosened her grip on me and left me on the floor panting desperately. She meanwhile went over to her corner and sank down on a chair in front of a table filled with files, telephones, sandwiches, bottles of beer and wine, and other things that I could not make out because the guards ordered me to stay where I was. I could, however, see that the woman who had beaten me was busy eating and drinking, all the while uttering uncouth things in French and expressions of utter disgust like "Yuk" and "Ugh"—all as a way of expressing her complete contempt for the effort she had had to exert in order to deal with a puny, lily-livered, and insignificant weakling like me. Sure enough, she soon started venting her spleen and mouthing her disgust.

"This is a total insult," she said, spewing spittle as she did so, "It's a crime! Here I am, having to deal with scum and idiots, most of whom faint as soon as I start torturing them. The general and his coterie can play around with drug cartels, terrorist bosses, and organized crime, using all sorts of funds and cash, not to mention the pretty boys and prostitutes. Equal rights for men and women! My ass, a thousand times, my ass!!!"

It was not enough for her to keep on talking about equal rights. She knelt down, bared her enormous backside, and then started doing the rounds of the room. She kept repeating the most disgusting phrases in Arabic; I was unable to block my ears and only record them here only with the greatest reluctance. But then, my only excuse is that it is not obscenity to repeat obscenity.

"Equality, equality!"

"Damn equality, my ass!"

"Equality, equality!"

"My ass to equality!"

All the while her assistants kept clapping as she made her way around the room.

"She's for real!" they kept chanting, and then they ordered me and all the other prisoners to repeat the chant, "She's for real . . ." None of us was in any position to refuse.

Was I in a prison or a lunatic asylum? What was clear enough was that in this case the difference between the two was as thin as a spider's web; above all, there were no signs or dividing lines to tell you when you were leaving one for the other. As an indication of that fact, no sooner had this woman finished dancing around and yelling with her backside exposed and then stood still again, sweating profusely, than she singled me out with a wine-soaked gesture. The guard rushed over, grabbed me from my corner and once again put me in her clutches. I decided to wear them out by running backwards and doing various feints and other stunts, but this time the female ghoul, duly aided now by the gigantic black man who was presumably performing another one of his functions, managed along with the other guards to grab hold of me and tie my hands behind my back. They placed a bottle between my legs and withdrew.

"Sit on it," she said in a lewd tone of voice.

The wine bottle test, I told myself.

"Sit on it?" I said, pretending that I didn't understand. "Sit on what?"

"That's right," she yelled after emptying the bottle of wine. "Sit on it so the mouth goes up your ass! God damn your mother's religion!"

"Don't insult my mother, I beg you. Seek refuge with God and his Prophet from foul talk and debauched conduct!"

She repeated her instructions, but this time as a final warning.

"I'll sit down, yes," I replied, trying to control my nerves, "but on a chair. That's only right and proper, Mademoiselle!"

The guards started laughing again, and the gigantic black man joined in as well. I laughed along with them, not because I was that naïve, but to try to keep the atmosphere as conducive as possible. However, I soon changed tack and became serious again. I tried as best I could to address her in such a way as to arouse her sympathy.

"Why are you insulting me like this?" I asked.

With chewing gum in her mouth, she chuckled and winked at one of the guards.

"Oh, no reason at all," he replied mechanically. "To kill the time, or maybe because the boss doesn't like your filthy face! Sit on the bottle!"

"Never," I protested, "my religion totally forbids such things!"

Mama Ghula responded to my protest with an outburst of abuse against my mother's religion, the like of which I have never heard in my entire life. Her assistants rushed over, still laughing, and attached one of my legs to a rope hanging down from the ceiling. The position I was now in promised nothing good; I looked like a slaughtered sheep about to be flayed. The ghoul now came up to me, with a cigarette between her lips, her features a tissue of hatred and disgust. She now started stubbing her lighted cigarette on the soles of my feet, my backside, my back, and my armpit. Even though I mustered the proverbial patience of Job to counter this onslaught, I still emitted some suppressed groans. However, she then spread my thighs apart and thrust the bottle hard into my anus; this time I could not help filling the entire room with screams of extreme pain. My torturess now seized the opportunity to tighten the noose by asking me over and over again about my cousin called Abu al-Basha'ir and his cell and my own involvement in what she kept calling a sleeper cell. When she did not get the information she was after, she leaned close to my ear and pleaded with me—for the last time, I reckoned—to tell her the truth and offer her my help. She told me that she was a widow with a family to take care of; she pleaded with me to take pity on her crippled daughter and other children. I could help by responding to their needs and guaranteeing their future lives. When she still did not get what she wanted, she showed me her dagger and started sticking various parts of my body, in simultaneous admiration and disgust.

"There's nothing to cut," she yelled in her foul French. "This sheep's got no flesh on him. He's all skin and bones."

How I congratulated myself on being so incredibly thin; I was so grateful! The torturess made do with scratching my backside and thighs with her dagger, then proceeded to pound me with a cane on the soles of my feet, which had been dampened with cold water. When she was exhausted and I was totally destroyed, it was time for the swing and seesaw routine, something that is infamous, even for prisoners who have the strongest possible constitution. Trussed up like a sheep for sacrifice, I was spun around horizontally in two directions while she launched insane attacks on my backside, stomach, and genitals.

If it had been a matter of swinging gently as in childhood days of old, it would not have been so bad, but in this case they were doing it to cause maximal pain and damage, flaying my body and making it bleed every time I crashed into a wall studded with sharp, pointed protrusions. No human intellect, no legal system, could possible justify such bestial activities.

One of the consequences of my gruesome and painful ordeal was that the bottle came shooting out of my anus, leading to the most incredibly intense stomach pains and severe internal convulsions and distress. My head, meanwhile, was finding it hard to tolerate the vertigo and the continual collisions with the walls, so that gradually I began to waver between a marginal consciousness and a sense of detachment from my surroundings. Even so, this fiendish woman kept up her crazy assault, kicking me savagely as she accused me of being hard-hearted toward her. In a bizarre twist, she was still insisting that I needed to stop torturing her and provide her with the information that would help her keep her job and look after her children.

All of a sudden she stopped and stood me up. She begged me to sign a piece of paper, accompanying the gesture with mechanical kisses that were rough and cruel—almost crushing my lips and chattering teeth.

Even though I was feeling dizzy, I managed to respond, "I've no objection to any woman kissing me on the mouth," I raved, "but not a barbaric ghoul-woman with foul breath and crooked artificial teeth!"

My torturess now completely gave up hope of using her normal methods on me, and put me back on the seesaw machine. This time it was even more vicious and insane than before. I now made good use of the disgusting meal that they had fed me before it all started and that was now causing me all sorts of intestinal pain. Taking advantage of the situation to have my revenge on this ugly fiend of a woman, I raised my head every time I passed by her shoes and used every ounce of energy I had left to plaster her face with a shower of thick, viscous vomit. By doing so, I hoped she would deliver a final crushing blow to put me out of my misery. In fact, the female ghoul whom I had insulted soon decided to prod my back with an electric stun gun and followed it with a savage blow to my head. I heard the other prisoners who were waiting for their turn utter cries of panic and fear, while the single girl among them started wailing and fainted away. In my semiconscious state, I heard the ghoul order her assistants to bring over some onion and throw some cold water on me, and she told me to remain conscious. However, the space around me started to become a blur, and everything turned head over heels. All my eyes could make out were vague shapes, all fuzzy, and a few other moving figures. Soon afterward it all disappeared down a dark and bottomless pit.

11

These Are My Injuries, and Then They Cut My Hair

When I woke up the next morning, I was aching all over. Everything hurt, but some pains were localized while others were everywhere throughout my body. With a fair amount of effort, I managed to sit up and felt a bandage around my head. My teeth were in a complete mess: three of them were only attached to the jaw by a slender bit of flesh. I hurriedly rid my mouth of them. Just then, I remembered the mirror hidden under my pillow. I took it out to take a look at the injuries on my face and body. My vision was impaired enough as it was, but the general sight was appalling: bruises and contusions everywhere; wounds, swellings, and scars. My nose was totally stuffed with phlegm, which meant I could only breathe through my mouth.

I need to piss, so I struggled gamely to my feet to go to the toilet. That made me aware of the fact that I was walking like a young boy who had just been circumcised. Once I had relieved myself, I started pacing back and forth in my cell and repeating to myself that my morale was still intact. I needed to make sure that I did not give way or show any weakness. They would never be able to take away my self-respect and pride, even if they broke my ribs and nose. This then was the routine I undertook for just a few minutes, and, when I felt exhausted, I collapsed on the bed. I wonder what day it is, I asked myself in a tone that, while weak, was still defiant . . .

When you are stretched out in bed the way I was, what can a patient do except think long and hard about the situation he is in and the possible outcomes that await. Once all thoughts have been exhausted or become too convoluted, there's a tendency to indulge in illusions, some of them fanciful, others more concrete and insistent.

Examples of the first type included women and more women, the majority of whom took the form of Nahid,* the secretary, her name and reputation being completely deserved. Within the second category I would see myself using my hands and whatever digging equipment I could lay my hands on to escape from this prison and go back to the place where I was picked up; I could disappear for a while and repair my body and soul under the protective eye of my loving mother. All kinds of frustration and roadblocks would stand in my way, but I was confident that I could either work my way around them or else jump right over them, inspired and guided by my determination and my burning desire to rescue my life from a deadly treadmill of futility and the clutches of a sudden oblivion.

These illusions started to pile up and reproduce, but all of a sudden the stream dried up as a result of my inevitable collapse into a place than which there is nothing more obscure and rotten—in fact, just like the one I am in, situated under the oppressive tread of its denizens and myrmidons, some of whom I met, others whom I never even saw.

These sessions involving contemplation and illusion had by now become addictive. However, on every occasion, I would lose track of things, either because I was struck by a crushing sense of impotence or because I would be interrupted by the arrival of a guard with food or a warder to take me for further interviewing and torture.

On one occasion the thing that bothered me was the din coming from the corridor of the cells next to mine. The reason for it became clear when three sturdy men invaded my cell carrying a spray machine and proceeded to spray every single corner of my cell, after which they aimed it at me, concentrating on my head, armpits, and crotch. When I asked what was going on, one of them told me that, by order of the higher authorities, there was a campaign in every part of the detention center to eradicate the ever-increasing insect population during the summer season. He went on to tell me that, as part of the instructions, the heads and beards of all prisoners were to be shaved and the hair was to be put in sacks for burning. The hairdresser advised me not to make a fuss and to let him shave my head.

Other prisoners who had resisted and made a fuss had had both their beards and moustaches completely shaved off as punishment. Watched by his two companions, he sat me down on a stool and started using enormous clippers to cut off hair wherever he found it, almost as though he were using a scythe to cut wheat sheaves or weeds. He then moistened my head, temples, and chin with foamy water and proceeded to remove any hair that was left with a razor. Before they left, one of the men spoke to me.

"Now you're ride of fleas, gnats, and cockroaches. You should be grateful!"

Here I am now with my mirror that I have taken out of its hiding place. When I take a look at my face, I can hardly recognize myself. All the bumps, bruises, and bald spots that used to be covered up by my hair, all the cracks in my lips—some the result of smiling, other resulting from incredible pain—are now exposed, as is the absence of most of my front teeth. May God grant me an even greater profusion of hair to make up for what has been shaved off and burned, and a bushy beard, too, which can accompany me on nights when I shall devote myself to higher things. When it comes to Your enemies, O God, those who abuse helpless people inside this place, send down upon them lice, flood, a plague of frogs, and blood, just as you sent down as clear signs of Your wrath against the tyrant Pharaohs of old.

Next morning, the guard woke me up with an invitation to a communal breakfast. I waddled my way after him to the usual prisoners' mess. No sooner had I set eyes on them with their heads and beards completely shaven than I remembered that I now looked exactly like them. It was difficult to recognize people and even more difficult to talk, particularly when, like me, you had no particular friends there. At the table to which I was assigned, I noticed that there were some prisoners with no eyebrows, and, when I looked round, there were others like them as well. I guessed that they had been punished that way for resisting yesterday's shaving routine and causing trouble.

A general mood of suspicion and caution hovered over the scene at the tables, not surprising in view of the fact that some of the so-called prisoners were actually plants among the real internees. For that reason, the major sound was the clanking of spoons, sipping noises, and the clearing of throats, all of which covered up the lack of any conversation. Beyond that, there were the usual suspicious movements going on close to and underneath the tables.

Once I had finished my broth and coffee, I started looking around, trying to work out who were the real internees and who were the plants. The shaving routine had not discriminated between the heads and beards of either group, but, like me, some of them had colds and catarrh and looked thin, while others looked perfectly healthy. The latter looked like violent skinheads, while the former now had all the bumps and bruises of their faces and skulls exposed. So where exactly did the bounds of truth come to an end and those of deceit and obfuscation begin? That particular question kept nagging at me, especially when one of the latter group leapt up on a table and attracted people's attention. Once everyone was watching, he lowered his trousers.

"So they shaved my beard and head," he yelled as they cackled, "but shit on all of them. My masculinity is still intact; they haven't been able to shave that off. Anyone who doubts that can take a look at my erect penis in my hands."

The guards came rushing over and tried to grab him as he leapt from one table to the next and then wove his way between the chairs, just like a well-trained clown. There was widespread chaos at this point, and voices were raised:

"Power to the man with proof in his hands!" they yelled. "Power to him!"

"Long live the stallion," others cried. "Long may he live!"

12

With the Investigating Judge and His New Secretary

Taking advantage of the security lapse in the mess hall, I slunk my way out through the kitchen door to the administrative wing and the investigating judge's office. I told the guard that I had some crucially important information to convey to the judge; it was really urgent, I told him. When he seemed reluctant, I threatened him with the dire consequences of not responding to my request. He went inside to ask the secretary about it, and I slunk in right behind him and shouted out the information that I had provided to the guard. The secretary upbraided me for my behavior and ordered me to be taken out. But, while she was still on the phone, she suddenly calmed down. Telling the guard to leave, she instructed me to sit down.

I took a seat opposite this woman, who seemed to be in charge but still to be showing some kind of understanding. I relished the fact that I had managed to inveigle my way into the administrative wing and grab the opportunity for a meeting with the investigating judge without an appointment. I gazed at this new secretary who was busy working, at the computer, on files, or other stuff. For sure she was not like either of her two predecessors, Nahid al-Busni and the earlier woman called Jumana. This woman was pretty and had her head uncovered, a pair of languid tawny eyes and silky black hair. Her clothes were contemporary but modest, and she was lightly made-up. Her facial expression was neither vicious nor flirtatious, and she seemed so serene and relaxed that the overall effect led me to nurse other feelings as well.

I felt a strong urge to talk to her, even though the fact that she was on the telephone made that difficult. When she started typing, I seized the opportunity.

"Which country are you from, Miss?" I asked her.

She did not answer, but instead asked me what was the purpose of my visit.

"The purpose of my visit?" I replied, acting dumb. "The purpose of my visit? Well, Miss, in your presence the purpose has gone right out of my mind. Maybe I'll remember in a while . . ."

"Are you intending to tell the judge about the events in the cafeteria?" she asked me. "If so, his excellency already has all the details."

I did not dare ask her whether the judge had a concealed camera somewhere with a private screen to keep him informed about everything going on in the mess hall, the game field, the exercise yard, the corridors, the cells, and every conceivable part of this complex. Perhaps he was well aware of the all the secret activities of my own life, everything that had happened when I was in the shock and terror cellar, not to mention my first and second cells. Perhaps he also knew about the terrible way I had been treated during that phony soccer game and the various types of torture that that female ghoul had inflicted on me—May God destroy her in this world before she even reaches the next!

The fact that the judge was aware of what had happened in the cafeteria just as soon as the events had occurred was extremely valuable information. It was not clear whether this modest beauty had revealed the information by accident or deliberately. Here I was sitting next to her, wishing that this situation could go on and on so that I could savor her feminine beauty, if only from a distance, and listen to her melodious voice.

"Have you remembered?" I heard her asking me.

"Remembered?" I asked. "What? My senses? My mind?"

"No, what you came here for."

I rubbed my shaved head as though pondering.

"Not yet," I told her, "but when I do . . . But let's get to know each other a bit better and have a chat. Please, let me kiss your hand . . ."

She pulled her hair back off her face and gave me an affectionate glance.

"I know everything about you," she said, "but, when it comes to me, you'll only find out what the judge allows you to know."

I presumed that the reason she was being so coy was that the judge was watching the whole thing on a screen in his office. With that in mind, I stopped pushing the point. Just then, a noise from the buzzer on the desk indicated that I was supposed to go in to see the judge. The secretary came over to do a body search, and I helped her by removing my clothing as far as my underwear. I was delighted to catch a few whiffs of her perfume, which enveloped my head and face. That done, she hurriedly helped me put my clothes back on and took me over to a dark corner of the judge's office. He was still busy on the phone, so she invited me to take a seat and take it easy for a few moments. She then greeted her boss and left.

While the judge was involved with his various phones, my mind kept swinging to and fro between an effort to pick up as much as possible of what he was saying and the thought of that lovely, gentle, and sweet secretary I had just met. The very thought of her provided a ray of sunshine and hope in the long night of my stay in this awful center—all of which calmed my much troubled spirit.

Here's part of what the judge was saying on the phone:

"Quite right, Your Excellency. What they're telling us is true: prisoner number 67 behaved in a disgusting and debauched manner in the cafeteria. He exposed his bottom in public and then started waving it around. He must be punished and made an example. But it shouldn't be by castration, something about which I've expressed my strong reservations to Your Excellency before. Above all, unforeseen consequences . . . Yes, that's true, there have been eunuchs throughout the course of history, and it's also the case that failures in such cases have been rare, and so you can't judge things on that basis. So your opinion in this matter is the one that counts . . . Exactly so, Your Excellency. So farewell, and my warmest regards to you!"

I have no idea whether this was a real conversation or the judge was faking it. At any rate, once it was over, the judge kept talking to himself.

"My predecessor in this job, Judge Faysal al-Hawi, declared castration to be legal and justified its practice on the basis of precedents whose only possible rationalization involved the use of entirely arbitrary judgment and coercion. He claimed that the arguments were definitive, whereas in my book they're speculative. The use of the tradition of castrating eunuchs in the harem and slaves goes back to an era that is long past. The fact that the Turkish soldiers brought in by the Abbasid caliphs decided to castrate the caliph of one day and night, Ibn al-Mu'tazz, is a decision that will work against them rather than for them on the Day of Judgment. In short, I don't go along with that judge's mode of reasoning or its application . . ."

He suddenly stopped his ruminations and addressed me directly.

"What about you?" he asked, staring straight at me. "What do you think of castration as a punishment?"

"Invalid both intellectually and legally," I hurriedly replied. "A heretical act that rides roughshod over the rights of men. Anyone who orders its implementation will go straight to hell—and 'evil is the resort.'"

"Bravo!" he responded. "So you agree with me and support my views. Na'ima, come back in here . . ."

The secretary came in with a washing bowl and started pouring water on to her boss's hands. He kept rubbing them with soap over the bowl. When he had finished, he dried his hands with a towel. She handed him a bottle from which he sprayed his bald pate, and his neck, back and front. She then carried the bowl out of the room.

The judge now noticed that I was there and told me to come over and sit by him.

"Wow," he yelled, "just look at Hamuda! Unbelievable! The new look Hamuda, I do declare! All praise be to Him who changes conditions and faces! What's brought you here? But first of all, tell me how the soccer game went. People tell me your star was in the ascendant during the game!"

"My dear Judge," I responded, unable to conceal my sarcasm, "my team used a good deal of bodily skill to score a large number of goals through clever passing and powerful shots at goal, but we were eventually defeated through an overwhelming force. My sandals were ripped apart, and I was subjected to all kinds of physical violence. You now see me before you, my body completely crushed and my feet bare. Only God is the victor . . ."

"I'm going to get you some Nike sneakers as a gift," he responded sympathetically, "and some vitamin pills to build up your strength again. Na'ima, come back in. Do you want tea or coffee?"

I indicated that I did not want either of them. She came quietly over with a nice smile.

"This young lady, Na'ima," he told me, pointing at her, "knows the language well—a bounty from God in person!—and does not pronounce words oddly. Thus far, Hamuda, you've met two secretaries, one of them debauched and fierce, the other modest and malleable. In this young lady I have at last discovered the prize jewel in the necklace—that center wherein lies my own faith and my legal focus. Nothing excessive or negligent, nothing too strong or too weak, neither recklessness nor cowardice. She is no spendthrift, but no miser either. And, Hamuda, something that concerns you a lot, she neither chatters needlessly nor remains silent."

He now stopped this flow of verbiage and busied himself lighting his pipe. I glanced at the girl and noticed that her eyelids were closed and her lovely smooth cheeks were blushing bright red because she was so embarrassed. Even so, I was able to enjoy looking at her until the pipe-smoking judge decided to resume his salvo of verbiage, projecting sentences in all directions without anyone having the vaguest idea about either the thoughts that were supposed to tie them together or the logic involved.

"Yes indeed," he said, "I mustn't forget. This girl and you are both fellow citizens of the Arab country of Morocco. If you asked her now to sing the national anthem, she could do it with a military salute and with unparalleled enthusiasm. She can remember by heart the names of hundreds of dancing and singing stars, both Arab and worldwide. But she's a believing Muslim, so she never hangs any pictures of them around her neck, or any talismans either. We're short of time, or else I'd allow her to tell you the life story of one of them . . ."

He paused for a moment to refill his pipe.

"Na'ima has a burning and defiant nationalist sentiment," he said as he continued smoking. "No sooner do I provoke her by saying something like 'Egypt is the mother of the world' than she immediately reacts by saying: 'And Morocco is its father!' I never argue with her. Today I'm an Egyptian on the surface, but an Arab nationalist in essence. A while ago, Egypt was indeed 'the mother of the world,' but today, well . . . oh dear! You're telling me that a country seething with downtrodden, unemployed layabouts is the mother of the world?! A country that fosters groups such as al-Takfir wa-al-Hijra* and Brotherhood this and that, a state that is in such straits, the mother of the world?! When a country shows no comprehensive growth and cannot present a democratic ideal, how can we term it 'mother of the world'? No, no, it's better to say no more. I can no longer enter Egypt safe and sound. I should go back to our sister land, Morocco. Now there's a country—all praise to the all-powerful Creator!—just a stone's throw from Europe but with roots firmly in Africa—both steeped in tradition and contemporary in its values, a land that can bring opposites together and reconcile the irreconcilable. Just to give one example, this young woman has two separate degrees, she prays the five daily prayers—even though she may do them all at once or delay them; she fasts during Ramadan, although, in accordance with the demands of her job or her monthly course she may arrange things as required. She does not earn enough to give alms and has never performed the pilgrimage to Mecca because of a lack of means. But, in spite of it all, Na'ima is not shy in seeking her share of this life on earth. Previously, she's worked in publicity organizations, danced at weddings and receptions, and embellished her résumé by being crowned beauty queen in . . . Remind me again, which city, Na'ima?"

I suspect that, like me, Na'ima was about to explode in anger. Even so, she managed to reply.

"Sefrou, Your Excellency," she told him. "If I remember correctly, it's in the southeast, in the province of Fez."

"Ah yes, Sefrou, with an 'e' vowel, not an 'i.' That right, Miss, Sefrou. But, before you get back to work, allow this fellow countryman to give you a kiss to congratulate you on being chosen as beauty queen. Come on, you lucky man, take what I have allowed you to take: a filial kiss between the man and woman from the same Arab country. They are siblings, a laudable custom, and there's no divine dictum that forbids it. Stand up and kiss her. You lucky man! But be very careful now, no straying beyond the cheek!"

I stood up to do what I was told, and planted a gentle kiss on the trembling girl's neck, desperately trying as far as possible to avoid committing the kind of sin that I was powerless to prevent.

"So, is everything okay?" the judge asked as soon as the Moroccan girl had rushed out. During the course of carrying out my duties, I've come across men who cry and ejaculate very quickly. Are you one of them? Can I be sure? Or will you recite the Qur'anic verse to me: 'O you who believe, ask not about things which, if they were made clear to you, would annoy you' [Sura 5, The Table, v. 101]. Okay, so you've understood?"

"From that particular perspective, Judge," I told him in a vexed tone, "you can be reassured. I haven't sneaked in here to hear your talk about castration and your attitude toward it, or about Egypt and whether it's the mother of the world, or about this Moroccan lady and her truly laudable qualities. I've come to see you about one thing and one thing only, something where I've come to the end of my rope. It concerns the woman known as the female ghoul, or Mama Ghula. The first time that barbaric female subjected me to totally evil and demeaning treatment, but I managed to tolerate it. But the second time the torture was utterly bestial and obscene. Now, Judge, I'm raising a complaint with you and recording it in the light of the fact that I've lost my front teeth and my body is covered in welts and bruises . . .".

The judge rubbed his bald pate and the back of his neck and took several puffs from his pipe, as though he were disturbed by my torture or found my account tedious. I gave him an inquiring look.

"Do you have an open mind? If so, then it can harbor secrets. I'm going to confide in you my personal attitude toward this female ghoul. It's just like my attitude toward castration: rejection and disapproval. She should be punished not merely for what she's done to you but also because, when it comes to monstrous conduct and illicit behavior, she has no peer; when it comes to terror and violence, no one else comes even close. But how can I be blamed when Uncle Sam has written her a blank check? What am I supposed to do? The Yankees have given her a green light—in fact, it's so green that there's nothing fresher and greener. And, if you've never heard of the Yankees and Uncle Sam, then let me tell you that it's the Americans . . .".

The phone rang. The judge mouthed some short, clipped phrases into it, the majority of which expressed agreement and support.

"Okay," he resumed, wiping the sweat off his forehead with a handkerchief, "let pick up where we were, since we're both of us fond of Na'ima. You have three choices, and no more. You can either open your heart to Mama Ghula and tell her all the secret information she needs about your cousin, Abu al-Basha'ir; or else you can do the same thing with me here; or you can continue defying Mama Ghula and playing the fool in her presence as you have been doing—this time you can imagine that she's a cow and circle around her repeating a whole series of threatening phrases like 'I'm a raging bull, and I'm going to put my horns into the female ghoul . . . ' The first of these three choices is a good one, and the second is even better. Both of them will get you safely to shore. However the third option can have no good consequences . . .".

With that he gave me an inquisitive look.

"My dear Judge," I replied, plucking up my courage, "what I know about my cousin consists of the things I put into the report that I submitted to your exalted self. There's nothing to add to it, and the only falsehood will come when torture makes me reveal things inspired by the devil himself."

"God, my God!" he interrupted, his eyes closed, "what lovely melodious speech. Let me relish it for just a moment! I won't even bother about the flattery behind it or the fact that it is so far removed from the truth . . ."

"Sir," I interrupted in turn, "even if my words are the way you have chosen to judge them, I have to tell you that whatever melody you detect is purely coincidental, not as the result of some artificiality. Above all, I don't intend to flatter. And my only intention is to tell the truth."

His beady eyes stared hard at me through his glasses.

"Every prisoner I have ever met, past or present, keeps playing the same old tape. Even those with a criminal record continue to claim that they're telling the plain, unvarnished truth; they're completely innocent of the charges leveled against them. They all make themselves out to be just the way their mothers bore them: innocent virgins regarding their actions, intentions, and natures. But, when we've conducted a patient and thorough investigation with them— using the best methods possible and, when necessity decrees, the most cruel and vicious, they finish up acknowledging their faults. At which point they start asking for reduced penalties; indeed, in the majority of cases they request permission to join the security forces and secret police. We usually grant them such requests, but only, of course, after they have gone through all the necessary psychological and physical tests. If you yourself might be interested in joining that particular group, then you should do your utmost to satisfy the preliminary requirements and not come back to talk to me again until such time as you have done the right thing. That way you'll be able to give both us and yourself some peace and quiet. As for now, retrace your steps and think things over very carefully. But before you do even that, I suggest that you rid yourself immediately of behavior that harms your interests and does you no good. Your nose and hands, for example, even if they have to be cut off. In fact, avoid using prophetic hadith out of their proper context, the most famous of which is: 'Grant your brother victory, be he oppressor or oppressed,' or 'He who offers a Muslim cover, will be covered by God on the Day of Judgment,' things like that. And don't cite verses from the Qur'an either. They're all merely pretexts you're using to protect your cousin, who insists on taking his own heretical path, following narrow interpretations and adopting extremist and fanatical views that are contrary to the moderate tenets of our tolerant Islamic faith. By so doing, he completely ignores the injunction of God and His Prophet to avoid all excess in matters of faith. Instead, he chooses to imitate the actions of the Kharijites, Sabeans, Barghwatis, and other fanatical extremists from Islamic history. This is my best advice to you: Don't pretend you don't know and don't spout heresy. Above all, don't play the infidel after being silent for a spell, and don't drink piss after so long being amiss . . ."

I could no longer stand to listen to this endless flow of verbiage from the judge who wielded such power over me.

"You mention piss, Sir," I interrupted.

"Oh, do you have an opinion on the subject?" he asked.

"No, Sir, but I do have an urgent need . . . to piss. I've been afraid of not being able to hold out while I've been sitting here. I might wet my trousers, and that wouldn't be fitting in your exalted presence . . ."

"Okay then, get up and go. But don't forget that, if you're stubborn and keep things to yourself, Mama Ghula will straighten your teeth for you . . ."

I pointed at the sky above.

"God alone created me," I replied. "He's the one who gave me straight teeth."

"But Mama Ghula will make them level with the ground," he yelled at me as the phone started ringing again.

In the secretary's office, Miss Na'ima thrust a piece of paper into my pocket, then took me to the door and handed me over to the guard, who immediately bound my wrist to his. He was furious and vowed a solemn oath that in future this would be the only way I would be allowed to walk anywhere with him. I paid no attention to his rants, but used my free hand to check on the piece of paper in my pocket. I was looking forward to the opportunity to open and read it once I was left alone.

13

The Letter That Is a Gleaming Light, and I Witness Executions

Back in my cell, I searched high and low to see if there were any hidden cameras or concealed microphones and made sure that at the very least nothing like that was visible to the eye or tangible to the hand. Even so, I decided to wrap myself up in my thin wrap and huddle up to read the contents of the thin sheet of paper.

And how amazing and wonderful were the things I read!

"My dear Hamuda,

"I have sensed in you the scent of my beloved home-land, coupled with your innocence of the charges leveled against you, charges in which you have no part. There is neither time nor need for me to tell you my own story. Yours is more noteworthy because it is more painful and bloody. Take great care. Every heroic act of defiance you perform, every resistance to torture, makes you a candidate for their designs: that you become a double agent to be inserted by the Americans and other Western secret service agencies into groups that they consider to be extremist or terrorist. Every single investigator at this center and its multinational directors have one aim, to create cooperative and well-programmed agents, and then to bump them off with deadly weapons if they should happen to go astray or resist in any way. It does not matter whether or not you reveal things to them; that's just a means whereby they can

*get you to be compliant and turn you into a convinced tool
in their hands ready to perform specific designated functions for them. Then they have you trapped in a deadly vortex from which the only escape is death. Through suffering
and bitter experience, the woman writing these lines to you
is well aware of what you're saying. I had no choice but to
enter this service—God curse poverty and unemployment!!
At this point I see no way of getting out of it alive . . .*

"So, my dear Hamuda, If you find it difficult to become
what they want, a willing servant of their devilish designs,
then you need to come up with a solution that may help
you escape if you can do it right: you need to pretend to
be crazy and sick. Shower your interrogators with every
conceivable kind of ridiculous and crazy talk; threaten your
torturers with your hacking cough and the risk of contagion
from your illness. Maybe they'll eventually give up and send
you back to your homeland or somewhere close to it. You
may well be drugged again, and, when you finally wake up,
you'll find yourself tagged with an electronic monitor and
permanently at risk of a bullet to the head, which may hit
or miss if you so much as tell your story to anyone else or
raise a complaint against some unknown entity.

"Time is short, and the danger is immense.

"Make sure you don't look for me or ask any questions.
If you should happen to appear before this same judge
again and I still happen to be in his service, bear with me in
silence if I'm forced to curse you and even hit you.

"This letter that I've written to you places my life in
your hands. By God, if it were to fall into their hands,
they'd tear me limb from limb. Hide it where no one can
find it or else destroy it completely. I pray that everything
will eventually turn out well for you . . ."*

I mouthed a prayer of fervent thanks to my fellow country-
woman, who had shown me such kindness, and immediately started

looking for somewhere to hide the letter. While I was searching and assessing the situation, the guard yelled to me to get my food. With that, I ripped the letter into tiny pieces, shoved it all down my throat and under my tongue, then took the broth and swallowed it all, along with everything I'd stuffed into my mouth.

"So, Na'ima," I told myself, "your letter's now become its own blessing!"

Yes indeed, a blessing that I had literally ingested, so there was no need to worry about its being discovered or disseminated. I've nourished myself on it so that I can now gain strength from its valuable advice. Now my path ahead is illumined.

Thanks to this short message from Na'ima—a kindred spirit who resides inside my heart and mind, I can now begin to make out some of the principal features of this cryptic labyrinth in whose infinite recesses I find myself wandering helplessly.

I'll confess that I once had a nagging suspicion, a devilish thought, one that made me think of that message as a poisonous ruse or trap. But I rapidly squelched the very thought and put it out of my mind, not least when I thought about the woman who had risked her job and even her very life in order to offer me some help. Her behavior and the message she had given me seemed to be totally truthful and trustworthy. And, if that were not the case and the opposite were true, then there was no hope for mankind nor anything else I could lose. A life of complete futility and death itself would be one and the same.

In my inner soul and being then, Na'ima was indeed my gleaming light and my support. Through God's power, the road to salvation lay with my own mind and its ability to come up with some cunning ploys, things that would involve concealment, deceit, duplicity, ambiguity, and outright distortion. Fair enough, then! Let heart and slate remain open to all eventualities, adjusting to the subtleties of circumstance and situation as may be necessary—and all following the dictates of mind and insight and the intuitions of the heart.

Some of the strands in this maze were now becoming clearer. What I had to do, but very gradually, was to uncover other strands that were still hidden or obscure. However, what was now completely clear and not subject to the slightest doubt was that this secret prison of unknown location was being directed by unknown foreign agencies. The policies were being implemented by people of a variety of nationalities (I had also encountered Arabs up close). Within that system I had been programmed to go through a variety of trials and examinations, duly labeled torture, abuse, and brainwashing. Once I had managed to survive the worst of these dreadful processes through my own endurance, I would then be a candidate for one of a number of disgusting positions that were in hot demand from the spy agencies that were clearly in charge. Those positions included agents who would infiltrate opposition groups, some who would collect valuable information, others who would become hired assassins, and still others whose functions I neither knew nor could even conceive.

The designers of this fiendish scheme can undoubtedly rely on a reserve army in the millions, one that only grows larger with time and is reinforced by the unemployed and people in search of a morsel to eat. The misery of such people is a positive boon for these forces; their misfortunes become the dung and poison needed to tame whole nations and terrorize their peoples.

So here I find myself facing one branch of a worldwide network, pyramidal in structure, and with tentacles that reach in every direction to grasp all kinds of false gods in their clutches and dogs of various breeds and specialties to implement their policies.

As I thought of dogs, I was suddenly reminded of a poem, "In Prison," written in the 1960s by the Egyptian poet, Fu'ad Nigm,* when he was being held in the Qal'a prison in Cairo. I could only remember bits of it, but recited them to myself and then yelled them out loud to the walls and bars of my cell:

Here in prison, good grief!
Death and suffering,
But suffering for whom?
They're all curs,
Guard dogs,

Hunting dogs,
Standing there with chains,
*Alongside 'Antar and Abu Zayd.**

So these dogs—God protect you, Na'ima!—and their masters have these fiendish schemes to subdue and enslave the earth's most wretched people in accordance with their tyrannical desires, and here am I, the one and only master of myself. Only I can come up with something to thwart their program and counteract their designs and calculations. My plan has to involve a combination of feigned idiocy and sickness. Yes indeed, I myself—and I ask God's forgiveness for invoking this "I"—am that one individual seed, weak perhaps in body and size, but yet strong in faith, something that in my current situation is the strongest and most resolute quality I possess. I will either save my spirit from imminent and dire destruction and emerge safe and sound, or else I will die a martyr's death. In either case, Na'ima, I shall raise the flag of victory as a shining point of light and significance, to be added along with all the others like it to the lists of revolutionaries who have risen up against tyrants, and equally against those who have allowed themselves to fall prey to thoughts of resignation and submission.

At first I thought about grasping my pen and some pieces of paper so that I could record my dreams and ideas and then hide them under my bedcover along with the mirror, but I postponed the idea when a masked guard suddenly entered my cell and tied my hands behind my back. He then escorted me along corridors and hallways that were unusually packed with guards and prisoners. When we reached a back yard that I had not seen before, he placed me in the middle of a crowd of other prisoners. He told me that we were there to witness the execution of five terrorist leaders who had all confessed to accusations of murder and other crimes that had been made against them. When I opened my mouth to ask a question, he ordered me to shut up.

The crowd was made up of scattered groups of prisoners. The guards who, as usual, mingled with them, prevented any individual conversations. The sun was high in the sky, which suggested that it was close to midday. The atmosphere was as heavy as lead. The only sounds were people clearing their throats, clanking chains, and general fidgeting. All of a sudden, speakers that were partially visible on the guard towers started blaring out drumbeats, and five men, hands and feet tied, came out of a steel door in one of the buildings facing the other prisoners. They were followed by two masked soldiers with loaded weapons. They ordered the five men to stop, spaced a few feet apart, with their backs to a dilapidated high wall

I was standing in a spot from which I could look straight at the faces of the men facing execution. There were no signs of panic or anxiety. I told myself that these were genuine heroes, willing to sacrifice their lives in the cause of their struggle, not showing the slightest fear in the face of death. As I took a closer look and focused more carefully, there was Ilyas Bu Shama standing to the far left of these heroic figures. His head was held high, his expression was clear, and he had a smile on his face. I can swear the oath that Ilyas himself would have me swear: "By the fig and olive, by Mount Sinai" [Sura 95, The Fig, vv. 1–2] it certainly was Ilyas. I yelled his name as loudly as I could.

"God is with you, Ilyas," I shouted as loudly as I could. "You're dying in the cause of the truth and will rise again in Paradise along with the companions and martyrs . . ."

The guard punished me by hitting me on the head from behind. He pointed out that Mama Ghula had just come into the yard on what looked like an inspection tour. She was wearing dark clothing and carrying a collection of black plastic bags. This time she was not accompanied by her gigantic black assistant or any other gorillas With her fat, fleshy body and stunningly ugly appearance, she was the only person who was walking around, strutting like a peahen at times and prowling like a leopard at others. She headed over to the crowd of onlookers and gave them all vicious looks full of contempt, chewing on gum and rubbing her thighs in a suggestive manner that managed to disgust even the most sexually repressed of the prison population. I noticed that she gave me special attention, just in case

I decided to surprise her with a lewd wink or salacious gesture. She may have realized that I was challenging her, cursing the day she was born and everything she did; either that, or else that my madness had worsened and intensified. But the whore turned away and ignored me. Then, all of a sudden, a primitive-looking prisoner came into the middle of the yard and galloped toward her like a horse.

"Long live jihad," he yelled. "Long live revenge! God is most great! He is the only victor . . ."

But before he could reach his target, a soldier shot him dead. Witnesses immediately pronounced the fourfold "God is great," while the man's killer removed his body from the scene.

Mama Ghula completed her inspection tour without batting an eyelid at what had just happened. She then headed over to the five men and conducted the same sort of inspection routine. Accompanied by a man wearing a clerical costume (which made him look like some kind of demon), she stood in front of each one of them, talking to him as though she was going to either cuff him or bargain with him. That done, she covered his head with a black sack, and the cleric pronounced what I assumed to be the statement of faith or the prayer for forgiveness or both. They both did the same routine with the other four men. When she reached the last man in the row, Ilyas Bu Shama, he resisted having the sack put over his head. He launched himself at her, and bit her on the ear, making it bleed. She cried out in pain, and the cleric rushed away to get help. Soldiers hurried over and rescued their boss.

Defying the iron grip of my guard, I yelled words of triumph and support to Ilyas, accompanied by a muted buzz from the prisoners, which soon became a crescendo of noisy objection and abuse. All the while, the soldiers were emptying their rounds into the bodies of the five men, following the orders of Mama Ghula, who gradually withdrew under the protection of male orderlies. When the guards set about loading the corpses into the back of a truck that was ready to take them away, a tremendous hue and cry arose and threatened to get worse. However, everyone promptly heard the whizz of bullets being fired into the air from some of the guard towers, and the yard was soon wrapped in a silence more profound and deadly than that of the grave.

There now prevailed a truly funereal atmosphere as the prisoners were led away under intensified guard to the communal cafeteria. There they sat down to eat a meal, the repetitive contents of which told me that it was lunch.

I had no desire to break into everyone's silent contemplation, but rather I needed to perform a religious obligation.

"My friends," I told the community, "men of profound faith with dreams as large as mountains have today died before your very eyes. We can do no less than turn, one and all, towards the *qibla*, say the prayer of the absent, and pray for them . . . My brothers, let us all say the four 'God is greats' . . ."

Nobody responded or even moved. At some tables, they started laughing out loud, and it gradually spread to other tables as well. The whole thing astonished me, and I was utterly disgusted. How could I not be? How? When things returned to their normal state, I happened to hear something uttered in my direction from one of the tables:

"Weeping over the dead is a waste, saint of God. With enough cares all you can do is laugh . . ."

I paid no attention to this comment, but started doing the ritual myself: first once, then again. By the third and fourth time, the sound of other tired voices could be heard praying along with me. When I sat down again, feeling aggravated and disgusted, my neighbor leaned over and whispered in my ear.

"I've the solution for you," he said. "It'll solve all your problems and provide you with a way out. It makes bitter things taste sweet, things that are tight open up; with it misery turns into a boon. Mama Ghula treats you like a lamb, or a cat even; the director like a cock, and the judge like a donkey. It's not wine I'm suggesting; that's forbidden. No, what I'm recommending is ecstasy, extracted from the purest hashish, and at a very reasonable price too. You can have it on credit or else you can perform a service for me. What do you say?"

Shying away in disgust, I rejected his offer. I put my tray back in its place and started looking for my masked guard to take me back to my cell. Once I found him, he told me that this was not a charitable institution for feeding the poor and needy traveler. I would have to help wash the cafeteria's pots and pans and clean the furniture and walls. I did just that, along with a whole group of other people, although I had no idea whether they were genuine internees or plants. Once that was all done, I again asked to go back to my cell. My guard accompanied me and for the first time asked me if there was anything I wanted to buy on the black market. He named them all: American cigarettes, French wine, a Japanese radio, Saudi toothpicks, Indian perfume, Moroccan hashish, local soap, and toothpaste and chewing gum from no particular location. Interrupting, I told him I wanted none of it.

14

Another Torture Session

Back in my cell, I noticed that my bedcover had been decorated with a pair of Nike sneakers, a prayer rug, a miniature bowl, and a bound volume that I assumed was a copy of the Qur'an. There were also some newspapers and magazines (in Arabic and Western languages), with their dates erased and some articles cut out. I assumed that they all went back several years. I immediately sat down and started leafing through the newspapers, reading some of the headlines and articles inside. Some of them made me pause: "Terrorist explosions all over Baghdad leave dozens of people dead and wounded," "Maghribi women are enslaved and sexually exploited in Gulf countries," "In Tangier a man from the Gulf deliberately infects his Tunisian companion with AIDS," "The AIDS virus threatens the entire continent of Africa," "Networks to transport Maghribi 'artistes' to work in Gulf and Middle Eastern brothels," "The rape of children in and out of schools is an ongoing nightmare in Arab societies," "Dozens killed and injured in terrorist explosions in the capital city of Algiers," "A family in Marrakesh sets dogs and snakes loose on their son's fiancée to force her to have an abortion," and "Spain keeps a watchful eye on Moroccan fundamentalists who have served in the army." The magazines were all pornographic, so I threw them into a corner to protect myself with the sheltering veil of modesty and devotion.

There was one article that I read all the way through, describing the incendiary threats issued by the authorities of the Zionist entity against the Arab resistance forces. It confirmed everything that not only I, but also all liberal and oppressed peoples of the world, already know: Israel's tyrannical regime, duly bolstered by comprehensive and unconditional support from America, is also supported by European regimes and even by certain Arab governments as well. The Palestinian and Lebanese resistance movements are fighting not merely Israel, but also all those other tyrannical forces. It was in that context that I read this article with great enthusiasm; I even jotted down some quotes from it and only wished that I knew who had originally written it.

I got up and washed my hands with the meager supply of water that was available so that I could handle the Qur'an, even though the process was hardly adequate. When I opened the cover and looked at the title, I was totally shocked: *The Perfumed Garden for the Heart's Delight* by Shaykh Muhammad al-Nafzawi.* My entire body convulsed, and I shivered at the thought of this utterly malicious and disgusting act aimed at me.

So, who had been responsible for sending me these "generous gifts," I wondered.

If it had not been for the lewd materials included with the rest, I would have assumed that they came from Na'ima, who still retained her place in my heart and mind. But, since I knew her own beliefs, I came to the conclusion that it had to be the investigating judge. It was a down payment on a pact between the two of us, something required to fulfill a need he had in his own vicious and evil heart. But I vouched to myself, by the Creator of the heavens and earth and in the name of my plan to resist and hold fast, that this judge, wallowing in his foul slime, would never be able to catch me in his snares or get the things he wanted. Praying on his prayer mat, I decided, would be corrupt and invalid; using the bowl to perform the ritual ablutions would not cleanse, just the opposite; and, as for reading *The Perfumed Garden* in my current situation, that would be the worst of all. Except for the Nike sneakers that I needed so badly, I tossed everything else—even the newspapers—into the corner where I had already thrown the pornographic magazines.

The next morning I helped clear and sweep the cafeteria along with a group of other prisoners. I was then escorted by a masked guard to a secret room in a cellar, one that I had not seen before. He tied my hands behind my back and sat me down on a seat facing a table and chair. After a few terror-laden moments, a huge, muscular man came in, clearly one of the detention center's major gorillas. Along with the guard, he stationed himself behind my back. Mama Ghula now came in, followed—what a nice surprise!—by Na'ima. The two women could hardly have seemed more different: one was like a compliant gazelle, while the other looked like a savage beast. There was Mama Ghula in all her proverbial ugliness and bestiality, while Na'ima was also there, infinitely attractive and supremely gentle.

Na'ima's boss instructed her to shine a light beam directly at my face. I now decided to show how crazy I had become, part of my plan that I've described earlier. I expressed my admiration for Na'ima, but without mentioning her name or referring in any way to her message.

"I'm delighted to see you here, lovely visitor," I declared. "Weren't you scared of the guards on the way?"

Instead of getting any reply from her, I received a blow to the neck from the gorilla standing behind me. That shut me up.

"No questions allowed," came a threatening voice as though coming from a machine. "No sexual harassment either."

He moved over and stood beside Mama Ghula, who was busy eating sandwiches and drinking bottle after bottle of beer. Every so often she would open her mouth, stuffed full of food, and whisper something in the gorilla's ear. He would then convey it to me as a terse question.

"The boss is asking," he would say in his mechanical tone of voice, "about the things you haven't talked about so far."

"Every arrow in my quiver I've told you about," I replied, my eyes watering because of the intense light focused on my face. "Prayers to God are all that's left."

"You've emptied one quiver, you son of a bitch," the gorilla replied menacingly, "but you've hidden another one. Empty it now, or else I'm going to empty your veins of blood. In your home city of Oujda, you were involved with books. Fine, but you also got involved in other things, too. A woman named Fatima al-Lozi, for example.

You installed her in your bookstore. The boss wants to know about your relationship with her."

"Fatima was a widow with little money," I replied immediately. "She was left alone and had had no children. Her life was utterly miserable. I gave her shelter and offered her as much help as I could in return for cleaning the bookstore and occasionally acting on my behalf . . ."

"The boss is asking if you had sex with her," the muscle-bound man demanded.

"Good heavens, no!" I replied. "She and I were both nursed by the same woman. That's totally forbidden."

That made Mama Ghula cackle.

"Your nursing sister, you fornicator?" she yelled, using a genuine or phony foreign accent. "My ass! Where is she now?"

"I don't know," I replied. "She disappeared two months before I did."

"No, no, you son of a bitch! Tell it right. She joined the maquis* in the mountains, along with her other suckling brother, your cousin, al-Husayn al-Masmudi."

The gorilla now received some more whispered questions from his boss.

"In previous interrogation sessions, you've never mentioned Fatima al-Lozi. Why not?"

"Because there was nothing to be gained from talking about her."

"Oh yes, there is! The boss is asking about your own sexual orientation."

"My sexual orientation? I don't understand . . ."

"In sexual matters," he interrupted, "do you favor women or men?"

"Women, of course," I replied, "because I'm a man. But not just any woman. If I could marry the lovely woman standing in front of me here in accordance with the practice of God and His Prophet, I wouldn't hesitate for a moment. But, if we're talking about this torturess, for example, death would be a preferable option. The gentler sex is totally innocent of her as a model."

With that, the female ghoul stood up and spat the entire contents of her mouth in my face, then sat down again and suppressed her fury with another bottle of beer.

"Your relationship with Fatima al-Lozi is of great help to the inquiry," the gorilla went on. "The fornication charge can be based on firm evidence and the dictates of the law. But that's not all you've kept hidden. There's also something far more serious: trading in gasoline smuggled across the Algerian-Moroccan border using different kinds of containers. At first, you were doing it on a motorbike, but later you used a car. It was butane gas which is highly flammable and could well have killed innocent people. Why have you kept that hidden?"

I did my best to conceal my alarm and responded slowly and deliberately.

"Had I been questioned about this information," I said, "I would have told you the following: It's true, I smuggled gasoline in small amounts from Algerian villages to Oujda and its environs. But I soon stopped, both because the dangers involved far outweighed the profits to be made and because there was an ever increasing number of 'withouts,' that being the term used to describe unemployed people who could only find work smuggling cans of gasoline. The only reason I used gas for my car was that it was fairly cheap and thus suited my meager budget. That's all."

Mama Ghula now signaled to Na'ima to turn the light up full. My eyes were so dazzled and disturbed that I kept seeing shadows and visions behind it. I looked away to give them a chance to recover and noticed that the guard was no longer behind me. She told me to look straight ahead.

"It's the boss's opinion," the gorilla's voice intoned, "that what you've told us is a pile of rubbish. So, for one last time, she's asking you the whereabouts of your cousin nicknamed Abu al-Basha'ir or even some of his men. If you cooperate, the charges of fornication, smuggling, and using a booby-trapped car will be dropped. You can add to all that the murder of your mother's husband as well. What do you have to say?"

I begged my Lord to give me the fortitude to withstand the violence and torture that were certainly to follow in view of my one and only response to her questions and threats. She gave another signal, and Na'ima came over to me, looked straight at my brightly illuminated face and repeated the question in a gruff voice totally unlike the one I had heard before.

"I'm delighted to see you here, lovely visitor," I said once again. "Weren't you scared of the guards on the way? By the true word of Him who created you in such a perfect form, I know nothing about my cousin's whereabouts, where he is, or who his companions are."

Na'ima gave me a slap on the face, and I enjoyed it. I turned my other cheek to her, asking her to do it again. She slapped that cheek too, not without a certain gentleness of touch. I really wanted her to keep on slapping me so I would forget this room and the people in it. I could imagine that the person slapping me fitted the old proverb that says: "One who loves a lot punishes a lot." However, my wishes were soon curtailed when the muscle man grabbed hold of me, dragged me to a dark circle, laid me down on my back close to a water bowl, and proceeded to stuff my mouth full of bits of wool and toilet paper. He then waxed it with a binding paste.

"Now, my stubborn fellow," he whispered in my ear, "warm suffocation is going to make you spit out the truth!"

Warm suffocation! What on earth was that?

The female ghoul now came over and sat cross-legged on my face. I could feel her press one of her orifices over my nose which prevented me from breathing and forced me to smell her foul gases and disgusting body odors. She only relaxed her revolting grip a little in order to ask if I was ready to cooperate yet. Once she realized that I was still maintaining my stance, she simply resumed her position. Her portable phone rang.

"Yes, Sir," I heard her say, "the dog's in our hands now. He's bound to talk. Yes, Sir."

When she felt my breathing slow down and my legs stop moving, she got up and went back to her place to continue eating and drinking. I stayed on the floor, groaning and spluttering.

Na'ima now came over, either prompted by a signal from the ghoul or on her own initiative. She took the stuff out of my mouth and untied my legs. I started coughing as never before and vomited up the entire contents of my stomach. I apologized to my rescuer, who moistened a towel from the water bowl and leaned over to clean my face and neck. Thanks to the attention of this sympathetic woman and her pure breaths so close to me, I gradually calmed down.

A few moments later the female ghoul came back, felt my neck vein and pulse, then signaled to the gorilla, who dragged me and sat me cross-legged in front of the water bowl.

"Now it's time for waterboarding!" he yelled. "The time has come. Either you confess, or else it's curtains for you."

So now it was time for the infamous waterboarding. People say that, as the person being tortured is deprived of oxygen, he can look upon his own death time after time until he confesses and cooperates or else dies without doing either. That is precisely what the boss now did with me, and in the most barbaric fashion. If she felt hungry or thirsty, or if the phone rang, she would hand things over to Na'ima, who started lessening the amount of time I was under water and pretend she was not good at it. The muscle man noticed the way she was behaving and told the female ghoul who was busy eating or answering the phone. As soon as she had finished what she was doing, she gave Na'ima a resounding slap that completely knocked her out. She kept complaining about the incompetence of these young female assistants and their lack of experience and knowledge. She gave instructions that her now-unconscious assistant be taken to the health clinic and then reprimanded for her conduct. That done, she set about subjecting me to more water torture and only raised my head out of the water in order either to heap all kinds of foul abuse on my father and my religion or else to threaten me with death by drowning if I did not open my heart to her and reveal all my secrets. As I struggled underwater, I had Na'ima's lovely face in my mind; as I strived to hold my breath, I kept asking for God's aid and hers. Then I started to feel a certain weakness creep into the female ghoul's curses and threats, also in the way she was holding my head under the water. I told myself that she was getting drunk. God willing, that would be my means of escape from this torment. My hunch proved to be correct, in that the guard came rushing in, looking very worried and helped his boss stand up and head for her bench. All the while she kept muttering snatches of incomprehensible nonsense. He returned to where I was and took me out of the room. He had to carry me to the health clinic on his shoulders, not only out of sheer sympathy but also because he did not want me to die in his custody. He could easily see how bad my condition was and that I could not walk on my own. In the waiting room he sat me on a seat fixed to the floor, tied my hand to it, then left to perform some function or other.

I was left on my own, waiting for the door next to me to open. Once the silence became pervasive, I could hear groans behind the door, noises that I assumed came from a wounded person being treated. However, those assumptions were shattered when my curiosity led me to take a peep through the keyhole. What I saw almost made me collapse on the floor. There was a doctor with her brassiere fully open leaning over Na'ima, hugging her, touching her naked breasts, and giving her deep-throated kisses on her mouth, exactly the way a man does with a woman. Seeking refuge in God, I went back to my seat, not least because I heard some footsteps in the hall nearby.

The guard appeared, removed my hand constraints, handed me over to the doctor, and asked permission to leave. Of Na'ima there was no sign! For that reason I refrained from showing any surprise by asking questions.

A middle-aged woman, foreign-looking, thin and flat-chested, with short hair and no makeup. She looked remarkably masculine. After giving me a smiling, self-assured welcome, she proceeded to conduct a variety of detailed tests with remarkable attention. With both a physical examination and through x-rays, she focused in particular on my chest and lungs and finished by taking for analysis a sample of my blood in a small capsule. She told me that Na'ima had specifically asked her to take good care of me, and then handed me a spray and some pills with a form telling me how to administer them.

She also gave me a set of empty plastic containers that she told me were a present from Na'ima. I asked her how Na'ima was, and she gestured to me that she was fine. With regard to our next appointment, she put her finger to her mouth and whispered: "If you start spitting blood . . ." She then escorted me to the door where the guard was waiting.

15

From the Crazy Block to the Shop for the People Practicing for Judgment Day

Can it really be true that I was carried asleep, put down on my bed, and then slept without waking for two solid days? That at least is what a voice emerging from a neighboring cell is telling me.

It was excruciatingly difficult, but even so I managed to stand on my two feet. As I did so, I noticed they had sores festering. I staggered my way over to the door, and it was then that I realized that I was in a different cell from the one I had been in. The proof was that this cell had iron bars on the door, through which I could make out a dark corridor and walls crisscrossed with cracks and a number of damp patches. Looking to the left I could see a dark hall whose precise dimensions were unclear, while to the right I found myself face to face with a man whose primitive appearance put me in mind of cavemen. Using his cane, he handed me a full bag.

"Your worshipfulness has enjoyed a long, deep sleep," he told me in a disgusted tone. "Meanwhile poor me has a stopped-up toilet. So empty this in yours and then give it back after you've washed it. There has to be . . ."

I was loath to respond to his request.

"Take it, and may God have mercy on your father!" he pleaded. "It's a whole week's worth, and that's a lot! One neighbor should look after another, as the saying has it . . ."

I tottered over to my toilet with the bag, holding my breath as I did so. All I could find in my own cell was a narrow-diameter hole covered with a brick and a water tap. I decided that the whole thing

107

was impossible, not only because the bag was so heavy but also because I was afraid that the stench would foul the air and expose me to disease. With that in mind, I wrapped up my bedcover and put it over all the furniture I could find. I then climbed up with the intention of emptying the bag through a skylight next to the roof. However, it fell out of my shaking hand and disappeared into some unknown vacuum.

I climbed down again and rearranged the furniture, then lay down to recover my breath. Focusing on the skylight, I kept trying to ignore the foul stench all over me and reassemble the various thoughts and ideas inside my head. I could recall that, before my profound period of sleep, I had been subjected to a concentrated period of vicious torture administered by Mama Ghula and her muscle-bound gorilla assistant. I kept seeing the lovely image of Na'ima, both during the torture session and afterwards in the health clinic, and the Christian female doctor who had subjected me to examinations that I now preferred to regard as special techniques rather than assuming the worst about them. That was particularly the case in view of the kindness and excellent treatment that I myself had received from her.

I automatically searched my pockets, and there I found the two sprays with Fontoline written on them as prescribed for asthma sufferers. She had given them to me at the time, along with empty plastic containers that she had said were a gift to me from Na'ima. While I was wondering about the meaning and purpose of such a gift, my neighbor asked me to give him back his bag. When I told him what had happened, he started yelling, banging the bars of his cell with his crutch, and threatening me with all kinds of perdition and misery. Many voices now rose from neighboring cells all along the hall, some of them demanding that I get the poor man his bag back and promise him a newer and cleaner one the next day, while others begged him to shut up, go to sleep, and consign my particular case to the Day of Judgment. As the din got louder and louder, my neighbor's hysteria intensified even further. Now he claimed that I had taken his property and deprived him of it, and all for a sinister purpose I had in mind. He proceeded to pronounce all kinds of foul and disgusting oaths against me, and with each oath the prisoners all yelled "Amen." This went on intermittently until early morning.

So here was yet another category of torture being imposed on me in this particular cellblock, one that was undoubtedly reserved for lunatics and the insane. I had either been put here on purpose, or else—as I dearly hoped and wished—by mistake or oversight.

I did not sleep for the rest of the night. Dogs kept barking, and the bedbugs were biting and sucking my blood. My only distraction was the thought of my Naʻima, the possible significance of her gift, and the last thing that the doctor had whispered into my ear: "If you spit blood . . ."

What is amazing is the way that, in spite of all the torture and suffocation I have been going through, my heart insists on beating and involving itself in life. The message that Naʻima sent me and the signs of her hidden affection have undoubtedly played a major role in reinforcing my resistance.

As morning dawned, I sat cross-legged, observing a guard who brought me some food or walked past my cell. I obviously had to inform the authorities that I was not in the right place, scratching my skin and pulling bedbugs off, warding off the effects of asthma by spraying my mouth, and waiting . . .

I was not disappointed, in that half way through the morning I heard the voices of guards by my neighbor's cell. I crawled over to the door and used the bars to stand up. Wearing masks, they were wrapping up my neighbor in a white shroud and preparing to take him away. The other prisoners meanwhile launched into the four-fold *takbir* and prayers for the dead. I joined them in this religious obligation as best I could. When things had died down somewhat, I drew a guard's attention to the fact that I had been brought here by mistake and asked to be taken back to cell 112. Raising his eyebrows in surprise and derision, he put his key in the lock, handed me my dead neighbor's crutch, and told me to follow him. Thus it was that I tramped behind the three men who were carrying the corpse while the other prisoners poked their hands through the bars in the block and poured all kinds of abuse and curses on me.

"You've killed someone unjustly," some of them repeated, "and now you're walking in his funeral procession? May God challenge you and consign you to hell for everlasting!"

When we reached a large space where a number of corridors met, my escort suddenly stopped me.

"How did you come to be in the lunatics' wing?" he asked.

I told him what I knew, but then he asked me what they all meant by accusing me of killing my neighbor. I told him about the bag and its contents.

"But they're all saying the same thing," he said after a pause for thought. "What's your response?"

"Officer, Sir," I replied, "I never even entered the dead man's cell. In law, the consensus of a group of lunatics has no validity."

He rubbed his neck as he gave the matter some more thought. Consigning the corpse to his assistants with instructions to take it to the gravediggers, he took me over to a door in a dimly lit block. Locking it behind me, he advised me to wait along with the people whom he called "people practicing for Judgment Day." Meanwhile, he would look into my case and the whole matter of the bag.

The shop where I now found myself consisted of a meeting hall with a high tin roof supported by wooden pillars planted in sandy soil. The whole place was teeming with people, young, middle-aged, and old. Some were standing in line while others—the handicapped and decrepit—were sitting down. I stayed close to the door, waiting for the officer to come back. An old man invited me to sit in his place, but I thanked him and pointed to the crutch I was relying on for support. When I asked him how he was and about this teeming mass of God's servants, some of them took turns in answering.

"Dear brother in God," one of them told me, "people here have been just as you see them now. For almost a month the weak ones have been sitting on the ground, and the sick have simply been laid out there . . ."

"Once a day," a second one added, "they throw us down some pieces of bread, dates, and bottled water from the roof. So we eat what we're given and wait here to be released by the One who is the only victor."

"Anyone who needs to relieve himself," a third one continued, "has to plough his way through the ranks and get to that facility with wooden screens and cloth awning around it. There's no water for ablutions, only stones. The prayers we perform fall far short and only involve fear. Those murderous tyrants make false claims about us: they say we're all heretical extremists. Their torture methods go so far as to train us for the Day of Judgment—that is, in accordance with their own hateful expression and their sickly imagination . . ."

"But we're all willing to put up with it," a fourth added. "We'll either emerge with our lives or else be resurrected as martyrs."

Just then a voice arose—I could not see who it was—chanting these Qur'anic verses: "You who believe, seek help through patience and prayer; verily God is with the patient. Do not say to those killed in God's path: 'They are dead'; rather they are living, but you do not realize it. We will test you with a taste of fear, hunger, and a lack of property, lives, and fruits. Give the good news to the patient, who, when afflicted by misfortune, say: 'Surely we belong to God, and to Him is the return.'" [Surat al-Baqara 2, The Cow, vv. 153–56]. Other voices responded, my own among them, with further verses. Just then, there was a hail of small bags and plastic bottles, and all of a sudden silence fell. I gathered up my share—bread, dates, and drinking water. The silence continued as everyone ate. Once that was over, a powerful voice was heard:

"Servants of God," it said, "the tyrants have prevented us doing ablutions and praying, so let's respond by performing chants and intercessions. That way we can at least remain pure and keep ourselves strong. Our noble Prophet—may God bless and preserve him!—said: 'God has ninety-nine names, and he who recites them will enter heaven.' He also said that any servant of God who encounters a problem or who feels sorrowful and then prays to God will have that problem or sorrow removed and replaced by joy and happiness. Servants of God, recite God's beautiful names with me. He is God, the only God, the Merciful, the Compassionate, the King, the Holy, the Peace, the Believing, the Protector, the Mighty, the Powerful . . .'"

Everyone in the room, whether Arabs or non-Arabs, joined the speaker in his recitation. The very sight of so many necks straining forward, so many throats reciting, was enough to send shivers down the spine and warm the heart.

Once the recitation, in which I participated as best I could, was over, silence fell again—that is, until the next phase:

"Servants of God, the Lord of Mankind has said: 'He who praises God thirty-three times at the conclusion of each prayer, extols God thirty-three times, and pronounces the *takbir* thirty-three times, then recites the hundredfold "There is no god but God, He is One alone with no partner; to Him belongs dominion and praise; and He is all-powerful," that person will have his sins forgiven, even though they be as plentiful as the foaming waves in the sea.'"

No sooner had this voice, that clearly belonged to a remarkable and effective imam, finished its exhortation than voices vied with each other to ask forgiveness, with exultations, shouts of praise, declarations of God's unity, all in the numbers designated by the imam. Once that was completed, the crowd started chanting texts eulogizing the Prophet, sections from the *burda* poem of al-Busiri* and extracts from the *Dala'il al-Khayrat* by the renowned Sufi imam, al-Juzuli.* Some of them went on to recite other Sufi chants and to perform the devotional dance. The whole atmosphere was fraught with an amazing sense of spiritual presence.

The various episodes in this profound and ever accelerating ceremony followed one another in inexorable progression. I joined in with both mind and spirit, although my body was exhausted by the need to lean heavily on the two crutches that by now had become an integral part of me. I was afraid that the officer would come back and not find me where he had left me, so I had to stay put near the door. I could not move away, even though my need to keep moving and my urgent desire to relieve myself were both becoming ever more insistent.

The group closest to me started reciting the famous poem in which the Prophet's companions welcomed him and his company to the city of Medina the brilliant:

The new moon has risen over us
from the folds of farewell.
We are obliged to give thanks.
Greetings to you, O best of summoners.

The sheer enthusiasm of their chanting spread to other groups, and then to the assembly as a whole.

The event that finally managed to calm their vibrant performance was when cold water started pouring out of gutters in the roof, all accompanied by a detached voice through the loudspeakers that kept repeating this slogan: "Cleanliness is part of faith. Clean yourselves without charge." No one managed to avoid getting soaked, even if it was only intermittent, and here and there some people started sneezing, coughing, and having runny noses. For my part, I started shivering uncontrollably; my teeth were chattering, and I started hacking so badly that I could not use my asthma spray.

Once the water stopped cascading down, everyone went back to the chants and incantations they were singing before. At this point even more people started dancing, and I presumed that they were trying to get some warmth back into their cold, soaked bodies. All of a sudden, loud techno music started blaring through the loudspeakers, so the chanters and dancers shouted as loudly as they could in order to drown out the music. However, they gradually became more and more exhausted, and little by little a powerful enforced silence began to take over.

Most of the people present now sat in clusters in the floor. The techno music stopped, and voices were raised to announce that there were some dead. I noticed an old man just by my feet; after checking his neck vein and closing his eyelids, I was able to confirm that he was one of that number. Accompanied by the people close to me, I said the fourfold *takbir*. I then noticed the door opening and a group of armed guards wading their way through the clusters of people and starting to remove the dead on rubber stretchers. When two of them came over to get the dead man close to me and put him on the trolley, I collapsed on top of him, holding my breath. They were forced to take me with the dead man, the assumption being that I myself was also in the Angel of Death's clutches. They transported me to the graveyard, while my ears resounded to the sound of gunfire, as the imam yelled out: "Remain steadfast, servants of God, remain steadfast!"

By now it was dawn. The guards made do with lining up the corpses alongside a wide, deep ditch in the graveyard. They went off to do something else or to use what was left of the night to get some sleep. Like a wounded crocodile, I slithered my way from this ditch that had obviously been dug for an indiscriminate corporate burial. Eventually I reached a grassy strip where I was able to breathe freely and rest for a bit. Holding my hand over my mouth to stop coughing, I was able to empty my bladder, something I had had to control while I was on top of the dead old man.

The sun rising in the sky shows no mercy on people trying to hide in this bare open desert, however much they try to scrunch up and make themselves invisible. Actually, the sun uncovers and exposes them, making them completely obvious to any wandering guard or person in a watchtower. As I lay there on the ground, I noticed a soldier's boot close to my eyes. Raising my head to look at him, I heard him threaten me and tell me to stand up. It soon became obvious to him that I could not do that. He asked me if I was trying to escape, and I told him I was not. He then asked me for my prisoner's number, and I spelled it out, quickly the first time, then more slowly. He was happy to carry me on his shoulders, as though I were hunting spoils.

"They've been searching for you all over the place," he shouted. "This morning you're my prize. Pray to God that, when it comes to salaries, you'll be the reason for my increase!"

I now told my rescuer the story of my getting misplaced in the lunatics' block, then in the hall for those practicing for the Day of Judgment. However, his mind was elsewhere, repeating the same thing over and over again and asking me to pray for him. Before he put me back in my cell and locked the door, he spoke about me to a number of soldiers and guards on the way—far more than required, and made them witnesses to the fact that he was the one who had discovered my hiding place and arrested me.

16

Between My Walls

The Christian Fayruz

How many long hours, or maybe whole days, I spent asleep, elongated periods that were interrupted only by abrupt episodes of wakefulness, about which I cannot remember any specific details but only the terrifying impact of their visions.

When I rubbed my eyes—it was noontime, I was appalled to see rats and mice congregating to consume the food that had piled up while I was asleep. What appalled me even more, however, was to see a woman's head poking out of the bedcover in front of me. When I tried to stand up, I found that I could not do it. I shooed the mice and rats away, and they went back down the holes from which they had emerged. I hobbled over to the toilet and put the stone over it, then towards the door and pulled myself up using the bars. I started yelling, pointing out that, contrary to the practice enjoined by both God and His Prophet, there was a woman in my cell. The only result of my yelling was to hear my voice echoing back weak and feeble. That was followed by a remark from the prisoner who was my closest neighbor:

"You moron!" he said. "They bring you a woman for your bed, and you turn her down! What are you, a man or a hermaphrodite? Fuck the harlot for free, you lucky man! If not, then give her to me, and I'll fuck her as I've never fucked a woman before. I'm so frustrated, it's unreal. Give her to me for a fair piece of hashish and a bit of spare change for the guard. What do you say?"

I paid no attention to such foul-mouthed drivel, but still decided to give my breath and vocal chords a rest for a while. I then resumed my yelling and shouting. This time all I got out of it was waking up my newly arrived cell mate, who proceeded to accuse me of being a plant and spying on her in her cell while she was asleep. I immediately denied her any ownership of the cell, pointing out that the number 223 coincided with my own number. In exchange, I expended some choice words on a counterattack, accusing her of being an informer herself, someone whose function was to tempt me with sex as a way of getting information that the female ghoul had been unable to do by torturing me.

I imagined that the investigating judge might be watching me through some hidden camera and laughing his head off at us. With that thought in mind, I leapt up, grabbed my blanket, and used it to cover myself as I squeezed against the back wall. I forced my mind and body to put God's protective veil between me and this woman and imposed all possible barriers between us. But no sooner had she watched as I calmed down and avoided looking at her than she too leapt to her feet and stripped off her prison clothes.

"Look," she upbraided me, "here's my body. See how they've carved trenches on my back! There's hardly a bone or muscle that the ghoul and others have not destroyed with electric shocks and various other torture devices. Now that you've seen all this, can you still accuse me of being a spy or infiltrator?"

"But you're the one," I responded bashfully as I looked at her cuts and bruises, "who started things by accusing me of evil intentions . . ."

She put her clothes back on and then sat down with a sigh.

"You're right," she said. "Suspicion and caution are both rampant, spreading like a cancer among us, even those people who have experienced the dungeon and humiliating torture. Those tyrant pigs have managed to completely subvert documents and roles. Companions in misery have turned into enemies—may God destroy them all and bring their own treachery down on them!"

From the way she was talking, this new cell mate of mine seemed both badly scarred and yet perceptive.

"By the way," she went on, "the fact that your number and the cell's are the same is not a pretext. The fact that this complex is packed with prisoners means that no prisoner can regard a cell as being his own. Many times they've put me in cells with women; and at other times with men. All too often men have used the situation to take advantage of my body and destroy my honor. Don't be scared. I'm not going to seduce you or rape you as hired female prisoners sometimes do. Like them, I may have syphilis or AIDS, but I swear by the God whom I fear, I'm not going to infect anyone with any disease I might have contracted. That even applies to my enemies and people who've done me wrong . . ."

She suddenly fell silent and closed her eyes, as though by suppressing her tears she could somehow control her emotions. At this point I took a look at her face, with its attractive but harsh features. She was forty or so, and her already thin body had clearly been worn out by starvation and violence. Her hair was streaked with hints of grey that gave her appearance and speech a staid and august tinge.

"So, my dear servant of God," I asked her as tenderly as I could, "tell me about yourself. Who are you, and what has brought you to this appalling center?"

She smiled as she wiped her eyes and then gave me a look filled with a profound sadness. Moving over to sit beside me, she took a pair of white gloves out of her pocket and put them on my hands.

"Rub my back for me," she said. "That'll give me some relief while I tell you part of my life story. My stage name is Fayruz, and my companions honored me by giving me that name because they thought I was the best imitator of the famous and much beloved Lebanese singer, Fayruz. My dear fellow believer, my situation is exactly the same as yours, except with regard to the particulars of our personal situations. We're both victims of injustice and dark times, oppressed and totally crushed until we are broken, at the beck and call of tyrants and subject to their Fascist projects and evil intentions. For reasons I don't understand they transferred me from the Abu Ghraib prison in Iraq to here. Their only question asks me to provide the names and addresses of nationalist, Shi'i and Communist resistance fighters to whose organizations I belong. My traitorous husband betrayed some of them, so I shot him in the head and left him dead. For two years now the very worst American torture experts have been wearing me out with their cross-examinations and torture, but my Job-like endurance has defeated them. With cross in hand, I have decided to be a martyr and to meet my Lord whenever He wishes and ordains. Is the river supposed to behave differently, I ask myself, simply because its source bursts forth and the distant sea pulls its course toward it?!"

I now understood that this woman was an Iraqi Christian resistance fighter.

"May God grant you long life, my Lady!" I told her with admiration, "and record you as one of those pious saints and freedom fighters who deserve respect in this world and the delights of paradise in the next. You mentioned that you were transferred here from the Abu Ghraib prison in Iraq. Where exactly are we here?"

"I don't know precisely," she replied, "but I get the impression that we're in a desert location either in the African continent or somewhere close to it. But God knows . . . I'm feeling tired and I need to sleep. God willing and if I'm still alive, I can tell you more about myself tomorrow and hear your story as well."

Hardly had she completed this sentence before the cell was invaded by four guards who grabbed her off my bed and dragged her forcibly outside, totally oblivious to my shouts and protests. They simply made do with swearing at me, calling me a fornicator, and threatening to come back for me.

"My name's Hamuda al-Wajdi," I yelled as they pulled her out. "Hang on and be strong; God is with you!"

"If God is not with people like us," she yelled back, giving me the victory sign, "then who is He with? Tell me, who is He with?!"

From the entrance to my cell and all along the corridor I could hear her Fayruz-like voice singing to the accompaniment of other prisoners' voices and applause:

Radiant fury is on its way.
    And all of me is a believer.
Radiant fury is on its way,
    And I shall forget about sorrows.

From every direction it comes,
It comes with fearsome steeds.

There followed a sudden silence. Stretching out on my side, I started singing Fayruz's glorious and defiant song; at the words "radiant fury is on its way" I kept punching my pillow and crying. But my chronic cough forced me to stop. I managed to suppress it by squirting spray into my open mouth, something that was especially necessary since some of my neighbor prisoners were vying with each other in urging me to ask for a transfer to the TB wing. With a good deal of effort I managed to get it under control and stop coughing. All I could think about at this point was what kind of awful things might be happening to Fayruz; I also thought about my own situation and the fact that, by dint of sheer endurance, I had managed to exhaust all the vicious and criminal activities of my torturers. It felt as though, according to their rules, I had now become a hopeless case, someone with no potential benefit or utility. Wrapping myself in my flimsy loincloth, I consigned some of these thoughts to my collection of notes, as follows:

I'm no Job, Hercules, or even 'Antara, the pre-Islamic poet-cavalier. In any case, if even people with their fortitude and endurance were to find themselves at the mercy of the ghouls and sadists in this rendition center where I've now spent any number of years, their sense of terror and oppression would be just as bad as my own. My body is broken and my soul feels shattered. Even so, I'm not defeated yet; in fact, I'm convinced that the only way they'll defeat me is with a single terminal blow—and that is something the higher authorities are hesitating to do in my particular case, because they're eager to destroy me and make me grovel and beg for mercy. As it is, staying alive in this virtual death situation doesn't bother me anymore. My only value and significance, I have decided, lies in putting a spanner in their works and a thorn in the soles of their feet. Dear God, thwart all their efforts to enslave me and crush my honor, and protect my mind from all harm and loss of control, even though I may at times have to pretend to be crazy for some particular purpose I have in mind.

This experience of imprisonment has taught me something I did not know. It has revealed certain proclivities and stimuli within me of which I was not previously aware and indeed never even supposed that I possessed. In those earlier days of my clearly mistaken sense of freedom, you could apply to me the words of a writer whose name now escapes me, but this is approximately what he wrote: 'Many, many are the rains and winds to which my body has been exposed in a quest for the sweet scent of sanctity and a modicum of happiness. But all their raging fury brought me was a severe cold and a bronchial cough!'

Hardly had I written down that last sentence before the four men who had dragged Fayruz away reentered my cell. I quickly shoved my notes under the bedcover and uncovered my face. The guard told me to stand up and accused me of fornication.

"We've just given that slut we dragged from under you a hundred lashes," another man said, "and we're going to do the same with you very soon."

I told them that their accusation had no validity because there were no witnesses, to which the third responded that they were the witnesses, four of them. In legal terms, that was quite sufficient. He now ordered me to collect my possessions and get ready, whereupon I showed them my swollen feet with their wounds, all the while cursing them for their false testimony and calling down God's vengeance on them. I gave them the choice: they could either carry me on their shoulders or else provide me with a crutch. However, I then recommended an intermediate solution that would work for everyone, if only for a while.

"And what's that?" they asked.

"That you leave my cell and let me be."

After a bit of argument they silently withdrew—wonder of wonders!—with heads lowered.

Accusations of fornication, threats of a hundred lashes, followed by the incredible way the guards had responded to my last suggestion, all those things were clearly part of the evil intrigues and games being played by Luqman, the investigating judge—May God never show me either his face or his shadow! He might well decide to send me another woman who would swing between promises and enticement at one point and curses and intimidation at another. But, through the strength and power of Almighty God, he would discover that I remained steadfast to the pledge and rock solid in my chaste behavior.

My thoughts now turned to Fayruz and the way in which the old scars on her back would have been inflamed by a hundred new lashes. I now recalled the wonderful words she had used: "Is the river supposed to behave differently, simply because its source bursts forth and the distant sea pulls its course toward it?" That's a saying that demands contemplation and interpretation; it's one that, if I ever manage to be rid of my suffering and escape from this diabolical center, I dearly hope to sit and explore in all its various dimensions and significances. And I am still thinking of cracking the code of the little containers that my fellow townsperson Na'ima had given me and understanding their underlying message.

There was a knock on the door indicating that I should take my lunch. I replied that I was not going to stand up or eat until they brought me two crutches and bandaged my feet. The guard came in, put down the plate by me, and then left, saying: "All the messenger can do is to convey the message."

I covered the plate with a cloth so the insects, rats, and mice would not smell it. I stayed there, flat on my back, staring at a tiny aperture in the skylight and gauging the passage of time by the way the light changed. I kept wondering what would transpire as a result of my request and my refusal to eat.

From the other cells adjacent to my own there emerged a variety of sounds: one person was reciting verses from the Qur'an; another was inviting his neighbors to listen to his tales as a peerless dormitory storyteller, and still another was suggesting that we all listen to his sex jokes with a particularly Marrakeshian quality to them. As the din grew louder and louder, a powerful, gruff voice with a tone like a bugle yelled: "Quiet!! Quiet! No more noise for the rest of the day. Time will tell, as the old saying goes. Democracy demands that people take turns to talk. Anyone who causes trouble will be shown no mercy or sympathy."

These words were the cue for a total silence to reign over the entire cellblock. I kept waiting for the storm to break, but nothing of the kind happened. As the atmosphere of silence spread, accompanied by a lacerating cold that promised a freezing, rainless winter, I huddled under my blanket and surrendered all my fears and concerns to a restless slumber prompted by Morpheus or some other sleep promoter . . .

17

Appointment with the Disciplinary Committee

When I woke up, my memory was still recalling snippets from a dream in which my cousin, al-Husayn, appeared and asked me to forgive him for the things that had now happened to me because of him. He told me that he had not given me any information about his resistance activities so that I could avoid any suspicion or complication that might have dire consequences. However, the blind, raging fury of the despots had managed to ruin his sincere wishes and intentions toward me. After calling down all kinds of eloquent and pointed curses on such people, he advised me to remain steadfast in the face of their atrocities so that the word of God should eventually emerge triumphant. He then disappeared from view, accompanied by a group of armed men who made for the forests of some daunting lofty mountain peaks.

My response to his image was one that I framed once I had woken up. I proceeded to write it down immediately:

"You're not at fault in what has happened to me, al-Husayn. You've done nothing wrong. You're so right: endurance is now my richest resort and patience in adversity is a natural instinct. So rest assured about me and concentrate your attention on your own situation and that of your men—and may God grant you all such success as He desires."

I wonder now whether it was just to pass the time or rather to suppress the rampant hunger I was feeling that I fainted or else fell asleep, but only after I had hidden away my notes.

The thing that woke me up again with a jolt was the noise of pounding feet in the cellblock as a whole squad of detectives arrived to search every cell, inside and out. The majority of them were for-eigners. When a group of them entered my cell, the senior one told me to stand up and face the wall, with my hands up. I showed them my feet, and they understood that I was crippled. They lifted me off my bed and used an electrical device to check all over my body. My pockets were emptied, and the contents were carefully examined. The man gave me back my spray, but kept Na'ima's little containers. Now everything around me was searched both by hand and with the same electrical device. One of them showed me my containers, mir-ror, notes, and old magazines and asked me in awful Arabic what else I had. Was I concealing hashish, a knife, a razor, bribes? I shook my head. Once they had left, I waddled over to my now rumpled bed and collapsed on it, thinking all the while about the fact that my notes had been taken away and what evil consequences might ensue as a result.

The fact that I was staying away from the cafeteria, the court-yard, and the recreation area may well have convinced the authori-ties that I was in danger of becoming completely paralyzed and that my hunger strike was serious. Only a few hours after this group of detectives had left, two male nurses arrived and transported me to the hospital on a stretcher. Someone started tending and bandaging my feet while another person force-fed me using a plastic tube that he stuck up my nose and down into my stomach. I had no choice but to endure the variety of pain that these twin operations caused me. Even so, I managed to spend some of the time thinking about Na'ima and her friend, the foreign doctor, about both of whom, as a precau-tionary matter, I had declined to ask for any information.

Once the two nurses had finished their task, they stood me up on two fresh crutches and handed me over to a portly guard with a shaved head. Looking at his watch, he took me to a lower level in the same hospital building and positioned me in front of a small table facing a huge dais. Two men and a woman now emerged from a door at the back and sat down on their chairs, whispering to each other. They were then joined by the female ghoul, who placed headphones over her ears, and Na'ima herself—yes indeed, Na'ima—who had a file under her arm. They sat at either end of the table. I assumed that the people whom I did not know had some particular function at the detention center. The guard whispered in my ear that I was in the presence of the Disciplinary Committee. After sitting me down, he stationed himself behind my back, holding on to my neck.

The woman was the first to speak, reading out a text that identified who I was. Once she had finished, she asked me to confirm the information that she had read out. I nodded my agreement, but the guard cuffed me on the neck and instructed me to stand up and respond "Yes, Madam President," so I did so. She asked me to remain standing and to observe a minute of silence out of respect for a dead lady who had passed away. I did as she asked. Once the minute had passed, I asked her to tell me who had died.

"Your mother," she replied gruffly. "We have the information from a reliable source."

I collapsed on to the chair, thunderstruck and grief-stricken. But then I got a grip on myself, deciding that the resort to this grotesque method of talking about my mother was clearly a pack of lies; the only purpose had to be to make me crack.

"We are members of the august Disciplinary Committee," the woman went on. "We've taken a look at the document about you and deduced from the investigative judge's report that you're a stubborn person, determined and resolute. You have displayed a remarkable ability to absorb blows and joined the hit parade in your willingness to tolerate pain; you deserve a gold medal for both. The judge actually characterizes you as a masochist, someone who relishes the thought of pain being inflicted on him. Such a group is as valuable as it's rare. For that reason your own cooperation is of extreme interest to the directors of this center. They are prepared to accept—indeed, they actually desire—that you should join the service. Your health would be restored; your accusations would be dropped, including that of murdering your neighbor, the man with the bag, and that of fornicating with the woman who calls herself Fayruz. We're willing to overlook all your crimes and faults, including your apparent craving for pornographic literature, your hunger strike, and so on and so on. All that would come in exchange for your signature on a document to join the service. What do you have to say?"

With the greatest imaginable difficulty, I managed to stand up and I raised a point of order in the usual fashion:

"Madam," I declared, "it may be that my dear mother has gone to her God, but I will only believe it if you can produce a proper death certificate. With regard to those accusations, I hereby proclaim my innocence, be they old or new. The accusations of fornication and a craving for lewd literature are a pack of lies, and . . ."

"And what about your role in the death of your neighbor, the man with the bag?" asked one of the two men, a frivolous Tirimmah*-like figure, tall and lanky.

"I only ever heard that neighbor's voice, Sir," I replied. "I never even saw him. The contexts of the bag were excrement . . . shit."

The guard now gave me a cuff that sank me to the chair again.

"Clean up your language, you ass" he yelled at me, "when you're in the presence of this distinguished committee!"

The Tirimmah figure and his dumpy colleague now proceeded to pin me down with a whole host of questions. Still seated, I proceeded to interrupt them with another point of order.

"I've been on hunger strike before, and they force-fed me with a tube. As a token of the determination that you referred to earlier, I'm now proposing to strike from any further discussion until you remove this gorilla attached to my back."

A moment of silence followed, then the woman gestured to the guard to leave, and he did so.

The woman now resumed her cross-examination, asking me a series of short questions. I duly responded, with corresponding brevity.

"What about those plastic containers?" she asked me pointedly.

Na'ima was busy recording the conversation, and I avoided looking at her.

"They were in the trash bin at the clinic," I replied.

"Why did you steal them?"

"To play with in my spare time."

"And the mirror you had hidden away?"

"To look at the bruises on my body from the torture and to count them."

The Tirimmah man now muttered something and then yelled at me, "Or was it for killing someone or committing suicide?"

"I have no right to kill myself, something that God Himself has forbidden, or to kill anyone else."

"No matter. Let's get to the important point. The investigative committee has come across an article by some unknown writer about the Arab-Israeli conflict. You've written on some of the pages. Do you support its findings?"

"The article is from a newspaper. It's one of the newspapers and magazines that someone put in my cell; I've no idea who. You've looked at it too, no doubt. I've scribbled notes on those paragraphs because I believe them to be important and correct. Remind me of some part of it . . ."

"Just a few parts, because of the time. 'From the Israeli stand-point Palestinians must choose between submission and obedience on the one hand and exile or martyrdom on the other. So how are we supposed to put any faith in Western concepts of justice and humanity and assess them according to the yardsticks of necessity and comprehensiveness?'"

"So," I asked eagerly, focusing on the quotation," how do you respond to that trenchant question?"

"We're the ones asking the questions," the Tirimmah person yelled.

I was totally unafraid to speak the truth at this point.

"Oh yes," I went on in a reproachful tone, "now I remember that the writer, whom I regard as a truly outstanding model of just and liberal ideas, goes on to say; 'I can see no reasonable justification for punishing Arabs for Nazi crimes, nor can I detect the slightest legality during the current crisis in initiating an expansionist movement based on references in the Torah . . . '"

"So you agree with all these assertions?" the dumpy man asked.

"Yes," I replied, "and I also agree with the way the article ends: 'The Arab struggle against Israel and its supporters is the other aspect of their struggle against their own weakness and backwardness . . .'"

"This writer of yours comes close to anti-Semitism and Holocaust denial. Do you also deny that?"

"I did not read any such thing in the article in question. If by the Holocaust you mean the massacre that the Nazis committed against European Jewry with the aim of eradicating them altogether, then Israel as a state, both before its creation and throughout the period of its existence, has been emulating the same massacre in their treatment of the Palestinians. It has involved repression and requisition, breaking bones, a continuous seizure of land, and destruction of houses and whole quarters. Every day the Palestinian sense of honor is belittled, and they find themselves thrust into detention camps. Their holy sites are desecrated, their ancient sites are Judaized, not to mention their trees and rocks. As the old battle lament puts it, 'O Mu'tasim!'"*

"That's enough nonsense, enough!" the Tirimmah person yelled, shouting me down and emphasizing it by beating his gavel on the table. "Let's turn to the most important point here: Your letter to your cousin who is a wanted man . . ."

"It wasn't a letter," I interrupted. "It was just some thoughts I jotted down from a dream I had in which my cousin, al-Husayn, appeared."

"Where did you see him?"

"On top of a high mountain with streams and trees. I have no idea where it was . . ."

"And what did he tell you?" the dumpy man yelled at me threateningly.

"The gist was that he loved me and thought about me so much that he had never told me anything about his personal fight. That was a way of saving me from suspicions or complications that might have dire consequences."

"How many fighters was he commanding?"

"I only saw him . . ."

"Can you swear that you did not notice any other people with him?"

"It was just a dream. What am I supposed to swear to?"

"True enough!" the woman commented. "Now you can return to your cell. You should think very carefully about our offer for you to join our service. You can communicate your eventual decision to the investigating judge. Don't burn all your notes. Use the ones you have left well, and there'll be more. The session is now concluded."

I could not help bursting into laughter.

"You talk about my notes, Madam!" I said. "Ever since I arrived at this detention center, I haven't had any notes to burn, not a single one or even several . . ."

I looked briefly at Na'ima, who was leaving the room by the back door along with the committee members. Leaning on my two crutches, I stood up and went over to my scowling guard. Covering his face, he asked me gruffly if I wanted to have my feet tended to. When I said that I did, he told me to follow him.

In the clinic, I was examined by a doctor who looked like a surgeon and was wearing a blood-stained apron. He might have been a butcher coming from a slaughter house or something like that. Arching his eyebrows, he spoke to me from behind his medical mask. He told me that my left leg was very swollen and purulent; gangrene was starting to show. In a few days it might be necessary to amputate. I begged him to do it immediately, but the guard who was standing next to me told him that would not happen till I have told them everything I was keeping to myself.

"By God," I told him, "I've told you everything I know."

The guard stood me up on my feet and ordered me to leave with him. Even though I was feeling dizzy and weak, I kept walking, my assumption being that the doctor's prognosis was yet another of the fiendish tricks and games being played on me by the investigative judge—may God never again show me his face!

If only it were possible for me to get rid of this heavy-handed and heavy-footed spy! Then I could go on my own and take a look at other wings and spaces in this center that I had never seen. I would be able to meet other human beings whom I had never met, even though I sensed their existence and surmised that they might be living in conditions that were even more foul and cruel than the ones to which I was accustomed. But my guard stuck close to me until he had delivered me to my cell, the very location of my weakness and frustration. Before he locked the door and went away, I asked him why he had covered his face.

"So I don't have to smell the prisoners' disgusting stench," he replied, "yours among them."

What curs they are! Worse than children with no faith or creator! When it comes to the water supply, they are particularly stingy: the daily ration is no more than half a bucket, and from that you have to drink, do your ablutions, wipe your backside, and rinse parts of your body. They then proceed to blame you because it smells bad, the stench of their very essence and elemental nature which is, by God, even worse; all the waters and perfumes of this world are of no use in getting rid of it. I thought about explaining such things to my veiled guard, but I felt so tired and disillusioned that I saw no point in doing so.

Once I had lain down on my bed, I discovered that my neighbors were asleep, which was very unusual. I could not hear any snoring, although maybe some of them were like me, concealing their pains and anxieties in either total silence or else in muted groans and secret expressions of misery.

18

The Condition of My Leg Worsens and the Block Starts to Sway

Next morning, I was sipping my coffee and chewing a few morsels of bread when I suddenly remembered a dream in which my mother had appeared alive and healthy. Standing in the middle of a group of women, she was weeping and wailing as she complained to God about her bereavement and misery. She kept begging Him to encompass her one and only son in His great mercy and forgiveness. When the women tried to calm her down and tell her that I was sure to come back, she slapped her thighs at times and raised her hands to the heavens at others.

"I know my son!" she groaned. "Even if he were in the deepest pit imaginable, he would never forget me and neglect to send me a card. Either the earth has consumed him or he's been swallowed by the great whale."

No, Mother, it's not that. It's the tyrannical ghouls of darkness who are doing their very best to rip me apart and destroy my resolve. Even so, I'm still standing firm, thanks to God's help and satisfaction with me, your son who has always done well by you and has never spoken ill to you.

My enforced incapacity made it difficult for me to move about the cell; some of my urgent functions involved my crawling. Even the guards preferred not to have to accompany me to the general refectory and the exercise yard. This same exemption also covered cleaning dishes in the main kitchen, sweeping halls and corridors, and

132

cleaning the cells of prisoners who were sick or incapacitated, except for my own cell, of course.

I now concentrated on the state of my left leg and trying to distract my mind from the overwhelming sense of frustration and claustrophobia. When the guard brought me my subsistence rations, I begged him to bring me pencil and paper. He asked for some form of compensation, and I promised to pray for him and his loved ones. He laughed in my face at first, but then asked me seriously whether my prayers were answered. I told him that, if intentions were good and came from a soul that was both believing and severely tested like mine, God might well answer them, He being the generous provider.

"I'll bring you what you've requested either with lunch or later," he told me earnestly. "But you have to say a prayer for me first. From my first wife I have a daughter who is still unmarried at the age of thirty. Pray that she may find a decent man to marry. My second wife has only given me daughters, but now she's pregnant again. Pray to God that this time she'll give birth to a boy."

I responded to his request as best I could, and he hurried off grateful and happy. On the positive side, I made a note that for the first time since I had come to this detention center, I had exchanged some genuinely humane words with one of the guards, even though at this point I still could not guarantee that there would be a good outcome.

In the cellblock opposite ours, there was now a good deal of unusual activity. I crawled across to the door to listen and look at what was going on. I noticed that the guards and supervisors were busy moving some prisoners—the sick or dead—and replacing them with others whose foot-pounding and general din suggested that they were many in number. They had all been given the task of sweeping and cleaning their new cells.

This new influx made me happy, since its sheer size was creating the kind of activity that might be able, if only to a certain extent, to eradicate the rust of utter boredom and stifling loneliness. It might also succeed in limiting the effects of a rainless and perishingly cold winter.

My hopes were not in vain, in that, at dinnertime, when the new prisoners had rested for a while, a loud voice invited the block's residents to come to their doors. Using my crutches, I did as the voice asked. Here is some of what I heard:

"Servants of God . . . these tyrants have decreed against us such things as God Almighty and all legal systems have forbidden. I and some of your new neighbors have spent two years and more in Block 7, known to its custodians as Olympic Hell or the Torture Hit-Parade Laboratory. In their warped view that place is enough to make Qays* deny his own Layla and 'Antara* abandon his 'Abla. Some inmates have died of illnesses, others have taken their own lives after going mad—may God forgive them! And, in full view of people susceptible to terror, still others have been executed in killing fields and forced to dig their own graves—may God shroud them all in the wideness of His mercy and install them in His heavens. Verily to God do we all belong, and unto Him is the return!

"Your humble addresser and his colleagues who remain alive have now been placed in this wing—for just a while perhaps— because our torturers have grown tired of us. They have preferred us to vacate the space so they can bring in other people who they think are less steadfast and strong in enduring the kind of hellish torture that I've just mentioned . . .

"Fellow prisoners . . . We new occupants of these cells are no angels, infallible and without sin, nor do we belong to any mystical fraternities or other ascetic communities. We're just like you. We've chosen to live a life of freedom and honor and have devoted our lives to that cause, even though it may involve pain and suffering for which we would seek no alternative. Our choice is the same as yours; for us, it is the balance that enlightens, the guarantor of eternal life, and the self-evident triumph. In times of trial and tribulation it alone transforms us into hot coals beneath the ashes and strengthens our resolve and our endurance, bringing our deeds into line with our aspirations . . .

"Dear God, I have come to an end. Let us make ready for our group the means of ease and contentment and for the time we have here that which will make it both tolerable and useful. As God Almighty says in the Sura of Joseph (Sura 12): 'We will tell you the best of stories,' while in 'Ali ibn Abi Talib's* *Durar* we find: 'Like iron, hearts can turn rusty. So you should offer them some pearls of wisdom.'"

The preacher's voice suddenly stopped. I realized the reason when a whole column of guards invaded the block and told the prisoners to remain silent and move back into their cells. We could then clearly hear their commander launching into a tirade of insults, from among which I managed to glean the following: "You lousy conspirator, you phony devotee, you promised me to stop proselytizing. Now you've broken your promise, so our only choice is to cut your tongue out. Gag his mouth and take him to the place where he'll get his just deserts in front of witnesses . . ."

No sooner had the guard troop left the block than a scary silence descended, only amplified by the advent of darkness. Prisoners now wrapped themselves up in their blankets in an attempt to ward off the icy cold of nighttime. I did as they did, particularly since it was now clear that we would not be getting any dinner. We had paid too much attention to the preacher, who was the object of such opprobrium and had failed either to confront him or use deterrent language and accusations of heresy to shut him up.

My diseased leg was now causing me pain all over, even though I did my best to suppress it. Added to which, O God my Creator, was chronic insomnia and a whole series of spotted images that crowded my mind, all of which combined to make me want to scream out loud and ask for help. The only thing that stopped me from doing so was my worry that I would wake up my neighbors and disturb their sleep. For that reason I made do with uttering a few low-keyed groans that were only audible to me, like someone struck low with diarrhea.

I stayed like this, with only God being aware of my sufferings, till night was almost at an end. Just then, a cry rang out: a prisoner was asking for a clamp so he could pull out a tooth that was hurting. I listened as a number of voices rounded on him, while others advised him to grin and bear it till the morning guard arrived. All the while, the poor man kept groaning in pain and mouthing deeply moving words to the effect that the chief nurse in the clinic had told him that he would only fix his tooth if he provided the names and addresses of a Salafi* mafia group that they claimed he belonged to, whereas in fact he did not. He kept on shouting and asking the prisoners who were yelling at him what he was supposed to do. Suddenly his yelling stopped abruptly, as though he had fainted or else he had been gagged and taken away.

"Some people's troubles are other people's boons," as the poet al-Mutanabbi* tells us. That was certainly the case with my present situation. My concern about this other prisoner in pain distracted my attention from my own problems, and the fact that he may have suffered dire consequences made me give thanks to God for suppressing my own pain. That was in spite of the fact that, according to my own reckoning and physical senses, my own pains were far worse than a mere toothache, even if it involved a molar. After such feelings of gratitude and the distraction evolved, I succumbed to a much needed slumber that felt for all the world like a drug-induced stupor.

19

Another of the Judge's Whims

My Appointment as Mufti

The way I woke up this morning was unusual—in fact, unprecedented. The sound of drums and clarinet echoed through the block, accompanied by the din as my neighbors jumped up and started asking questions. I was totally stunned and amazed when a music group made up of two men invaded my cell, preceded by the gigantic black guard carrying two platters on his head. I was sitting there with my two crutches beside me as he put them both down in front me. No sooner had his two companions stopped their playing than one of them came forward, cleaned my hands, then placed my right hand on a copy of the Qur'an on a platter, and asked me to swear. I asked him what about.

"Swear first," he replied, "and then we'll tell you why."

When I refused, the second man had no choice but to take a document out of his sleeve and hand it to me, using a duly gruff tone to claim that it was an official document licensing me as mufti and signed by his excellency, the judge. No preacher, whether of the mystical or orthodox variety, would challenge it. He went on to tell me that the two platters and the clothes, food, and drink on them were all a gift from the judge to the newly appointed mufti, a celebratory gesture on the occasion of my promotion and the bestowal of such bounty on me.

I lowered my head and swallowed hard, both astonished and annoyed at the extent to which this idiotic and corrupt judge was prepared to take things. I said nothing for a while, as I made ready to give a trenchant answer to this sinister and self-interested proposal. All the while, my neighbors were spreading the word, reacting angrily to what the ones closest to me were telling them about the goings-on inside my cell. Loud voices were raised, some accusing me of being a spy and agent, while others confirmed the impression by noting that I regularly spent long hours with the judge and received special treatment. I had a single cell to myself and now had been given two platters with who knows what kind of good things on them. Another one protested that he had once spotted me wearing a decent suit and tie, not to mention the Nike shoes he had seen me strutting around in. All their voices were now united as they proceeded to curse all traitors and informers like me and promised me that God and His servants would wreak the very worst punishment on me . . .

I used my two crutches to stand up and informed my visitors that this new promotion demanded that I make a tour of my neighbors.

"Not until you swear the oath," the platter carrier objected.

"The tour first," was my response.

The two musicians argued with each other at first, but then they and the giant black man went out ahead of me. I walked the entire length of the block on my two crutches.

"God is sufficient for me," I yelled as loudly as I could, "and good is He as a trustee! The people I'm helping are letting me down."

I kept repeating these phrases as often as I could, and eventually they stopped their taunts and curses. I now uncovered my swollen, pus-filled leg.

"My fellow prisoners," I told them, "how can your accusation possibly apply to someone like me who has to use crutches to walk and whose leg is supposed to be amputated? Our torturers are making my treatment conditional on cooperating with them and being a spy. I stand completely innocent of the charges you are leveling at me! I pray to God to give you all forgiveness and pray to His almighty power that he will save us all from this dire experience that tyrants have imposed on us all, using all kinds of tricks and subterfuges to sow suspicion and dissension in our ranks. O God, protect us with Your mercy and forgiveness. Lessen for us the trials of aspiring towards You. Grant us the necessary strength and fortitude, but do not make us reliant on our own feeble and troubled souls. O God, intensify Your punishment for all those who tyrannize and do evil on earth. Carry out Your threats against them on this earth before the next world. Amen! Our final prayer is one of praise to God, the Lord of the two worlds!"

All the prisoners were by the doors of their cells, clinging on to the bars. As I pronounced each prayer, they all said "Amen!" They stretched out their hands in greeting and asked me to forgive them. Some of them had tears in their eyes. The gigantic black man kept looking back and forth between me and his two companions, and I noticed that signs of emotion, and even tears, were clear on his enormous face and his reddened eyes.

When I thought it was time to bring this manifestation to an end, for fear of dire consequences, I made my way back to my cell, followed by the three men. The clarinet player stopped me and reminded me breathlessly about the oath.

"I will not swear any oath," I declared in a clearly audible voice that undoubtedly would reach as far as my closest neighbors. "I reject the post and will have nothing to do with it. I also refuse to accept the two platters and their contents. Inform your master that prisoner number 112 protests against his current situation, citing in the process the most important figures in jurisprudence where they say: 'Those who try to render legal judgments without learning are like people who pick grapes before they're ripe.'"

Many voices now relayed what I had just said, either directly or from the prisoners closest to me who had heard it. Their tones varied. Some of them chose to acknowledge and value its rectitude; others to explicate its context and significance; still others to ask what the word *tazabbab* (pick grapes) meant in Arabic. I decided not to get involved in these issues, but went into my cell, giving the giant black man an affectionate glance, especially since he stopped the two men from taking the gift away and stuck closely to them as they left.

After a few moments to recover my breath, something that I presumed all my fellow prisoners were doing, I leaned over to take a look at the two platters. I noticed that there was a megaphone on one of them, presumably something that the judge wanted me to use to announce my opinions.

"Fellow prisoners in this block and the entire wing," I said, grabbing it with delight, "in order to fulfill the pledge I made to you, here is an account of what is on the two platters. One of them contains various kinds of hors d'oeuvres and fruit, both fresh and dried, and bottles of milk and water; the other has a copy of the Qur'an and the two great volumes of commentary,* a prayer mat, rosary, cloak, headcap, shawl, house clothes, sandals, a water pipe along with pieces of ambergris and incense, a perfume bottle, and lastly, a transistor radio. The entire gift is now at your disposal, to distribute among yourselves amicably and with all due liberality."

I now heard several voices declaring that the items in question were clearly my property, fair and square. One single voice could be heard above the others, praising me for my unequivocal refusal to accept the position of mufti offered by the administration. However, on behalf of his fellow prisoners he asked me nevertheless to avail them of my advice and counsel, all in fulfillment of the statement of our blessed ancestors: "religion as counsel . . ."

When the guards made their rounds, the voices stopped and silence prevailed once again. I took advantage of the situation and lay down on my back, relishing the relaxation and looking at my cache of gifts on the tray, with its eats and drinks. As I was testing the smallest transistor radio I had ever seen and picking up a fuzzy, weak signal in some foreign language, I happened to notice a cavity at the bottom of the wall opposite my bed. At first I thought it must be a mouse looking for a way out, but there soon emerged a reinforced cardboard tube, through which I heard the voice of someone who introduced both himself and the tube as a telephone linking the prisoners in the cells. When he asked me if I was on the air, I replied that I was. No sooner had he made sure that the line was good than he told me that he had a whole cluster of questions about the situation of the majority of prisoners. He had collected them all and selected the most intelligent ones. The thrust of some of them was to ask whether it was legitimate to mention God's name—may He be exalted!—in a prison such as this one, polluted as it was with some many outrages and enormities, not to mention stenches of every conceivable kind.

"The mention of God's name," I replied, my mouth close to the tube's aperture, "is not only permissible, it is required, and frequently at that; all in order to bolster the soul in its steadfast resistance to the trials and tribulations we are all facing. It was the same way with the original Muslims in pre-Islamic times when wine, gambling, idols, fortune-telling, animism, and female child burial were all common practice . . ."

The same voice now continued in a quavering tone, asking questions framed by the notion that there should be no bashfulness where religion is involved. The brunt of the question involved prisoners who were suffering from diarrhea, constipation, and hemorrhoids, and others who were ejaculating whether asleep or awake. Some of the latter—God forbid!—could not control their sexual instincts; no sooner did they set eyes on a female prisoner, guard, or typist than they ejaculated. Another group, whose questions were closely related to those of this last one, was asking about the law's view of their need to masturbate as a way of relieving their feelings of frustration and sexual denial. In all these cases and others like them, the primary issue involved the meager supply of water they were getting, which made it impossible for them to wash themselves and remove their impurities, something that in turn nullified both their ritual ablutions and prayers.

I proceeded to answer these questions one by one, projecting them through the tube to the person who was now virtually the communal communicator. I recited Qur'anic verses about times of anxiety and hardship, and others dealing with kinder and easier moments. I mentioned the need to keep such difficulties to oneself; in times of hardship and cruelty, necessities could render undesirable conduct legitimate. I counseled them all to remain devout, to perform the prayers of fear, illness, and imprisonment. I categorically forbade any of them who were either ill or incapacitated to fast during Ramadan and other times in case they subjected themselves and their health to potential danger . . .

"It's the messenger's task to pass on what he hears," the other voice said. "By God's power I'll convey your words to the people who asked the questions. I can hear guards' footsteps. Cover up the hole with soil. If they happen to notice it one day—heaven forbid!—then blame it on mice and rats. That'll be a good excuse, and you'll be safe."

That was the last thing the voice said before the tube rapidly disappeared. I followed his instructions about the hole, then stayed where I was, staring at my surroundings. The food distributor looked in and stared at the platter in a way that suggested that the gift I had received would last me for days and days, lucky me!

The giant black guard—God grant him a good reward!—had wanted me to have the platter of food and drink for myself alone. If I left it untouched, it would undoubtedly be eaten by the rodents and insects. I had to assume that the food and drink did not contain any deadly poison because the judge who had ordered it sent to me still wanted me alive so he could implement his fiendish plan to use me as a co-opted spy, mufti, and so on. I lunched on some bread, dates, and milk, then poured some water over my face, and stretched out to performed such prayers as I could, training myself in the process to get some rest and peace of mind, both of which I genuinely needed.

While I was relaxing in this way, I remembered the guard who had promised me to bring me pencil and paper, and for whom I had uttered the prayer he had requested of me. I found it odd that he had stayed away and felt sorry, hoping that there was a good reason for it. While I was indulging in these and other obscure thoughts and illusions, I fell into a deep, troubled sleep, which lasted well into the night. I was awakened by noises in the block, as a prisoner tried to appeal to the consciences of the nurses or anyone with an ounce of pity in him to rid him of the hemorrhoids that made it impossible for him to evacuate his bowels or sleep.

Some voices started shouting out my cell number, asking me to shut this prisoner up, by delivering a fatwa or offering him advice.

Through the megaphone I responded that I had no knowledge of medicine and pharmacology. Instead, I cited for him the story of the Sufi, a renowned advocate of modesty and salvation, who acquired his own share of hemorrhoids which became acutely painful. He managed to tolerate them till nobody heard any more about them and no one ever bothered to look at his private parts. He told some of his closest devotees that, before he was to die of some other disease, he had gone along with the tales of people and nations who had perished in times of yore, 'Ad, Thamud, and Pharaoh. Every time his pain became unbearable and acute, he had used their stories as a cooling fan . . .

Various voices now competed with each other to pass this piece of information along. Some of them termed it implicit advice on my part, and counseled the sick man to follow the advice so as to relieve himself of the pain and his colleagues of the sound of his groans. And that's what happened! Only a few minutes went by in the block—amazingly enough!—before absolute silence prevailed, and everyone was able to get back to sleep again. All of them thought that the solution was the consequence of my noble heart, but that was not the way I saw things. I lay there in my cell, consigning the last vestiges of darkness to their distant resting-place and awaiting the first signs of light.

When morning came, the guard whom I had been long awaiting finally arrived. He put breakfast down in front of me and kissed my head in thanks. I asked him why, and he responded delightedly in a loud voice that I begged him to lower.

"You, by Almighty God, are a genuine saint. Your prayers have been answered. My unmarried daughter has been married to a nice man, and my second wife has had a baby boy after only giving me daughters!"

"That is all from God's own bounty alone," I replied. "He alone deserves the praise. He is the Generous Giver."

"I'm giving you this bag of pencils and paper to fulfill my promise to you. You can expect even more from me if you can make another prayer for me . . ."

"Is it for something good?" I asked anxiously.

"It's all good as far as I am concerned. I want God to give my boss a heart attack so I can be rid of his violent ways and take his place."

"That's a nasty prayer to ask for, and the consequences are far from clear."

"Please don't say no. I kiss your hand . . ."

"I would need to know a lot more about you, your boss, the site of the center, and the identities of its bosses and directors."

"I only know a little bit about those things. If I revealed even that little to you, Saint of God, my head would roll before your prayer had even a chance to get rid of my boss . . . I have to go now before our relationship arouses suspicions . . ."

"Go then and think carefully. Let me do the same. However can you give some help to the sick people on this block?"

"I'll tell a female doctor whom I trust and some other nurses about their condition and yours. God be with you!"

I was longing to ask him if the doctor was the same one that I'd met in the clinic and who has treated me so kindly, but, before I could do so, the guard kissed me on the forehead and hurried out. I now turned to the breakfast tray and ate everything before it went cold. When I checked on my leg, I noticed that it was even more swollen; congealed blood in the veins was making the dark blue area spread even further. I hurriedly wrapped it in the mufti's scarf to protect it from the chill of the morning air, then took the undergarments from the table, put them on with a good deal of difficulty, and wrapped myself in the mufti's cloak under the blanket, where I decided to wait and see what would happen next.

As torture experts are well aware, boredom and routine are types of psychological torture that can be applied to break prisoners' wills, reduce their self-esteem to zero, and destroy them—all with the goal of making them compliant and submissive in mind and body. However, as I look back in time, I can see myself having cultivated a resistance, endurance, and steadfast posture of defiance. Now that I had been through so much and traveled so far, it was no time to crack up and give way. My leg might well have to be amputated, so let them do it! As for my asthma, well, it might hit me at any time. So, by the true work of the Creator, I shall either move forward to rescue and victory, even if it means crawling; or else I shall perish and surrender my soul, happy and sufficient, to its Creator.

I noted these thoughts down on my new notepad, and added some further comments in which I condemned lust and the humiliation of slavery and extolled the pure air of emancipation and liberal existence.

My activities were interrupted by noises through the tube from my neighbor. He began by thanking me on behalf of all the inmates in the block and himself for all the kind words of advice I had offered yesterday. He told me that they had all asked that I give them some of the dates and raisins from my platter to eat so they could all sweeten their own mouths and stomachs and share all the benefits with me. I was glad to do as they asked and passed as much as I could through the tube until only a little bit was left. A few moments later voices were raised, promising me dates and raisins in paradise; still others wished me well for interceding with the guards so that the sick people in the block could be transferred to the clinic for treatment—particularly those who kept screaming in pain and others who kept making vain attempts to suppress their agony. There was one voice, sounding like a bugle, who asked me to respond urgently to a series of questions that he described as being difficult. When your endurance is at an end, he asked, and your body is totally destroyed by torture, does the Shari'a law allow you to commit suicide? And, with the reference to God, is He with the crushers or the crushed? Are people allowed to listen to dirty jokes as a way of lightening the burden of weary and oppressed souls?

The entire place fell suddenly silent, as though the entire group was waiting for my responses. I paused for a while to think, then used my crutches to move over to the door, holding the megaphone.

"My brother," I said, "Shari'a law forbids outright anyone killing himself. 'Do not kill yourselves; God has been merciful to you' (Qur'an, Sura of Women, 4, v. 29). God Almighty's mercy demands of human beings that they endure suffering and misfortune. The idea that God should consort with wrongdoers and tyrants is abhorrent—Heaven forfend! God stands far above such a notion, He who never wrongs the slightest thing. He it is who addresses His prophet Noah who has to confront his rebellious nation: 'Do not address Me regarding those who have done wrong. They are drowned.' (Qur'an, Surat Hud, v. 37). With regard to jokes, the idea is to make time pass easily, not to kill it. The general purpose is to provide the soul with some solace and benefit. So, if someone has a store of tales that are disgusting, then he should let people know that his jokes are going to be like that. Modest and bashful people can then block their ears. If time and place were different, I could provide you with more elaborate answers . . ."

Hardly had I finished before a watchman whom I had never set eyes on before grabbed the megaphone from me and told me to stop talking and withdraw. I decided to do as he asked, whereupon he frowned threateningly at me and retraced his steps. I assume that his colleagues must have done the same thing with the other inmates of the block, because for a while everything suddenly went silent, interrupted by occasional throat-clearings and coughs. After a while another voice could be heard, chanting the Sura of Yasin. After cleaning my hands from the bottle, I followed the text in my copy of the Qur'an. When the voice finished chanting, I continued reading some other chapters from the Qur'an, using them as sources of divine inspiration to rid the soul of its dross and carry it aloft to the realms of contemplation and reflection.

20

From the Hospital to My Involvement in a Communal Burial

When I woke up and looked around, I saw the gigantic black guard leaning over me. He had a sympathetic look on his face as he removed the Qur'an from my chest and placed it on the platter with the thurible and perfume bottle. He then gave me a series of signals from which I deduced that he wanted me to accompany him to the hospital for treatment. His expression gave no other indications besides what he had just communicated to me, but nevertheless I indicated how delighted I was. He helped me get up, but I was so weak and giddy that he had to carry me on his shoulders, with my two crutches under his armpit. As he carried me slowly along the block, my neighbors stood by the cell doors, enthusiastically shouting my name and wishing me well: "Long live the Saint of God, Hamuda! Long live the hero, Hamuda! May he live long!" Some of them even prayed that I would be able to endure the torture that awaited me in the female ghoul's torture chamber, while others prayed to God and his faithful saints that they would help me endure my sufferings and bring me back alive to their quarters so they could benefit from my advice and I could explain to them what the word *tazabbab* meant in Arabic.

In the hospital operating room, my carrier put me down on a high bed on wheels, then left. He handed my crutches to an orderly and gave me a very affectionate glance. The orderly removed all my clothes and tossed them into a basket. He then washed every part of my body, dried it off, and sprinkled it with eau de cologne. He took my temperature and felt my pulse. With a penlight, he examined

147

my eyes and my mouth and felt the most sensitive parts of my body. While he was finishing his work and recording the results on a chart, a foreign-looking doctor came in wearing a mask. After checking the record and putting on a pair of gloves, he started taking a close look at my leg and giving it a close examination. It seemed as though he were deciding on its fate: either amputation or drugs and antibiotics. Eventually he whispered something to the orderly, which I did not hear, and then left without saying a single word to me.

The orderly gave me an ambiguous look, which I interpreted as meaning bad news. He gave me an injection, which I assumed was intended to make me unconscious. He now set about cleaning the swollen parts of my leg, then rubbing special ointments on it and cotton swabs soaked in liquids with a powerful smell of alcohol. Contrary to my expectations, I remained fully awake, and it occurred to me that, since my leg was receiving this kind of treatment with concentrated drug therapy, it implied that—Thank God!—there was no danger of amputation, even a partial one. When my savior proceeded to wrap my legs in copious bandages, that impression was confirmed. After he had dressed me in an orange-colored garment and transferred me to a bed in a small room nearby, I felt even more confident. He told me that I would be staying in the room for a while under medical supervision until my leg was cured. I thanked him profusely and asked him for his name and that of the members of the medical staff. I hoped thereby to be able to get him to tell me who was the foreign female doctor, Na'ima's friend, who had been so kind to me. However, he told me in the accent of someone from the Eastern part of the Arab world that I was here to be cured, not to ask questions. He then ordered some pills for me that I was supposed to take with some fruit before going to sleep. With that, he left.

Among the pills that I was supposed to take there was likely to be one that was a soporific. They obviously wanted my leg to get better using medicines, while my mental state stabilized with some sound sleep. I woke up in the middle of the night needing to piss; I had no idea what day of the week it was. I could not find my crutches anywhere, so I had to crawl with my leg in bandages and look for the toilet. It was so dark in my locked room that I could not find it. I could not decide whether to yell for the night-nurse or evacuate my bladder against a wall. Reluctantly, I decided on the latter, and then went back to my former position, where I lay on my back, sleeping part of the time, and waiting for dawn to break for the rest of it.

When night was replaced by daylight, a portly, menopausal nurse with olive complexion came in. She cursed whoever it was had spread such a foul stench in the room. Taking a bottle out of her apron, she proceeded to take a sniff from its contents. Standing on a chair, she opened a window that I had not noticed before. Disappearing for a moment, she came back with breakfast on a wheeled table and put it in front of me. She asked me if I were the one who had covered the wall with piss, and, without even waiting to hear my reply, she poured a liquid down my throat and give me an injection, instructing me all the while to eat. Before she left, I asked her about the toilet, and she pointed to a corner in the back with a plastic curtain.

Truth to tell, breakfast consisted of a variety of food, rich in proteins and vitamins. As I ate it all with gusto, I kept wondering to myself what might be the reason for such plenty—this display of truly Hatim-like generosity.* Were they trying to compensate me for all the evils things they had perpetrated against me; or was it some cunning plan either to get me well again or bring it to a crowning conclusion through assassination? With me in my current condition, the best thing was obviously to leave things as they were and let the fates do what they willed. I had to hold on; that was my plan and my surety till either victory or death.

I finished everything on the plates and still wanted more. I looked at my leg all wrapped in white bandages; it was as if I wanted to know how things were going. Everything seemed to be pointing to improvement and the possibility of a cure. I then took a look at the window above me. The sunlight and blue sky were so intense that the bars seemed to be illuminated. I stayed this way for a while, looking at my leg at times, but then staring upwards, where occasionally I would spot flocks of migrating birds. When yesterday's orderly appeared, I greeted him warmly, and he reciprocated. He proceeded to clean my leg with fragrant liquids and medicinal ointments, then changed the bandages. Once he had finished, he told me to practice walking, but I told him that that would be difficult. I asked him to get me my crutches so I could avoid falling down and harming myself. He brought me one of them.

"Now walk!" he said.

I managed to take some steps around the room relying on just one crutch. The orderly was impressed and put me back in bed. He told me to take some pills after lunch. Before leaving, he gave me a time when I would be taken back to my cell that evening.

The lunch that the same portly woman brought me was just as delicious as the breakfast I had eaten earlier. She reminded me to take the pills, and I did so. I did my very best to have a pleasant conversation with her, but she gestured to me to the effect that the walls had ears. After giving me another injection, she left, taking with her the tray and what was left on it. I now felt very drowsy, anticipating that my eyes and senses would soon give way to slumber, but I was mistaken because a masked guard now came into the room.

"Time for a stroll first!" he insisted.

I pointed out to him that I was in recovery; my condition made me exempt.

He started cursing and threatening me.

"Just say a prayer to the Prophet!" he said.

I begged him to postpone things till later, but he banged my bandaged leg and told me to hurry. I got out of bed so as to avoid an even worse blow and followed him, hobbling along on my single crutch. We now passed through a variety of halls and blocks along with others of various categories. When we eventually went outside the building, he attached me to a group of prisoners. Guarded by a troop wearing medals and helmets, some of them apparently foreigners, we made our way in a terrifying procession. I asked the person closest to me what was going on.

"They're taking us," he told me falteringly, "to dig our own graves or those of our brothers . . ."

I started shaking, and my remaining teeth chattered. My cough came back, and I did my best to suppress it. If the prisoner to whom I spoke had not lent me his spray, my condition would have drawn the attention of all the guards close to me.

When we arrived at a flat, dusty spot, they handed us axes and spades and divided us up into twos and threes. We were told to dig graves two feet deep and no more. With no other choice but to obey, I set my crutch aside as best I could and started digging up the soil to the extent that my injury allowed. A guard spotted me and threatened to throw me into one of the graves and pile the earth on top if I did not work seriously enough. I redoubled my efforts, and now and then other diggers who sympathized with my plight helped me.

When the officer in charge had counted the number of graves dug and blown his whistle to stop work, his aides told us to sit where we were. They allowed us to rest for a while and drink some water. Time went by, as heavy as lead, and our heads roasted in the boiling-hot sun. Some people had sunstroke, and a young prisoner, who they told me was actually a doctor, was allowed to help them as much as he could, which meant spraying their heads and bodies with cold water.

All of a sudden, everyone sitting down started whispering about the thing they could see in the distance, which they called the death caravan. The man next to me said that some of them had died of some illness while others had been condemned to death. We all strained our necks to get a glimpse of the people coming toward us. Two of them were carrying a stretcher, with a shrouded corpse on it, followed by all the other prisoners with stretchers. Once they reached us, the soldiers pointed each stretcher-carrier toward a particular ditch, where they deposited the corpse. We were then ordered to put the pile of soil back where it had come from and level the ground. Most of us were very reluctant to undertake such a task, and many voices were raised, which I joined at the top of my lungs, pronouncing the four paeans to God. I declaimed the prayer for the dead, to which everyone responded "Amen." We only proceeded with the burial when bullets started whizzing through the air and close to our legs. Hardly had we finished the task that had been forced upon us before, wonder of wonders, we spotted a prisoner attacking two soldiers with an axe. He left them both dead, then used the axe to split his own head and fell to the ground in his own blood. Soldiers rushed over, stood him on his feet to show that he was still alive, then threw him into an empty ditch and covered it with soil. After we had witnessed this appalling spectacle, the guards hurried us back to our quarters.

My guard caught up with me and told me the stroll was over. He urged me to walk in front of him, so I did so, leaning on my crutch which, thank God, had not been mislaid.

Back in my room in the hospital, I found the portly nurse waiting for me. She sat me on the bed and took off my prison clothes. After covering my genitals with a cloth, she proceeded to wash my body in rose-scented water. She then removed my leg bandages, cleaned the remaining scars with an alcohol rub, and put on a minimal bandage. She advised me to leave my leg exposed to the air, and then put the clean and scented mufti's cloak on me. She gave me some delicious food to eat, before laying me out on my back and injecting my buttocks with something that soon had me slipping into a deep sleep.

21

In My Torturess's Bed

A Night of Debauchery and Terror

"For several years now, my esteemed male spouse, I've always slept with one eye open. My fear has been that, if I fell fully asleep, innumerable hands would extend in my direction, to pluck my eyes out, chop off my breasts, and insert needles and skewers in every aperture of my body. They would then pour ammonia over me and empty a can of gasoline so they could set me on fire and reduce me to a pile of dust. You would be the person selected to toss it into the foulest toilet. Isn't that the dream you have in mind, you who, as of today, are my resident male spouse?"

The first time she used that term, "male spouse," to describe me, I thought the female ghoul was using a term whose meaning she did not know. But the second time, I retorted to my strangler: "No, I'm not your spouse!"

"Oh yes, you are," she replied, "duly signed according to law. Here's the marriage contract with two witnesses. Tonight was our wedding night. You had sex with me so I could bear you a son of your own kind. Pretty soon, Hamuda, I'll be able to fulfill your dream and tell you that I'm pregnant . . ."

The very self-confidence of this woman hit me; it felt like poison and made me feel dizzy.

"You're a disgusting slut!" I yelled as loudly as I could. "I would never be your husband, even if your gang sat me on an electric chair or tore me limb from limb . . ."

"Listen, Honey," she went on, "don't judge my age by my weight. I'm still under forty. I haven't given up hope of getting pregnant and having a baby."

O Lord, rid me of this foul female ghoul and the power she has over me! Now that You have enabled me to outwit both her and her scurrilous minions, Lord, she's trying to destroy my mind!

O Lord, relieve me of this calamity, loosen my chains, and bolster me to confront this new trial, one I have never encountered before and have no way of resisting.

O Lord, my shield and helper, You are my only guardian and resort!

She asked me what I was rambling on about, but I said nothing. When it came to the question as to whether or not I believed that we were truly married, I indicated disgustedly that I totally and utterly rejected the possibility. She planted a rough kiss on my mouth that prompted in me a strong desire to vomit. She then put two fingers to her mouth and let out a powerful whistle. Four men now appeared, among whom I recognized a preacher although I could not remember exactly where I had seen him before.

"So, august legal authority," she said, keeping her clutches on me, "is my marriage to this man legal according to the law or not?"

"Legal, definitely legal," the man replied, duly accompanied by the other three.

"Did he have sex with me or not?" she went on.

"He certainly did," they all replied in unison.

I managed to get my head free.

"My brother," I yelled at this pseudo-authority, "what have they done to your mind? Drugged it, shaken it? Is it even conceivable for a man to have sex with a woman without knowing about it or even being aware of it?"

"Yes indeed," he replied immediately, like some programmed machine. "It can happen in dreams. If a woman is lying next to a man, he can dream things and project his desire into a female's vagina. She may get pregnant and bear a child. In God's creation there are indeed many wonders and signs!"

I screamed out a prayer cursing all phony jurists and purveyors of falsehood. The ghoul now signaled to the four of them to leave. Once she was alone with me, she tied my other hand to the bed and my leg (once she had splayed them apart). She now climbed on top of me with her foul, heavy body.

"Now, my lover," she said, "you're going to know for sure and be fully aware of everything. She then proceeded to do things with me that I could never have conceived, even in my wildest nightmares. In fact, she assaulted and raped me, showing superior skill and a whorish professionalism in the process. I kept screaming in shame and begging for help, but she stopped me by kicking my bandaged leg, which had not fully healed yet. Once she had finished, she lay down beside me, panting heavily as though she had just emerged from a particularly brutal fight. Once she had recovered her breath, she started singing in a coarse tone. I could not make out what the words meant.

If I had found a way to plunge my fingers into the eyes of this debauched songbird, I would certainly have done it without a moment's hesitation or any concern about the possible consequences. The fact that I could not caused me pain, as did the fact that I had no choice but to listen to her singing such trivial nonsense. She then clutched a pillow that she called my baby, my child, and started singing the same stuff again.

She now told me that she had learned these songs from a female Moroccan Arab prisoner before she had died of a massive heart attack. She asked me if I would be bringing her child peaches and pomegranates. I said nothing and did my best to block my ears to these disgusting details about the love affairs she had had previous to what she was now terming our own beautiful story together, one that was so unique. She started talking about her intention to resign from the tiresome job she had so that she could follow me wherever I went, even if it was to a desert island. There we would build our little nest, love each other, raise our child, and cull such meats and animal milk as we wished from our little paradise. She then elaborated on the scenario with yet more detail, while I struggled to ignore what she was saying by considering my new plight and the dreadful consequences that might emerge from it.

A few moments later I reemerged from my ruminations with a jolt and found myself in my actual dire situation, confronting an explosion of abuse and complaint from the ghoul because I was refusing to consort with her and kept myself apart. This outburst was accompanied by nervous cigarette smoking. From time to time she forced me to smoke it too and to light others. When she had had enough, she threw the butt away and pulled a tray full of sandwiches from under the bed, along with two bottles of wine and some fruit. She sat up and put it down in front of us. She tried to get me to start eating, but I refused; when she offered some wine, I pressed my lips together to show clearly that the very idea was repellent. She now used her teeth to open the bottle.

"By God, you're going to drink the wine of love from your bride's own hand," she said.

When I refused point blank, she hit my bad leg. When she grew tired of my resistance, she grabbed my testicles and swore that she was not going to let go until I did what she wanted. The sheer pain left my mouth open, and within moments my torturess had thrust the bottle into my mouth and started pouring the liquid down my throat. I tried spitting it out but had to swallow to avoid choking myself. She used the same method to empty a second and third bottle down my throat, accompanying her actions with foul language and the grossest of insults:

"God curse your mother's religion! Here I agree to marry this despicable groom, folks, and yet we're not getting drunk?! So, you little creep, you prefer heaven's wine to mine? Whoever said you're going to heaven, you little bastard?"

All of a sudden this disgusting routine came to an end. Maybe she had had enough or felt tired. I watched as she smoked and drank with her usual frenzy, while the effects of all the wine I had drunk—something I had never even gone near before—gradually became apparent in me.

"Now the night is ours, my man," I heard her say as she swallowed some more wine, "and ours alone. Tell me some jokes . . . I kiss your mouth and hand . . . Really good jokes, no holds barred. They're the only kind that make me laugh and feel like sleeping. If you do that for me, I'll divorce you tomorrow morning, then I'll be rid of you and you of me."

"God," I said, "the Blessed and Almighty, may tarry but He never overlooks anything . . . His punishment for wrongdoers, male and female, is severe. He will decree a painful punishment for you, far more severe than what you have meted out to me and others as well . . ."

"To the contrary, Hamuda, you're the one who's punishing me with your steadfast refusal to cooperate and your rejection of me. You deprive me of your knowledge and secrets; all you show me is your stubborn negativity. It's you that God is going to punish. Now keep your eyes wide open, and I'm going to tell you something to develop your taste for jokes. There was a prisoner who died in my custody when he had a massive brain hemorrhage. He used to come to this bed of mine and tell me wonderful jokes in exchange for my dealing with him less severely. My aged midget servant used to attend those sessions as well, and he can remember all the jokes.

She now whistled three times, and a person smaller than anyone I had ever seen in my life immediately appeared. His silver beard reached down to his knees, and he was wearing a suitably sized clown's cap on his head.

"I heard my mistress call," he said, "and immediately interrupted the prayers I had to do in order to make up for the ones I had missed all week because I've been so busy with other things . . ."

She now told the midget to start telling stories, and he did so with all due deference to her.

"Your favorite joke-teller—may God have mercy on him—used to start a session by saying: 'Once upon a time it so happened . . . ' and you would tell him, Madam, to cut the cackle and tell the joke straight away with no beating about the bush . . . There was one joke that always made you laugh whenever I told it to you. The teller described it as being real because it actually happened to him in person. 'My wife, God curse her,' he said, 'is very partial to all penises except mine . . . and at the mention of the word 'penis,' he told another story about an Egyptian from the south who took his wife to the gynecologist. When the doctor was alone with her and told her to take her undergarment off, she ran out to her husband in the waiting room screaming and complaining. He scolded her and told her to do as the doctor asked. When she went back inside and the doctor asked her again to remove her undergarment, she replied flirtatiously: 'Take yours off first.' On the way home, the husband told his wife that the doctor clearly had a big brain, as big as this . . . To which his wife responded: 'Yes, and his penis is that big too!' 'Did you do it with him?' he asked her. 'You told me to,' she said. 'As of tomorrow, you're divorced,' he replied."

The debauched woman tapped my eyes to stop me falling asleep.

"The same jokester," the midget went on, "and may God fight him!—tells another story about a woman who found out only a month after her marriage that her husband was getting drunk in bars and having sex with prostitutes. Even worse news arrived soon afterwards, that he was buggering boys. She was furious, but offered a peaceful solution to the problem: she would let him enjoy himself by exercising his legitimate rights and functions inside the house. By way of experiment, the husband agreed. When the agreed-upon night came, she consorted with him as required and allowed him to have intercourse with her in the usual way. However, when he started to do the other thing with her, she started screaming out in pain. He rounded on her. 'Listen, woman,' he said, 'now you're supposed to be a man!'"

The ghoul cackled and punched me to make me laugh too.

"More!" she told the midget.

"Let it be the farewell joke then, Madam," he said. "Once upon a time . . . There was a young man who worked all day in a factory. Every day when he went home, he found his mother looking sad and depressed. When he asked her what was wrong, she said nothing. When he lost patience with the situation, he asked his only friend for advice. The latter gave him some counsel, the gist of which was that, when his mother was in this particular mood, he should sit with her and imitate her till he managed to discover what was causing it and work things out. So that's what happened. No sooner did the young man sit opposite his mother looking utterly miserable than she turned to him.

'My dear boy,' she asked him, 'why are you behaving like me. Haven't you found anyone to fuck you?'"

The ghoul cackled again and shook me to do the same. She then asked the midget to do what he normally did at the conclusion of each session—namely, to delight her with some details about himself.

"God be praised and thanked!" he said. "I have been compensated for my short stature by having both a capacious memory and a huge penis, one to make even an elephant jealous—it being an animal proverbial for its memory and long penis."

The ghoul, who was still cackling raucously, now regaled the midget with words of praise and approval. At the same time, she reproached me for not telling her any lewd jokes, they being the salt of life in her view, and not joining her in appreciating the ones the midget had told. She threatened to punish me for that when morning came. With that she started eating and drinking again, then started spouting some drivel that I ignored. After that, she lay down, belched, farted, and started puffing a lot.

One of the weirdest things I now witnessed, with a due amazement—was that the midget did not retrace his steps, but instead climbed on to the bed and started hugging the ghoul. I signaled to him to withdraw.

"I can't do that," he whispered in reply, "until my mistress allows me to do so. Otherwise my head and beard will be consigned to the devil."

I gestured to him in other ways, but his response was to the effect that his mistress could see and hear everything, even if she were asleep; I needed to say nothing and go to sleep. With that, he fell into her arms, and they both let out a series of pants and groans . . .

O Lord, what crimes and misdemeanors can I have committed against You or Your servants that I find myself being tortured and kept awake by two such utterly disgusting creatures? Now their foul deeds are followed by thunderous snoring, the female ghoul herself and her compliant, debauched midget. O Lord, are You testing me with enforced drunkenness, migraine headaches, and a veritable cascade of hallucinations and dark visions?

I remained in this state, asking my Lord about myself and projecting my pains and agonies to Him, till the first light of dawn appeared. The whole place rang with the sound of the ghoul's voice, objecting to the smell of urine in her bed and cursing the mother and father of the perpetrator. The midget leaped out of the bed, his mouth showing through his quaking beard as he swore a solemn oath that he was not the culprit. She ordered him to send for the black guard and shoved me away after untying my bonds. She then removed the sheet, blanket, and counterpane from the bed and tore up the phony marriage contract, threatening me with a humiliating punishment at the hands of the giant black guard.

When the guard arrived, she ordered him in a gruff tone to throw me back in my hole and do with me as he wished. She described me as a drunkard and said that I was now divorced. She specifically noted that her status as an unmarried mother had made the prospect of marriage to male excrement like me seem attractive.

The guard took my crutch, picked me up, and carried me rapidly out of the room, as though he were eager to get away from his boss and her foul tongue. He stopped by the toilet and indicated to me to go in, hand him my cloak, and wash; he would come back after a while. And that is what happened. Once I had cleansed myself after such a night of debauchery, he returned, wrapped me in a warm blanket, and carried me back to my cell, where he put me down on my bed along with my crutch and two bags. He then went away, although I could see that his bloodshot eyes were welling with tears of sympathy.

My fears and hallucinations, combined with the effects of dizziness and exhaustion, all came together to make me feel so drowsy that it felt like a swoon or even entry into some black hole or deep trench.

22

I Have No Choice but to Sleep and Wake Up to the Vestiges of a Fire

When body and soul are both in the furthest possible stages of decline, the only stratagem available to the person so afflicted is to replicate the dead by remaining still and training mind and senses to be as self-denying and abstemious as possible. I listened as two guards standing close by my bed speculated as to whether I was actually dead or merely close to it. They were on the point of laying bets on it when a nurse arrived to feel my pulse. The two guards asked him to tell them which one of them was right, but he replied that neither of them would win the bet because I was half-alive and half-dead. He then gave me an injection which he told them might keep me alive rather than dead, if only for a while. They all left suddenly, and there was an all-pervasive silence in the block, as though either the cells had no one in them or else the same thing had happened to them as to me, although the modes and circumstances might be different.

I have no idea how long I spent in this drink-induced compulsory slumber: a few hours, or a couple of days and more. The effects of the wine the ghoul had forced down my throat were still making me dizzy and giving me terrible headaches, but even so I began to feel myself getting gradually better and recovering both breath and clarity of thought. As far as I could make out, it was close to midday. While I had been asleep, the food on the platter had obviously long since disappeared inside the various members of the insect population, but the other platter still had the copy of the Qur'an, the thurible, and perfume bottle on it. There were also the two bags

162

that the kind black guard had left for me. I checked on their contents and found one full of bread, olives, dates, boiled eggs, and bottles of water, while the second had clean underwear and a fresh blue suit. Dear God, be kind to this servant of Yours and liberate him from the clutches of the corrupt people of this earth and the battalions of rogue criminals.

As a way of testing how awake I really was, I put my hand in the food bag and ate some of it with all due deliberation. After taking a few swallows of water, I got to my feet, still wrapped in my blanket, and tried walking on my leg without the crutch. To my delight, I noticed a distinct improvement in my bad leg and made myself walk up and down the cell a few times. I concentrated my mind on a variety of ideals and lofty values, using them as an antidote—or rather, a total block—to the specter of the female ghoul and the evil physical and psychological abuse to which she had subjected me. As I sweated and panted profusely, I was purging my body and faculties of the pollution caused by her barbaric actions, foul tongue, and disgusting odor . . .

When I felt tired, I lay down again on the bed panting heavily. Just then a thought occurred to me: I remembered the hole in the floor by which I was connected to my neighbor. I removed the earth with my crutch and started sending some muted messages down the tube. Once I had repeated them several times, it became clear that there was no one there to listen. I looked down the tube in case I could see a shape of some kind—a foot moving or standing still, but there was nothing. My neighbor had either been killed or transferred somewhere else, and the same might be true of the other people in the block, whether close to me or further away—God alone knows!

So was I now alone in this cellblock, with no one else living there?

Previously, people had envied me for having my own private cell; some people regarded it as a boon, a kind of preferential treatment. However, the torturers themselves adopted it as a form of revenge that they used on people when they wanted to drive them crazy through a crushing total isolation. If I was now the only inhabitant in a cellblock that had previously housed some one hundred prisoners, then that was undoubtedly something much more sinister. But they could dump me down a well or in the desert, and yet—by the God who has created and trained me so well to mention His name and call on His familiar saints—I shall never allow myself to give in to hallucinations and delirium, nor will I plunge into a bottomless labyrinth.

In a spontaneous gesture of defiance, I went over to the door and looked out through the iron-framed aperture. There was not a soul to be seen or heard, merely a profound silence steeped in humidity and a graveyard atmosphere. The whole situation seemed highly problematic and augured ill. I was utterly amazed when I pushed the door and it opened. Perhaps the kindly black guard forgot to lock it, I surmised, or he left it that way as an act of generosity and release for me. I wrapped myself up in my blanket, grabbed my crutch (for which I now had other uses), and leaned on it as I entrusted myself to God's care. I made my way out into the dimly lit corridor and made a quick tour of inspection. I was shocked, or rather shocked and saddened, to see that all the walls were coal-black, as though they had been eaten away by a roaring fire. The cell furniture and people's possessions had all been reduced to piles of ash, which gave off a few wafts of smoke from time to time.

My assumptions were confirmed by an aged prisoner whom I spotted sitting cross-legged at the back of a cell. I looked down at him and offered my greetings, then asked him what had happened. He did not move, but merely gave me a tired look. He then muttered some phrases in a quaking voice, from which I gathered that a prisoner in one of the neighboring cells had set his cell and himself on fire. The fire had spread to all the neighboring cells, with the exception of the one on the end and another one opposite it. I asked him when precisely this had happened, and it emerged that it had been on the night I had spent in debauchery with the ghoul. When I asked about casualties, he told me all the prisoners had either died of asphyxiation or suffered terrible burns. I asked him about his own situation, and he responded that what the fire had not taken away from him was now being done by hunger and thirst.

"Ever since it happened, my son," he told me, "they've forgotten all about me, or maybe they think I'm among the dead."

I hurried back to my cell and brought back half of my provisions. Since he could not stand up, I threw them down for him. He took them and thanked me profusely. I asked him to wait till I returned, and then went to look for a doctor or nurse. I walked through corridors, halls and lobbies in the direction of the hospital, with people staring at me in amazement because I was clad in my blanket, as though I was from the land of the Eskimos or else afflicted with some kind of heat deficiency.

In one courtyard that I had to cross, some prisoners decided to provoke me. They made fun of my clothing and the fact that I was so flustered. Some of them stretched out their hands to remove the blanket and expose me naked. I took refuge with a guard.

"Sir," I asked him, "would you escort me to the hospital, please?"

He asked me for my number.

When I told him, he rubbed his neck.

"112, you say! How did you escape from the fire?"

"A miracle, Sir, a genuine miracle!"

"So you've lost all your belongings? Why do you need the doctor?"

"There's still a prisoner in the block. He's still just alive but is close to death."

"Go back to your cell at once. I'll look into the problem. Now go!"

I could not disobey the command of a man whose black uniform and medals made clear that he was an officer of some kind. I retraced my tracks, avoiding the glances of the other prisoners. When I reached my cellblock, I looked in on the old man and found him stretched out fast asleep. Rather than disturbing him by waking him up, I went back to my own cell and hid my bag of new clothes under the bedcover. Then I too collapsed on the bed, waiting to see what would happen next.

From the Penitents' Wing to a Debauched Nightclub

One cool and cloudy morning, I woke up to the banging of hammers and pickaxes. The intensity of the activity and the orders being issued by the guard made it clear that the cells were being repaired and rebuilt using prisoners with professional skills. Putting on my new outfit, I walked over to the door of my cell and happened to spot the officer guard whom I had met the day before. After greeting him, I asked first about the sick old man whose sorry state I had brought to his attention. He issued two orders, but managed to tell me that the old man had been buried. While I was feeling personally sorry for the old man's demise, he continued to chew his gum. He asked me which trade I myself knew best. I raised my eyebrows hesitantly, but, before he left, he instructed me to get ready to help the plasterers. The next day I spent close to an hour helping prepare buckets of gypsum, but the professional workers soon excused me, not only because I had no training but also because of my general weakness and crippled condition. Their boss advised me to go back to my cell and abide myself in patience till the work was finished and things in the block returned to normal.

For someone like me who was now inured to hardship, this kind of advice from the boss was not hard to follow. By now I was more than able to cope with whatever harsh blows were aimed at me! I got used to the noise the workers were making all day long, and at night I came to appreciate having my door blocked. I had the strong impression that I was now totally forgotten in this cellblock, perhaps the last one; there were no meals or water. If it was not for the food and drink that the kindly black guard brought me to keep me alive, I would have been starving and suffered severe stomach problems. I read verses from the Qur'an in the dim light and, when darkness fell, recited such proverbs and poetry as I could remember. Those things provided me with another kind of more spiritual sustenance which helped me overcome my loneliness and disillusion—all in an attempt to connect to loftier values and ideals.

The repairs went on for several days, during which the gigantic black guard came to visit me at night and bring a bag of food and some water. Once the work was finished, there was activity in the block that indicated that some new prisoners would be arriving and entering the cells. The process was accompanied by drums and clarinet. A megaphone announced that from now on the block would be known as the Penitents' Wing. To mark the occasion, the new occupants received bags of food and bottles of milk and water. Although I had been in the block for a long time, I was included in this largesse which obviously was not in any way inspired by any kind of God-given principle.

Once the ceremony was over and the guards had left, a voice near my cell was raised in objection.

"No, people," it said. "I'm not supposed to be here. I've not murdered anyone, nor am I a thief. I've never harmed anyone. I've spent six years with political prisoners, and they've imposed all the very worst kinds of punishment on me. At night they intentionally deprive us of sleep, using what they term 'nonstop Qur'an recitation.' Even so, they're hoist with their own petard since the verses have given us welcome relief and transported us to realms of peace and paradise! I'm a salafi* counselor; I want to go back to my companions. I have no regrets over my choice and my commitment to the cause. I seek no forgiveness from anyone. God alone is the Merciful Forgiver."

"Oh no, Shaykh!" yelled another voice from the other end of the block, although it was still audible. "Pedophilia, raping innocent boys, is a foul crime forbidden by the laws of heaven and earth. Punishment for such a crime occurs in this life even before the next.

Isn't that so, people?! Listen, you faker, your previous pedophilia has caught up with you here and now. It's a blot on your character and a disgusting crime that completely nullifies your debauched and phony claims to be a popular Muslim figure."

The fundamentalist paused for a while, maybe to catch his breath after such a deadly assault on his character.

"That man with the foul tongue," he yelled at the top of his voice," the one you've all just heard, is a secret policeman who's tracked me wherever I've gone. He's been picking up snippets of information about me and other people in order to pass it all on to his bosses and employers. I have material proof of what I'm saying, and I'm asking those of you who can hear me to pass it on. You in cell 112, did you hear what the other person said about me, even though he's in a cell far down the block?"

I replied loudly that I had indeed heard, and my response was passed along to the prisoners, one after the other.

"If the spy's voice can be heard from one end of the block to the other," the accused man continued, "then it must be because he's using a secret electronic microphone, one supplied from the arsenal of miniature devices that are used by informers among us to carry out their devious functions. If anyone can get close enough to him to carry out a search, he'll be able to confirm what I'm saying and prove that the man is a slimy and corrupt character; one of those people who make a living by trashing the reputation of devout people and practicing all kinds of scandal-mongering—may God fight them and thwart their intentions till the Day of Judgment!"

Voices were now raised in support of the shaykh, while others cursed the informer. It was only when a unit of the rapid response force arrived that things calmed down. They went around brandishing their truncheons and threatened the inmates, all to the accompaniment of their barking dogs. Some of them stayed behind for several hours to reimpose order, keeping prisoners on their toes with unexpected probes. I myself had my share and more. There can be no doubt that the state they found me in, lying on my bed, was enough to convince them that I was behaving properly and had no evil intentions; that made them stop observing me and flashing lights into my cell. They simply left me in peace.

I took advantage of the fact that they left me alone to remove the earth from the hole in the floor and whispered through the tube to my new neighbor. I was delighted when he responded. I rapidly gave him my name and the principal details of the accusations leveled against me, swearing to God that I had no part in them. He did exactly the same, with the fundamental difference that in his case the charge was correct and there was no question of appeal or invalidation. When I asked him to explain, he counted off for me the number of murders he had committed, including his mother and daughter, both whores, a pimp, and three of their customers. He told me that all the inmates in the penitents' wing had committed similar or even worse crimes—robbers, con men, and murderers, drug dealers, sex- and wine-retailers. He made an exception when it came to the *salafi* counselor about whom he knew nothing and whom he had never set eyes on before. He went on to say that public law criminals such as himself were being asked to join the secret services and to work as contract killers, all in return for pardons, cancelation of indemnity, and payment of a paltry salary. Before his voice completely disappeared, he warned me to be careful when it came to the other prisoners in the wing.

Evening fell. When the night was far advanced, a harsh voice could be heard.

"Listen, you people in this cave," it said. "While you're waiting for your regrets to ripen and ferment and for your repentance to result in pardon and forgiveness, why don't you lighten your nights with some jokes and stories? When you want to have a good laugh and take the weight off your mind, the best ones are the dirtiest, the ones below the belt. So search your own repertoire so we can cancel our worries and kill the time. Be generous, all of you, and tell them well, or else you'll all become depressed and time will kill you. In order to sharpen your talents and inspire you, I'll start. Have you heard the one about the man from Marrakesh who was a homosexual? He used the mountains as his base and went on sex raids through forests and plains. His targets were young boys, teenagers, and even older men. This homosexual managed to outwit both the police and the national guard. One gorgeous spring day, a senior officer was walking across a mountain slope when about a hundred meters or so away he spotted three men praying, with their backsides in the air. He discovered that the three were some of his own men. When he asked them to explain what they were doing, they all stood up and saluted. They told him that, since every attempt to arrest the elusive homosexual had failed, they had decided to lay a trap for him by using the method he had witnessed. The officer told them all to get dressed again and ordered the detachment accompanying him to put them in prison and open an investigation into their sexual orientation."

The entire wing burst into laughter, all of which encouraged the disgusting storyteller to move on to even worse jokes. I used pieces of bread to block my ears, anxious as I was to protect my own space which contained a copy of the Qur'an. I now ate a little bit of supper and hung my food bag on my crutch, which I placed horizontally between two holes at the back of my cell. Did I not say that my crutch had other uses?! I used the toilet and checked on the area before wrapping myself in my blanket and lying down on the bed. I whispered a few phrases to myself in praise of sleep, hoping that my eyes would be closed.

I was abruptly woken up in the middle of the night by a voice begging for help and groaning. I removed the bread from my ears and went over to the door.

"O God," I heard from somewhere in the block, "I give witness that I'm being killed, I have not committed suicide. I witness that there is no deity but God and Muhammad is His Servant and Prophet. I witness . . ."

The voice suddenly grew weaker, then disappeared completely. As loudly as I could, I begged the other inmates who were asleep to help the poor prisoner who was being murdered. There was no response. When I tried again—it still being pitch dark, a hand reached through my door-window and grabbed me by the neck. A voice now threatened to strangle me if I said another word. I found myself being pushed back to my bed, where I lay quivering.

After what I had heard and what had then happened to me, I did not sleep a wink. When the cackling of some winter birds announced the arrival of dawn, there was a din of voices in the block close to my cell. Some of them announced that the *salafi* preacher had committed suicide by slitting his left wrist, only confirmed by the fact that a bloody knife was still in his right hand, which proved the veracity of the findings. Peeping through the window I could see a doctor in a white apron, guards, and a number of the new prisoners.

"The *salafi* has committed suicide," one of them said. "It's a pre-Islamic kind of death, so we should not pray over him or ask for God's mercy on him. To avoid any contamination he should be buried like an animal corpse."

"His cell should be thoroughly cleaned of his blood," another voice commented, "not only that, but his bed and sheets as well. Witnesses have given their testimony and the file is closed with official legal signatures. Break it up now and return to your cells."

It occurred to me that I needed to pronounce the fourfold praise of God and say some prayer for the poor man who had been treacherously murdered. The facts of the matter were clearly the exact opposite of what the false witnesses had testified, but I found myself having to assess the consequences of reporting the matter when I was housed among a whole cluster of professional killers. With that in mind, I resorted to silence and said nothing.

After eating some breakfast, the inmates in the penitents' wing were ordered to leave their cells and go to the exercise yard. I hesitated to come out, but a guard came into my cell, forced me out, and thrust me into the midst of my new neighbors whom I was now able to see in person for the first time, albeit without their knowing who I was. Every one of them had a paunch and bulging muscles, as though they were former boxing champions or Sumo wrestlers. The thin ones looked for all the world like giraffes in height and stride; some of them had long beards that hung down like poisonous stinging scorpions. They were wearing earrings, and their bodies were covered with tattoos in weird shapes. As I walked as part of their moving column, I looked like a monkey or a young boy. Some of them decided to have some fun, yanking my beard or cuffing me on the neck and head; they kept laughing at me and poking fun at my crippled gait. There was no way I could complain or protest, so I simply tolerated the whole thing as long as the exercise session lasted, something that now seemed even more taxing than usual.

When the group reached the wide yard, it broke up into separate groups, one to play basketball, another to wrestle, and a third to lift weights. It was members of this third group that took me and started using my body in various ways, as though I were one of the weights, tossing me around as they saw fit and exercising their bulging muscles.

I was not of a mind to let them use and insult me as they wished, particularly when I heard them negotiating as to who would be using me as a bags of skin and bones to toss around; anyone who failed to catch it (meaning me) would have to pay his dues, implying a round of drinks or hashish. I took advantage of this chatter and their rest time and slunk away. I ran around the courtyard, hither and yon, looking for somewhere to hide or escape. When some of the men I had run away from caught up with me, I managed to avoid them by slipping out of their reach and getting away. Just as my breath was beginning to run out, I hurled myself at a guard and told him my name and cell number. I begged him to protect me and take me to see the investigating judge. How I rendered praises to God when the guard ordered the men who were chasing me to go back to their exercise.

"You're Hamuda!" he yelled at me. "What a lucky chance! The judge has been asking me about you. Let's go to see him now. But first you need to shower, shave and put on some fresh clothes. Follow me."

Duly amazed, I followed him. My only hope was that, now that I had escaped from the bulging-muscle brigade and was on my way to see the judge who would decide my fate, I was not simply going from the frying pan into the fire. To convince me that nothing worse could possibly happen, I obeyed the guard's three injunctions. A few hours later I had washed my body and mouth, shaved my beard and head, and put on a black suit, white shirt, and red tie, keeping my Nike shoes to help me walk.

For hours, the guard kept me in a narrow room that was locked, but I did not mind; quite the contrary in fact, I was enjoying the quiet music that emerged from speakers in the ceiling, not to mention other services being offered by a beautiful, dark brown hostess: refreshing drinks, a splendid lunch followed by cups of decent tea, and a variety of delicious sweets. I tried to get the hostess to talk and gathered that she was Filipina and only spoke English. In a few broken phrases I communicated to her how grateful I was and that I did not know much English. I apologized for my awful accent.

As I sat there alone in this room, I spent several moments in front of the mirror, staring at my body and noticing how incredibly thin it was and how bad my face looked: Few teeth in my mouth, sunken cheeks, a jutting nose, dark eyes with little glow to them, hair and beard flecked with grey. Escaping from the realities of the miscreant mirror, I sat down on the bench, unable to decide whether to stop thinking about things and relish the current moment, or else to try to guess what was going on in the judge's mind; what new tempting offers or unpleasant surprises would he be springing on me if I stuck to my guns or, as he would term it, my stubborn behavior.

I remained in that state until the hostess returned in the evening and invited me to accompany her at once. With her, I got into a jeep with its armed driver. For about five kilometers we crossed the desert at high speed. The jeep stopped in front of a sturdy-looking building with fences all around. I followed the hostess inside, where the air conditioning gave one a sense of relaxation. After I had gone through an electronic screening machine, a foreign soldier subjected me to a detailed manual search of my body. He told me to remove my shoes and put them in a basket, and I did so. After he had disappeared into a side room, he came back and handed me some moccasins to replace my own shoes that he was going to keep for reasons that I could not ask about because of the language problem. Putting the moccasins on, I followed the hostess through lobbies and halls with American décor and furniture till we reached a bar with the name Zemzem Bar written above the door. She told me to sit on a separate bench that she pointed out for me, then said her farewells and left.

The bar had an American design, at least as far as my knowledge of Western movies made me aware. The majority of the people in it were Americans; theirs was the only language that was to be heard. I tapped out a rhythm on the low table and whispered the tune sung by the late Husayn Salawi: "All you hear is Okay, Okay, come on, bye-bye."

One of the barmaids caught my attention, not just because her breasts were almost naked and she was extremely beautiful, but also because she looked very much like Na'ima, the judge's secretary, the woman who had been so kind to me. Without even realizing what I was doing or thinking about the possible consequences, I rushed over to her and whispered her name. She pretended not to know me and told me that she would be bringing what I ordered. I went back to my spot as quickly as possible so as not to disturb her or arouse suspicion in any prying eyes. A few moments later, when I realized that no one was paying me any attention, Na'ima came over and put a glass of orange juice on my table.

"If you talk to me," she whispered, "you'll ruin my entire life."

And with that she melted rapidly away.

"No, a thousand times no, Na'ima!!" I told myself. "I'll never ruin your life. It's quite enough already that my own life is in ruins, quite enough . . ."

But how could I keep quiet about these soldiers and foreign detectives, strutting around so arrogantly. Dear Na'ima, they will never make you an exception to the way they treat waitresses and other barroom girls. One of them taps your backside for pleasure, while another squeezes your breasts, puffs his cigarette smoke all over them, and raises a toast to their beauty. Yet another pulls you toward him and gives your mouth a passionate kiss.

So, tell me, Na'ima, am I supposed to say nothing as I watch these disgusting goings-on? Should I simply swallow my fury, or do I have the right to pounce on these Yankees and curse them for fooling around with you? Should I tell them: "Listen, you pig, don't touch any Moroccan girls, or else . . ."

Or else what, Hamuda?! You're so weak, so sick and completely crushed; a surefire candidate at any time for murder by a knife thrust or fatal blow to the heart or head. You're a total nonentity, a flea. By God, all you can do is cower in your chair and grovel. You're dreaming if you think you can put up a fight. So you disapprove of the lewd behavior you're watching and giving this haven of debauchery the holy name of the Zemzem well in Mecca. Fair enough, but you had better keep it all under wraps. If you so much as air it in public, it will be the end of you.

A large number of people of both sexes began to populate the bar. As I watched, mouths and bodies started responding to the glasses of alcohol, not to mention the music, which attracted more and more people to the dance floor. Hands and legs intertwined, and the dancers rocked and swayed as they kept up the bump and grind, and so on and so on . . .

Na'ima came over to me as I sat there at the edge of this scene. She gave me a glass of water that I smelled but did not drink. My expression showed how much I disapproved of the whole thing, but the words that she whispered in my ear had the opposite effect, bringing me a sense of warmth and serenity:

"Here's a vial of blood. Hide it. When your interview with the judge comes to an end, break it open and spit the contents out. Complain to him that you have a bad cough and think you may have contracted tuberculosis. But don't mention me. Farewell!"

It was only a few minutes after my adviser, Na'ima, had disappeared into the crowd before someone tapped me on the shoulder.

"Get up and follow me," they said.

24

A Final Meeting with the Judge, Then the Dormitory with No Sleep

The person who had instructed me to follow her was wearing a military uniform; in all likelihood she was a foreigner. As I followed her through corridors and halls, the din from the nightclub gradually diminished. She took me through one door, then a second and a third and made a telephone call on her mobile. After a few minutes' wait, she was authorized to enter. I followed her into a wide lounge with muted red lighting. I spotted the judge sitting cross-legged on a wheeled couch, his face showing all the signs of an advanced state of drunkenness. My escort sat me down on a chair, gave a military salute, then left.

I sat there like a statue, waiting for the person who had summoned me to say something and let me know why I had been invited to appear before him in such a luxurious environment. But he seemed distracted; something weird was going on underneath his table. Just then, a half-naked girl emerged and went out of the door. I watched in utter disgust as the judge pulled up his trousers and poured himself a glass of whisky as though it were water. I found it necessary to let him know I was there, so I let out a cough, all the while fingering Na'ima's vial. I coughed louder, but then suppressed it when he started spouting nonsense:

"Fantastic things: fucking in water, using pregnant women as permitted by law, menstruating females, having clusters of gorgeous whores under tables . . . I've done it all—no stake involved and no pretense either . . ."

He started rocking to and fro on the bench, eyes closed and utterly drunk. I started coughing again, and he sat up and asked who was coughing. I told him who I was, and he was surprised to find me there. I reminded him that he was the one who had summoned me. After a moment's thought, he told me to sit down close to his table, but only on condition that I did not cough any more. I managed to stop.

"So, Hamuda from Oujda," he told me between gulps of whisky and puffs on a cigarette, "this is your very last chance. If you take it, you'll be set free; otherwise it's the end for you. All the long years I've been working, I've never encountered anyone as stubborn and resistant as you. But let me be totally clear: I'm not going to let you be a thorn in my foot or a rock in my path. I've devoted a lot of my valuable time to you, even though you're not worth it. I've stopped the female ghoul from torturing you even more; I've given orders for you to be washed and cleaned; I've seen to it that your leg has been cured; I've appointed you as mufti and given you all kinds of gifts on the two platters. But here you are, you ungrateful bastard! All my kindness and gifts have been rewarded with stubborn resistance and recalcitrance. You've closed your heart and soul in my face! You revealed a number of details to the Disciplinary Committee that you've kept from me. I've a feeling—in fact, I'm certain—that you're still concealing information, most importantly about your terrorist cousin, al-Husayn al-Masmudi, and his gang. So now the final hour has struck: either you tell us what you know in return for which you'll join our service, be pardoned and have your previous crimes wiped clean; or else you'll carry on rejecting this and that, in which case you'll go back to the penitents' wing, where you'll be killed by one of the professional murderers. Once you're back there, there'll be no guarantee that you'll remain alive. Anyone who issues such a warning is forgiven if things go wrong. Your fate is now in your own hands. Make your mind up and don't delay!"

As I listened to these words, my heart was in my throat.

"Sir," I told this debauched and totally drunk judge between coughs, "I've told you about my cousin a thousand times. I've nothing to add to what I put in my report for you, or do you want me to make something up? That would be wrong, and in both religious and moral terms. My state of health makes it impossible for me to enter the service. The atmosphere inside your center does not agree with me; as you can tell, it's had a negative effect on my health."

I watched as the judge's face altered in fury. He came round the table and attacked me with a series of blows. He told me not to cough, then lifted me up and delivered a savage blow to my head that sent me reeling; I almost lost consciousness. When he went back to his bench and took another drink and puff from his cigarette, I took advantage of the moment.

"No to violence!" I yelled, "no to violence! Isn't that part of your personal credo, Judge?"

While I was expressing those words, I put the blood vial in my mouth and did what Na'ima had advised me to do. Getting a good amount of blood mixed with my spittle, I went over to the judge, started coughing, and splattered a glob of blood into my hands. I protested that I had tuberculosis and was afraid I might be infecting him too. The judge leapt up and moved away. He covered his face with a handkerchief, then pointed to the backdoor.

"Get out of here, you tubercular creep!" he yelled. "Get out of my sight!"

At first I did not obey his order. I decided to play the fool a bit so this raving judge would have another pretext for ruling that I should go back to my homeland. It now occurred to me that I no longer had anything to lose in this detention center. My tuberculosis was my weapon, whether I actually had it or not. With that in mind, I started chasing the judge all around his wide lounge, coughing all over him and spitting blood and threatening to pass on my disease to him. All the while he kept maneuvering his elephantine body around the copious supply of furniture, holding his handkerchief over his nose and mouth. So here we are, Na'ima! Your boss is behaving like a scared child, running away from a genie or ghoul who's chasing him. If you happened to see him looking so scared and panting for all he's worth, with sweat pouring off him, the pretense would fall away completely, and you would realize that this would-be lion who determines the fate of tortured souls in this facility is merely a paper tiger, someone who is as afraid of death as any other poor wretch.

When I noticed that his esteemed excellency had taken refuge in the toilet and locked it, I decided that it was time to close the circus and leave the lounge by the door that his now vanished eminence had pointed to. It opened out to a cement cellar with dim lighting suitable as an escape route or some such thing. At the end it led to a sandy area with hills and mounds of earth. The light of the full moon showed clearly how vast the space was and how closely packed and well-arranged its sections were. For a few moments I stood there wondering what to do, trying to make out the direction that would take me back to the detention center buildings. One thing I knew for certain: wandering around in the desert without food or compass was guaranteed to result in my demise, either buried under mounds of sand or else as fodder for birds of prey and other rapacious animals.

Not wanting to die in such an undignified manner, my mind—or what was left of it—led me to work out that the jeep that had transported me to the spot where I was standing had not traveled more than five kilometers or so. So I had to walk in the opposite direction, invoking all my senses to pick up any noises, smells, or lights that might guide me. And that is precisely what I did.

A fair amount of time went by, and I covered a distance that I could only assess by how tired and cold I felt. Just then I heard dogs barking, and, as I increased my pace and overcame my fear, the sound grew gradually louder. Before long, a patrol appeared with their dogs. They shined a powerful searchlight in my face, surrounded me, and learned my identity and cell number. They had a shackled prisoner with them, and their leader asked me in the light if I recognized him. I pursed my lips so as not to say his name—'Umar al-Rami—and for caution's sake pretended I did not know him. However, 'Umar hastened to remind me of the night he had spent with me in my cell before the female ghoul had ordered his second testicle removed. They now allowed him to give me a hug and kiss.

"In front of these people, my brother," he told me tearfully, "I confess that I've tried to escape from this prison. I now accept the death sentence that has been passed against me."

"No, 'Umar," I replied distractedly, "that's an unjust verdict. You must demand an appeal!"

"The law's the law," the leader interrupted loudly. "It'll be applied to you as well, since we've caught you trying to escape. In your case I'm going to ask for an accelerated decision because, unlike 'Umar, you've donned a nice set of civilian clothes and were obviously trying to deceive people and put them off the track . . ."

In some distress, I made a statement to the effect that I was wearing these clothes, which were not normal prisoner's garb, because the investigating judge had invited me to pay him a visit. Hearing that, the entire troop of soldiers burst into laughter, and the desert echoed to their guffaws. The leader was now forced to issue an order to carry out the death sentence. They bound 'Umar's eyes and stood a few meters away, with their rifles pointed at him. The leader made me stand beside him and asked what was his final statement of wishes.

"I want you to put Hamuda from Oujda in my cell," he said. "He is to inherit my belongings and preserve my memory."

With that, he pronounced the statement of faith, fearlessly and without flinching. The men who had taken me over to him now pulled me back. The leader gave the order to fire. My poor friend fell to the ground, soaked in his own blood, which could be seen in the brilliant moonlight.

Shivering with both emotion and the bitter cold, and holding back my tears, I begged them to bury him with the four prayers in praise of God and a personal prayer for him. The leader rounded on me and told me to go with them and keep quiet. I had no choice but to do as he demanded.

"No praises of God and prayers for people like him," I heard him mutter to himself. "Too bad for them! That's the law when it comes to people who try to escape and fail. People who run away don't get buried. It only takes a few hours for only bones and skull to be left, and they'll be covered by the sands for evermore . . ."

We reached the gate of a prison building whose number I could not make out. There the soldiers handed me over to a gorilla-like guard. The leader told him to put me temporarily into the cell of the deceased prisoner, 'Umar al-Rami, in the dormitory where no one slept. The corridor leading to my temporary new abode had cells with iron bars on either side so that you could see what was going on inside. In this particular block the level of privacy and personal intimacy was zero or even less! Once the guard had locked the door, all I could do was throw myself down on the bed and try to sleep off the trials and tribulations of the previous day.

It was not daylight that woke me up, but the sound of a variety of song and dance tunes that reverberated in my cell in continuous clashing waves of noise. Even though it was still night, I opened my eyes and realized where I was now. I got up to investigate and discovered that the cell opposite mine was occupied by the figure of someone wrapped in his bedsheet, most probably asleep. I yelled to him several times, asking him what was going on, and requesting that he let me sleep and have some peace and quiet, but there was no response. Going back to my bed, I lay down and contemplated my new misfortune, the noise that was now emerging from transistor radios and the loudspeakers on the walls and ceilings. I was anxious to find some distraction for my senses and nerves, so I started checking on the late 'Umar al-Rami's belongings. All I found was a medium-sized radio that I immediately hid, a circular-shaped comb, two tubes of toothpaste with no brush, and a blue prisoner's uniform, which I put on over my Western suit so as to give me extra protection against the cold. My sense of smell told me that there was some food in a sealed bag, so I opened it and proceeded to assuage my hunger with some bits of bread, olives, and boiled potatoes. I then used water through a thin tube to clear the mucus from my nose and cleaned my teeth by putting some toothpaste on my finger. I lay down to get some rest, but the deafening noise of the music made that impossible. As time went by, it never let up.

Late at night, there was a sudden silence. I seized the opportunity to get some sleep, but almost immediately a ringing voice could be heard intoning the phrases "In the name of God" and "Thanks be to God." That was followed by a homily and advice concerning the proper way to perform ablutions, wash the bodies of the dead, and say the necessary prayers over them. The devout Muslim was enjoined to practice that prayer is better than sleep and reminded to consider night and day the punishments of the grave inflicted by the two questioning angels, Munkir and Nakir,* not to mention the Day of Gathering and Judgment. This was the kind of sermon that put you in mind of the poor and stupid preachers you might encounter in the desert or the countryside. This particular preacher of the end of time included in his premonitions certain verses from the Qur'an, our sacred text that is far too lofty to be soiled in this foul and demeaning place. The dreadful way he was pronouncing the verses was even worse than a donkey braying. Once he had finished and his voice had turned hoarse, his words were immediately followed by some recorded songs with lewd lyrics. It was totally impossible to get to sleep. I noticed a guard passing by, so I hurried over to the bars at the entrance to my cell and yelled my complaint to him. He signaled back to me that he could not hear what I was saying, then left.

I was left on my own to mutter angry words of complaint to myself. I used moistened bread to make some earplugs and held them in place with my tie, but they did little good. This incredibly loud noise, completely nerve-shattering was another means that the people in charge of the prison were using to torture prisoners and drive the weaker and more sensitive ones to breakdown and madness. I turned to my own devices, invoking whatever help I could to protect myself against their evil and thwart their devilish schemes—God is enough for me, and good is He as a trustee.

Dawn is the time for prayer for those who will. As I did so, the situation in the wing was no different from what I have already described. It was only when morning broke that things calmed down. A guard brought me breakfast. I begged him to ask the inmates to lower the volume on their music at night so people who wanted to get some sleep and relax could do so. In a gruff tone he informed me that the basic principle of this wing required that prisoners inure

their bodies to being deprived of sleep or to get whatever they could
to the accompaniment of popular verses and contemporary songs,
interspersed with sermons on Fridays and holy days. When I asked
him why the noise happened during the night rather than daytime,
he scoffed.

"You idiot!" he replied as he locked the door, "It's at night that
you're sleepless. The music you've been hearing is merely a warm-up
for the even greater soirée tonight. Haven't you heard about it?!"

"The even greater soirée tonight?" I was still asking as he left.

If I am invited to attend, it will be certainly easier than staying
in this block, which seems to be inhabited by people who are not
actually alive—human specters with God knows what problems and
afflicted with how many scars.

Apart from performing my prayers—something that by now has
become my fondest activity, the only way of passing the time of day is
what I have been training myself to do: huddle in a corner in a lump
and withdraw into myself so I can engage with my inner being. Then I
can probe and search, hold conversations, recollect and recall things,
battle against fancy, and declare victory. I can pose those ultimate
questions and seek the remotest of signs; I can broach the discourse of
the impossible, that elusive elixir that is so hard to grasp; I can circle
around myself like a snake and chew the soles of my feet, and all in
search of a small amount of sleep and quiet. Perhaps I can also indulge
in still deeper contemplation and replace my current, horrendous reality with a more luminous dream. But fat chance of that!

The entire corridor is ringing with the sound of feet and voices
chattering. The stretcher-bearers are taking the sick and dead prisoners out of their cells. Among the latter is the prisoner opposite me
who was always wrapped in his blanket and two of his neighbors.
As I watched, I prayed to God to grant them all mercy. Through a
megaphone, a loud voice then kept announcing that the major soirée
would be happening and encouraged all healthy prisoners to attend.
To make sure it was a success, they were told to get themselves washed
and remove the foul stench from their bodies. The same voice went
on to say that the people who were invited had to get rid of any

weapons—knives, razors, and the like. Anyone who did not do so would be caught by the electronic screening devices; the punishment would be twenty consecutive days in the dungeon.

The man making the announcement looked into my cell and urged me to wash myself. The sound of his voice kept babbling until it faded away down the block. I struggled to my feet, telling myself that the gang in charge of the center seemed to be claiming to have plenty of machines to collect foul stenches! As I took off my clothes, the whole idea forced a reluctant chuckle out of me. I went over to the water tap and discovered that there was plenty of water to be had, something very unusual. I washed my shirt, sprinkled water over my body, beginning with my armpits, buttocks, and pubic region, and, as a crowning gesture, performed a ritual ablution that was worthy of the name. After performing the obligatory prayers, I sat cross-legged on my bed, waiting for my shirt to dry and to see what happened next.

There was a weird atmosphere of silence in the cells and the corridor, and I had no idea what kind of din might follow it. As a way of passing the time, I decided to make a kind of perfume as best I could, one I could use to rinse and scent myself. I squeezed some toothpaste into a glass of water, dissolved and shook it, till it was a liquid suitable to my needs. At the same time I prayed to God that He would look on 'Umar al-Rami with His mercy, he being the one who had given me two tubes of this priceless commodity—may God reward him with something yet more precious and valuable in His eternal paradise!

While I was wrapped in my blanket and still putting my shirt where it could catch the breeze from the upper window, I heard some other voices—some shouting, others merely muttering; they were complaining and protesting. How could he attend the soirée, he was asking, when he was suffering from penile dysfunction? Whenever anything emerged from his penis, it came in painful spurts. Another person was asking for some soap so he could wash properly and remove the filth from his body. Still another said that it was very unlikely that he would attend the soirée since his clothes were filthy and he had no incense or rosewater to perfume himself. The other voices were too far removed or else their voices were not clear, so I could not hear what they were saying.

Just before sunset, I was fully prepared. Putting on my modern suit and tie first, I had then put the prison uniform over it. I had used my own special perfume again and brushed my beard and what hair I had left. A few moments later a guard called out my number and took me via some empty cells to a hall where a large number of prisoners had gathered, although I did not recognize any of them. The majority of them looked grim and downcast, as though they were either going to their own deaths, or else to a funeral, rather than a major soirée. The gestures and affectations of any of them who looked happy and contented made it clear that they were either hashish addicts or mentally deranged.

A whistle was blown to indicate that the group was to move on, and the guards started hustling people along like a herd of cattle. As the group made its way through halls and lobbies, the number grew. When we left the building and headed via courtyards and squares to another one, a soldier took me aside and, avoiding my questions, told me to walk ahead of him. When we reached the side of a sandy hill that was deserted except for two soldiers and a man wearing a jurist's cloak, the last of the three pronounced the phrases "In the name of God" and "Only God has the power" and then addressed me. He asked me first to confirm my name and prisoner number.

"The list of your crimes and sins is a lengthy one, man from Oujda," he said. "Most recently you've tried to escape and then occupied a cell that does not have your number on it. So answer me swiftly: Do you seek repentance?"

"I have done nothing wrong that would require repentance," I replied. "I did not run away. I was with the judge, and at his request . . ."

That made them all guffaw.

"This claim—in fact, this utter falsehood—is yet another crime, which only makes things that much worse. Tell me, aren't you afraid to die?"

"God Almighty has said: 'Every soul tastes death, and We test you with good and evil as a temptation. Then unto Us do you return" [Sura 21, Anbiya, v. 35].

"So that's how little value you place on your own soul?! Is it because you can't find a job? At a time when massive unemployment is spreading like a deadly plague, why aren't you looking for work?"

"I would certainly look for work if it were legitimate and honorable and provided me with a living wage."

"I can see that you're both coarse and stubborn. You deserve neither forgiveness nor mercy. So now prepare to die; you can either be buried alive or be shot. The method used is not by compulsion— Islam forbids such a thing, but rather one that the explicit texts of our righteous religion do not forbid, either heads or tails. It's up to you, so which one do you choose."

"In God's name," I replied, utterly stunned, "I . . . I . . . choose . . ."

"Very well then," he went on, "here's a coin. I'll toss it in the air, and let it fall into my hand. I'll make the choice instead. Do we agree?"

This phony jurist did as he said. When the decision was made, he came over and kissed me.

"You're so lucky," he yelled in congratulation. "You're to be shot. That's much kinder than burying you alive. I'm so happy for you! There are also two different ways of doing the shooting. The first has the soldiers in charge, in which case they fire either live rounds or rubber bullets that do not kill. The second way involves us giving you a revolver with a silencer, which you yourself point at your head; either it fires a live round or else there's nothing that kills and the only noise is the sound of the firing pin. So which do you choose? This time you have to make the decision."

"Let's do it the first way," I replied, my head still spinning with his dreadful words.

He now instructed the soldiers to take their positions at the legally sanctioned distance, while I recited the Islamic statement of faith. The man now came over to me.

"I'll exempt you from this imminent threat of death," he told me, "provided that you accept the judge's offer. You know it by heart."

I signaled my refusal, and he moved back to his former position.

"Three, two, one, zero," he yelled.

The bullets struck me all at once. I sank to the ground, but was still alive. When I spotted blood splattering my chest, I had no doubt that I was bleeding profusely and about to die. When that seemed to be taking a while and I was still waiting, I heard the people who had carried out the sentence guffawing with laughter and poking fun at me. From the ground I saw two shoes, the owner of which ordered me to get up. As I stood up slowly, my entire being was completely shattered. The person addressing me was this so-called jurist.

"We're postponing even your death for a while," he told me, doing his best not to laugh. "That's so you can think seriously about things and make the best decision. How lucky you are! The blood on your chest is actually tomato ketchup. Wipe it off and go to the soirée. Good-bye!"

I obeyed the order of this soldier who had disguised himself as a jurist and followed a soldier to the place he was indicating.

25

The Major Soirée and Its Disgusting Surprises

My escort halted me and then told me to go in. Once inside, a guard told me to sit on an empty chair at the back of the hall. I was surprised that no one had used an electronic device to search me for weapons or check on my bodily odors; maybe because I had come late or stories about the electronic scanner had been a pack of lies. I asked someone sitting opposite me where we were. He seemed perplexed by the question, so I specifically asked where this detention center was. He pointed his finger at his head and turned away. I stayed where I was, although I resisted the temptation to fall asleep by looking at people's backs and watching the prying eyes all around the hall.

The hall where the soirée was taking place was actually the dining hall that had been turned into a kind of theater. The audience consisted of the various types and categories of prisoner, surrounded by guards and a few soldiers who kept going up and down the rows. Everyone was facing a wide stage lit by flashing strobe lights that pulsated to the soft rhythms of some jazz blues. As the prisoners sat there and waited, various salesmen wandered up and down the rows with bags and baskets: one offering cold drinks, another snacks and sandwiches, and a third—who was most successful at flaunting his ware.

"Listen, folks," he shouted, "if there are no more beans, don't blame my means!"

A short while after I had taken a seat, a girl got up on to the stage. Her bodily attributes made it obvious—but God knows best—that she was none other than Nahid Busni. She started singing in a

188

thoroughly suggestive fashion, and her reddened lips spoke into a handheld microphone. Here's some of what I managed to pick up:

"What to drink when you're thirsty? What can you drink that will make you feel happy and vigorous again? What lets you feel young all over again? Drink what I do, Pepsi Cola! Young folk only drink Pepsi. Pepsi Cola makes girls feel sexy and men strong. And here's the last thing I have to tell you: When my boyfriend and I are feeling bored and start quarreling with each other, we lie down on a Rich-bond bed and that makes us happy and loving all over again! Rich-bond, Rich-bond . . . wow, what a bed!"

This girl waved at the crowd. By now I had no doubt in my mind that she was Nahid Busni, the only difference being that, whereas she had previously been pronouncing the letter "r" as "gh," now she was turning the "qaf" into a "hamza." My assumption was confirmed when the prisoners started yelling her name out; as she sashayed her way off the stage. Some of them even invited her to try a straw bed where she would find some real men.

Once she had left the stage, her place was taken by a fat, bald man with a yellowing beard who started leaping and charging across the stage. He was wearing a yellow suit and carrying a microphone in one hand and a red handkerchief in the other which he waved at times and used to wipe the sweat off his forehead at others.

"Dear audience," he shouted, "may your enjoyment and delight last forever! The girl in that part of the show with the lovely voice and perfect shape has now left the stage, but she'll be back, thanks to your polite reception. I'm the master of ceremonies this evening, and I'll be back to let you all know more about this wonderful evening, one that will break the ice and remove all the nasty disputes between brothers. All that will happen according to the sacred verse that says: 'You are all Adam's descendants, and mankind comes from Eve.'"

A number of voices were raised to correct him, and the emcee hurriedly apologized.

"Oh, I'm so sorry!" he went on. "The tongue has no bones in it! We've been looking into the complaints that some of you have raised against others and propose to use either consensus or majority vote to come to decisions about them on this stage—all with a view to being absolutely fair, reconciling people with each other, and being totally impartial. There's only one complaint remaining, and it's been raised by prisoner 19, who is present among us against prisoner 112. I see a hand raised . . . maybe the defendant. So let him come up to the stage along with the plaintiff. Be quick now; time is not on our side. You are Hamuda from Oujda, correct? You're a cultured man, right? This man, 'Allal Munkhar, accuses you of causing him to receive sixty lashes because you encouraged him to applaud you during a previous cross-examination. We can give you a choice: do you want to receive the same number of lashes as he did in front of this crowd, or would you prefer to kiss his head and beg him to forgive you?"

To bring closure to this farce, I had no choice but to accept the second option. As I used the microphone to ask the man's forgiveness, my eyes happened to fall on two men sitting side by side in the front row. The emcee came back on to the stage, and both he and the plaintiff urged me to leave.

"Praise be to God!" the emcee said. "The kiss has taken place and the file is now closed. Why are you standing there like a statue, Oujda man?"

I pointed to the two men.

"That man and the other man beside him, I know them both," I declared.

"Do you have a complaint to raise against them?"

"That one is Ilyas Abu Shama, who was killed in the main courtyard a while ago in front of witnesses, but here he is now, alive and kicking! The other one is 'Umar al-Shami, who was killed in my presence only yesterday, and yet here he is too, alive and kicking!"

The emcee used the microphone to relay my comment, and the whole place erupted in laughter.

"Time's short," he told me. "Choose one of them, and we'll see if things go for or against you."

I pointed at 'Umar al-Rami, and he came up on stage. I tried to embrace and kiss him, but he refused and pushed me away.

"By what heavenly miracle are you still alive?" I asked him as affectionately as I could while the emcee kept switching the microphone between the two of us. "I watched the soldiers fire a fusillade of bullets at you."

"None of what you say ever happened," he replied in a dry tone. "You're certainly mistaken . . ."

"My dear brother," I went on, "don't you remember the night they put you in my cell? It was after you'd been brought from the torture chamber with the most dreadful wounds. I saved you and looked after you. Please remember, I beg of you . . ."

"Listen, everyone," he replied, "this man's spouting nonsense. Everything you're saying is a pack of lies!"

"We need to get back to the program," the emcee interrupted. "Can anyone suggest a way forward or a solution . . . ?"

Some voices were raised, suggesting that Shari'a principles be applied: the burden of proof rests with the plaintiff, and those who wish to deny it have to be prepared to swear. Someone else demanded that I describe the body of the now resurrected dead person in detail. The emcee obtained my agreement to the proposal. When I pointed out that the prisoner's uniform that I was wearing was actually 'Umar's, he objected that all uniforms looked the same. I then whispered in the emcee's ear that he should investigate whether 'Umar had been castrated or not. He gave me a weird look and let out a series of guffaws that sounded like women at weddings. The effect spread to the rest of the audience.

"No, no!" he chuckled. "That's impossible! This is a prize, something you'll never forget even if you manage to forget all about this soirée. Listen, everyone, and bear it in mind for later. Now as before, words count and the verdict will be carried out. This lad here claims that his rival has been castrated, and he wants it checked. Can you imagine such a dreadful accusation?"

Laughter echoed around the hall, and some inaudible questions were asked.

"You've all freely posed a number of dreadful resolutions to this matter," the emcee commented. "I propose to appoint this audience member from the front row to assemble them all in a single opinion. Take the microphone and proceed to announce in all clarity what it is to be."

This assistant now took the microphone. I immediately recalled that I had met him in the penitents' wing; I had forgotten him and the fact that he was one of the men who had used my body as a punch ball! However, I did not wish to make my situation even more complicated, so I said nothing about that.

"From what this august assembly has decided," he said, "I deduce that they wish to elect a commission of upright men. Its task will be to investigate the charge in detail. If they find that the defendant indeed has no testicles, he will stand accused of concealment and lying. If on the other hand the charge is not found to be correct, then the plaintiff will be partially castrated in accordance with the circumstances involved. That's the way it will be. So be it!"

The emcee now asked if both parties agreed to the proposal. My opponent immediately agreed, but I demurred. Instead, I admitted into the microphone that I was wrong and the person in question merely looked similar. I actually had no doubt that 'Umar was the person involved, but he now grabbed me by the tie and heaved me across the stage twice, while the emcee kept on yelling that there should be no violence and ordered us both to return to our seats.

"Before you sit down, Oujda man," he went on delightedly," kiss this innocent man on the head. In that way we will be purging the atmosphere of all evil, with God's assistance, breaking the ice, and removing all the nasty disputes between brothers. Now our nonstop soirée will continue. I can communicate to you all the happy news that in a short while our soirée will be honored by the presence of the senior officials at our center, except, that is, for the judge, who has been compelled to travel abroad for some routine medical tests. Now, I want to repeat what I told you all earlier: this stage, this party, with its dance music and musical dance, it's all part of our motto, our desire to see everyone feeling better. So that's our slogan. Now let's give a big hand!"

There were enormous speakers at the top of pillars and corners of the hall, and mechanical applause resonated through the space. The majority of prisoners did not join in until the guards made it clear through their looks and gestures that everyone should participate. I did my part, feeling absolutely delighted that the judge had found it necessary to have a medical checkup. My prayer to God was that the reason was connected to my last interview with him and the way I had pretended to be ill.

"Thanks for that warm and sincere applause," the emcee resumed. "Now, before anything else, this American expert on Islam wants to share with you, in Arabic, the results of his research and archeological digs. Do you agree? Fine, then I now gratefully present to you Doctor George Levy."

The man in question who was wearing a civilian suit and bow tie now came forward and positioned himself behind the static microphone.

"Gentlemen," he said tentatively with a nervous smile, "I'm honored to be able to address you all in your wonderful language, the one in which the Qur'an was revealed. Please forgive me if I make any grammar mistakes or use inappropriate words. To avoid such pitfalls I'm going to rely on the well-known proverb, 'Where there's a will, there's a way.' That's all based, of course, on the sound Islamic doctrine of tolerance, mutual understanding, facilitation, and kindness. You should all be aware that 'the Kind, the Forgiving, and the Merciful' are all beautiful names of God! Surely you have all read in the text of the Qur'an where God Almighty says: 'He has not imposed on you any restriction regarding religion' [Sura 22, al-Hajj, v. 87], and 'God wishes ease for you and does not wish hardship' [Sura 2, al-Baqara, v. 185]. People claim that Islamic fundamentalism in its various guises is the reaction of a wounded creature, but only advocates of extremism, violence, and hatred would want to wound not only themselves but also others, to the point of murder. Islam forbids such behavior and anything else resembling it. Islam is a religion of peace and reconciliation, as the Sufi tendency clearly demonstrates. It's a religion of compromise, one that encourages harmony and debate over ways to make things better. Muslims follow the better way, albeit based on the Qur'an, which certainly allows for adjustment with the requirements and necessities of the age, from which to reformulate doctrine. Islam is anti-war and anti-weapons, except enough to protect society against internal enemies. It disapproves of weapon ownership, because at base Islam is a faith system that advocates malleability, adaptability, meekness, kindness, and a general inclination toward peace and quiet. I'll explain this in more detail in my next lecture. Farewell."

Protests were heard all over the hall, and the speaker was compelled to stop talking and hurry off the stage under a positive hail of shoes. Some of the prisoners were arrested, but one of them managed to elude the guards and, like a genie out of a bottle, made his way to the stage.

"It's easy to counter this nonsense from the Americans," he yelled into the microphone. "Just listen to a recent statement I managed to get from my transistor radio before they took it away from me. The prime minister of Israel, Ehud Omert, had this to say: 'If Hamas does not stop terrorizing our children and old people with its homemade bombs, we're going to destroy Gaza and leave it a total ruin.' The two major political parties in America and other groups also have been falling over each other in their rush to declare Israel a strictly Jewish nation, implying the need to strip Palestinians of all their weapons, including religion. The secretary of state, in fact, has spoken in the name of all the groups and on his own behalf. What he has had to say is even worse and more vicious in its intent. Just listen . . ."

He was not able to finish his sentence because Nahid Busni approached him on tiptoe and sprayed his eyes with pepper spray, the smell of which spread all around the hall. As she went back to her seat, two guards picked up the speaker, who had fainted, and took him out through an emergency door—all to the accompaniment of protests from the audience.

The soldiers and guards now imposed quiet again, and the emcee returned to the stage, accompanied by a group of men who looked like ascetics and dervishes.

"Oh dear, oh dear!" he said nervously, tapping the floor with his foot. "I said from the start 'No politics, none!' Politics tear people apart and sow the seeds of dissent and conflict. Our goal here is to clear the air, break the ice, and remove all the nasty disputes between brothers. Now that I'm feeling a bit calmer, let's go back to our soi-rée. As I said before, brothers, our slogan tonight is dance music as a way of feeling better. This is a group that has devoted its talents to a blend of Sufi séance and well-known techno songs. The same thing has happened with jazz and the traditional music of the Gnaoua.* This group's known by the initials, TTI, Transtechno-International. They're here to entertain you with some of their works. Anyone who feels moved and transported and wants to join in the dance is wel-come to do so. Three, two, one, zero . . ."

Ear-splitting music now emerged from the speakers, and the group did a crazy dance in a circle, necks extended, heads and bod-ies swaying, and eyes closed in the sheer emotional intensity of the moment. Voices competed with each other to shout out phrases, but the only one we could hear was "God is with us, God is alive!" While some people in the audience joined it, others—including myself—did their best to ignore the whole thing by reciting verses from the Qur'an and repeating the beautiful names of God.

The music stopped all of a sudden, and the group left the stage to applause, most of it artificial. The emcee now came back.

"Thank you, thank you to the TTI group," he enthused. "Now this wonderful soirée will continue. It's time now for humor and jokes, something that'll make us all feel so much better. This is the way things were in the past, those fortunate people who imitated the behavior of our Prophet—the purest of peace be upon Him! The story is told about him that, whenever he attended a ceremony of some kind, he had it recorded. So no scowling and frowning, people!"

While his enormous body was swaying and dancing this way and that, another group came up on to the stage, singing in the rap-style:

"Take it down, folks, take it down,
Take a good look, folks, a good look!

Watch and be watched,
Have a good time and sing,
Sing, O sing again,
Life goes by so fast,
If you don't have a laugh,
Things'll get you down, and you'll be dead!"

"So then," the emcee went on, "it's time for some good old-fashioned laughter. Our center's clown for the evening is a master at telling jokes and humorous stories—the salt of life and the best cure for depression and anxiety. So a round of applause, please, for our witty midget with the long white beard and experienced penis. He comes from a family of jokesters and inherits the talent from the old masters of racy humor, the ones to whom the well-known slogan applies: 'There's no modesty in faith.' There are countless examples who could be cited—al-Jahiz, al-Tawhidi, Ibn al-Jawziyya, al-Suyuti, al-Tifashi, and many, many others as well—God's mercy on them all!* We have all benefitted from their mention and memory, and both they and we are thereby forgiven. Everyone say 'Amen!'"

Some people responded enthusiastically, others less so. At this point, a group of senior officials at the center came out through a door at the back of the stage. There were seven of them, including the same ghoul with her amazing body clad in black and her usual searing glances. The emcee leapt up to welcome them and escorted them all to their special seats with a welcoming bow. He then turned and told the assembly to stand up and greet them all with applause. Some groups did as they were asked, but others refused. The guards went over and started hitting and threatening the recalcitrant prisoners, so all were eventually on their feet and clapping. The loudspeakers added their own mechanical applause to the noise, along with some weird military band-music—may God never empower such people! Once this particular farce was over, the officials sat down in their seats and so did everyone else. The emcee now thanked everyone for welcoming the senior officials so warmly and displaying their genuine feelings in this way. He then called on the official clown to perform his act. The midget came forward and bowed to each of the officials one by one. His beard looked long enough to serve as a broom for the stage.

"Dear prisoners, our beloved in God," he said, grabbing the microphone to a chorus of hysterical laughter from the audience, "have you heard the one about the smart young dandy? He kept on saying wonderful things about one of his singing-girls and her sexual performance in a whole variety of rarely encountered positions, all with a professional approach that was unrivaled. Is this slave girl of yours going to enter heaven or not, he was asked. 'No, she won't,' he replied, provoking all kinds of laughter and applause, 'By God, not unless I hide her with me on the Day of Judgment and cross the narrow path to heaven with her. Then she'll be able to make it under my cloak!'"

Mechanical applause emerged from the loudspeakers.

"May God preserve you all from collective repression and inadequacy! So here's another one, about an old monk sitting on a crowded bus. Standing next to him is a beautiful and attractive young girl. When the bus brakes suddenly, she loses her balance and her lovely backside lands up in his lap. When she gets to her feet again, she's blushing furiously and asks him to forgive her. 'My dear girl,' the monk replies, 'I totally forgive you. All you've done is to arouse the church keys from a prolonged slumber!'"

There was some feeble laughter, followed by more when people finally understood the symbolic meaning behind the joke.

"So now you're enjoying my jokes," he went on, "and you want more. However, the program is a busy one, and time's short. So just one more as a farewell gesture. Here's one about a shaykh who liked boys. One day he spotted a truly lovely boy, so he followed him and decided to use every means possible to seduce him. The boy got on a bus, so he did too. Standing right behind the boy, he started whispering in his ear. The boy indicated his agreement, but the shaykh started rubbing the boy's backside hard. 'Enough!' the boy told him angrily. 'We've agreed already, so why are you tickling me like that?' 'Just to remind you!' the shaykh replied."

That was followed by a lot of lewd laughter, led by the female ghoul, who had a microphone right in front of her. The loudspeakers duly amplified the laughter and applause, which grew louder and louder. She stopped laughing all of a sudden. The midget stood in front of her and proceeded to perform some amazing gymnastic tricks, as though he were dedicating them to his only acknowledged patroness and guardian. Once he had finished, he disappeared behind her.

"God fight you, master clown and midget!" the emcee now said, faking a broad smile. "Now it's the enormous black guard's turn. He's a loyal servant of this center and needs no introduction. From time to time you've undoubtedly heard the sounds of tom-tom drums that trace their origins to deepest black Africa. However, you'll never have heard anything as loud and superb as what our African giant can do. The amazing thing is that, as he's playing, he can actually hear nothing—whether it's soft or loud—because, as you all know, his hearing and speech are both impaired—we seek refuge in God from such calamities! He'll be coming up on the stage, so please give him some applause to encourage him. Count down with me . . . three, two, one, zero . . ."

True enough, the giant black guard now came up on the center stage. I got up from my seat to look at him; in fact, I was one of the first to do so. In this case, the applause was heartfelt and genuine, not compulsory or under threat. People were yelling support for him and offering prayers for his continent, his people, and his tribe. The guards now started interfering to get people to stop yelling and take their seats again. The giant guard bowed low to the audience, then sat there with the drum between his knees. With taps and drumbeats he started creating melodies that were at turns soft, medium, and loud. The feelings of joy and rapture that they aroused made everyone want to shake and dance. And that is precisely what happened: as the atmosphere intensified, people started standing up and dancing, soon followed by others. Feet, legs, heads, hands, and bodies all started moving in crazy, swaying circles. One of them asked me to join in, but I excused myself because of my bad leg. He did not hear me. I was pulled toward him and did my best to imitate his movements.

This went on for a while, and the emcee was not able to do anything about it. The dancers were clearly totally absorbed. It felt as though they were not yet rid of their feelings of filth and repression and were using their sweat, shouts, and frothy moans to expunge it all. The emcee did his best to rewind things and used the microphone to ask the assembled company to stop; there was a still a lot to go in the soirée's program. He reminded them all that the crowning touch would come when new groups and ranks of recanting prisoners would be presented, people who had now seen the light and were going to cooperate in a spirit of true devotion, to root out extremism and terrorism from all quarters of the globe. When this announcement totally failed to achieve any result, he went over to the black guard and signaled to him to stop playing and leave the stage. But the guard refused and hit him so hard that he fell to the floor.

At this point the female ghoul staggered to her feet in disgust and walked unsteadily toward her servant. She indicated to him by mime that he should put the drum away. He did so, showing his obedience by bending down and kissing her feet. She now asked for her microphone and proceeded to announce in a mixture of French, English, and Arabic that in her previous life she had worked as a circus trainer of lions, tigers, and other wild beasts. Training the African slave who was now bowing in front of her and kissing her feet was easier than training a monkey or braying ass. Turning to the audience, she threatened them all with time in the dungeon with no limit, and torture chambers. The punishment would apply to anyone who continued to subvert order and refused to obey instructions.

However, no sooner had this thundering, frothing woman stopped talking to recover her breath before launching into another tirade of insults than the entire audience witnessed something utterly amazing. The black guard suddenly leapt to his feet, with the female ghoul perched on his enormous shoulders. He walked all across the stage while she, obviously stunned, waved at the audience and showed the victory sign to a wave of artificial applause. Everyone's astonishment only intensified when, in front of the entire assembly, the black slave threw the female ghoul to the floor. As her eyes widened in sheer amazement, he leapt on her and put his fingers in her eyes, while she screamed for help. He aimed a series of crushing blows at her head and started ripping at her stomach, as though he wanted to tear out all her organs and innards. No sooner was the stage emptied of the emcee and other officials than the soldiers and guards fired a hail of bullets at the black guard, who fell to the ground to take cover. He then stood up, holding the bloody body of the female ghoul. Once the armed men realized that their female boss was either near death or already dead at the hands of the man who was holding her up, they were told to attack the stage and aim at the black guard from every direction. That is precisely what they did, firing a hail of bullets at the target while at the same time not missing the dead body of the ghoul. The two bodies fell to the floor in a pool of blood.

At this point a whole series of protests and fights broke out involving groups of prisoners on the one hand, including me, and on the other, guards and other prisoners. The soldiers now started attacking the former group, firing live rounds into the air and at their feet, along with tear gas. Panic ensued, and everyone tried to get to the doors and windows. I suffered a blow to my neck from a rifle butt. Along with many others, I lost consciousness and fell to the floor.

26

My Return to My Beloved Land

I woke up to find myself in the clinic along with a whole host of other wounded prisoners. I made a huge effort to remember what had happened some time ago, a period I could not even estimate. I was able to recall a few details, but I stopped trying because I was suffering from a chronic migraine. I pretended to be asleep, but then I noticed Na'ima approaching my bed with her friend, the Christian female doctor and a foreigner—all of them wearing surgical masks. They were all talking in English, but I managed to understand that the doctor was trying to convince the man that I was paralyzed and spitting blood. Na'ima told him the same thing and suggested that I should be returned to my homeland because my health made me useless for any kind of service, and I might cause contagion in the center that would affect everyone. That was the last I heard before I felt Na'ima's hand touching my face and watched as the three of them moved on to other beds and then left.

I was delighted by this chain of events, although I still felt a bit cautious. The possibility of my release came closer when the foreigner did not demand that I be subjected to any further medical examination. It never even occurred to me as a possibility—but it's what actually happened!—that one of the other sick prisoners in a bed beside mine stood up on his bed and yelled as loudly as he could; "Listen, you people!" he said. "This man's paralyzed. They've sent him here to infect us all with his infectious disease. Either take him away now or else get us all out of here!"

These words of warning were followed by complaints and protests from the other prisoners. Most of them were getting ready to run out of the room, and they would have done so if the emergency intervention squad had not come in and resolved the issue in their own unique fashion. Once their commander realized what the issue was, he gave orders that I was to be put in a secure room. I praised God for this series of events and assumed that it augured well.

A masked visitor arrived in the middle of the night, grabbed my left arm by the wrist and put an electronic monitor on it, one that would tell the personnel and staff at the center everything I would be doing on a series of high-tech screens. He advised me that I would soon be on my way and advised me strongly not to let anyone or any other entity know that I had been in prison or why I had been away for so long. If I did so, the electronic device would administer a deadly electric shock even before I had a chance to open my mouth. If there were to be any technical problems, a fully trained sniper would fire a silenced bullet at my head. This visitor administered an injection, then left. With that, I lost consciousness . . .

They must have re-injected me with a powerful, long-lasting sedative several times during my transfer; I had not the slightest sense of its mode, method, or duration. I woke up to find myself in the shade of a palm tree with a bag containing some conserved food, bottles of water, and some Moroccan money. I was able to confirm that I was back in my beloved homeland when a camel driver came up and asked me in the purest Moroccan Arabic if I needed any help. After thanking him for his offer, I asked him what the date was. He told me it was Wednesday in the Muslim month, Rabiʿ ath-thani 1425; in the Western calendar, the 17th of May, 2006. So, I muttered to myself, I've been in prison for five years. The man looked worried and asked me again if there was anything I needed.

"Yes," I replied. "What's the closest village with a mosque?"

"'Abw al-Akhal" he replied. "It's a short distance away. I'm going that way."

I stood up and mounted the camel behind him. With a shout of praise to God, he urged the animal into motion.

On the way he asked me what had brought me to this deserted spot.

"A sheer love of my homeland and its desert," I replied, conscious of the monitor on my wrist, "and a desire to see the moon and pearly stars from close up."

He approved of my opinions and recited these Qur'anic verses in a melodious tone: "God has made the earth for you as a carpet, so you may traverse its pathways and valleys." (Sura 71, Nuh, v. 20)—God Almighty has spoken the truth.

I told him that I was heading eventually for my hometown of Oujda. He replied that, praise be to God, there were a number of trucks, cars, and buses that went there. Once we arrived, he took off his outer coat and put it on me, then left me by the only mosque in the village. With that, he continued his journey, but not before asking me if I needed anything else.

I entered the mosque where I first performed the ritual ablutions, then prayed the requisite prayers and some other litanies, thanking God for my release and safety. I spent the night inside the mosque, along with a group of strangers and other travelers. Next morning, I used of a number of different modes of transport as I made my way back to my hometown.

27

Conclusion

1

Oh yes, my gracious Na'ima, may God be gracious to you and comfort you!

Since returning to my homeland, I've chosen to live on the Angad Plain, a hilly farming area with clean air, fresh, pure water, the sounds of birds, domestic and farm animals, and a sweet refreshing breeze that blows in from the Bani Sanasin hills. It is springtime, and the whole scenario coalesces in a way that manages to distract me, if only from time to time, from the horrendous years of imprisonment and the physical and psychological injuries I have suffered.

A genuinely pious and generous man, Hamdan al-Mizati, who owns the farm where I am staying, has arranged for me to be looked after by a widow and her unmarried daughter. They are taking good care of me and feeding me nourishing food and various herbs. Thanks to the ministrations of these two women, I have been able to resume my normal sleep by gradually ridding myself of the patterns of nightmare and sleeplessness that afflicted me in prison. For a whole month I have managed to spend daylight hours in the shade of a spreading leafy oak tree, while the evenings have been spent by lamplight in the wide-open house, committing to paper the chapters of my prison narrative and recalling as far as possible all the painful memories and residual consequences of such a physical and psychological trauma.

Between prayers, and especially in this wonderful month of Rajab, I find that my mind catches fire and my talents explode into creativity. By means of my pen, words and images move from my tongue to the page. Whenever I rest or eat something, my hostess, Khaduj, and her daughter, Zaynab, ask me what I am doing. When I give them some snippets, the mother throws her head covering to the floor and launches into a tirade of prayers against the tyrannical monsters who have committed such things against me, while the daughter's reddened eyes weep copious tears, which I hasten to wipe away, either with my handkerchief or my hand.

One fine day I decided to sit in the hollow at the top of the oak tree and put the finishing touches to my manuscript with some editing and corrections, all to the accompaniment of the fascinating logic of the bird population. I did just that, but I had hardly involved myself totally in my task before I had to stop, having noticed Zaynab running hither and yon, like a gazelle that has gone crazy. She kept yelling my name and begging me to show myself. Her mother kept telling her to calm down and control herself. When I scrambled down the tree, Zaynab rushed over to me, panting and out of breath, and looked at me with tear-filled eyes. It has been ages now since I have come across anyone with warmer and deeper feelings than hers. As she ran away, I saw her mother coming towards me with my breakfast tray.

Once I had finished work on my manuscript, I folded it up and put it in a box. I told Khaduj that I wanted to use her mule to go into Oujda and deal with some urgent business. She and Zaynab both prepared a travel pack for me and stuffed it with food, baskets of vegetables, and fruit for me to give the jurist, al-Mizati. As they both said farewell, they made me promise not to stay away too long. I went on my way, feeling free and easy; with my beard duly clipped; I was wearing a *jallaba* and a turban on my head.

The five days I spent in the city were filled with activity and success. First thing, I went to the blood laboratory, where I gave some blood so I could check on my immunization status. I then headed for the dental clinic, where my few remaining decayed teeth were extracted with anesthetic. I was promised a new set of false teeth made to measure so I could forget all about my messed-up mouth.

I spent that same night in my bookstore, using candlelight to collect the books that I could save, ones that had not been eaten by mice and bookworms. I put them all in a box that still preserved some of my personal possessions, clothes, and civil-status documentation. That done, I did my ablutions and said the prayers before surrendering to sleep, still dressed in my *jallaba*.

Next morning, I woke up with a start, having just emerged from a nightmare in which all the personnel in my terrible prison experience and all the dreadful events had followed one another in relentless succession. I leapt up and made for the mosque, where I performed the ablutions again, prayed the dawn prayer, and asked God for guidance. None of the other worshippers knew who I was, and the same thing applied to passersby when I exited the mosque. My traditional garb, my graying beard, and the years I had been away all combined to make me seem a stranger or a new arrival in the city. For my own part, I barely recognized anyone as I made my way through the markets, bazaars, and other crowded places. People had changed: health problems, the inexorable advance of time, and old age had all had their effects, but this was all part of God's practice with His creation—and to that there was no alternative.

I hastily ate my breakfast and then headed for the blood laboratory to get the results of my test analyses. I asked the senior nurse to reassure me that I did not have AIDS, and she told me that everything was fine; that made me very happy, needless to say. Once I realized that God had saved me from the dire ministrations of the female ghoul and that the way now lay open for me to get married, I kissed her hand. Now there was no need to hold back or delay, particularly in view of the fact that I had wasted many years in prison and was now close to fifty years old. As evening fell on my second day in Oujda, I went to visit the home of the virtuous jurist, Hamdan al-Mizati, and broached precisely this topic. As I did so, I handed him the basket of food from the woman who, I hoped, would become my mother-in-law. His face immediately lit up, and he told his wife to prepare dinner.

"By God, my boy," he told me, "your intentions show that what your plan is indeed an act of charity. You'll be sheltering and looking after a good woman; you'll care for her and she for you. You will enhance your religion with a God-sanctioned marriage. Yesterday an official from the Angad region came and asked me why you were staying on my farm. The things I told him set him back on his heels, and he apologized profusely. But now that you've made this decision, you don't have to worry about him or anyone else."

He noticed that I was hesitating before saying something else. But just then his wife came in to welcome me and offer congratulations, and I stood up to greet her. After setting a number of plates on the table, she told me that her husband, the Hajj,* had told her wonderful things about me and I was to treat their home as my own.

"I have two sons," the jurist continued after she had left. "One died in obscure circumstances, and the second travels a lot to apply his modern knowledge and experience. So you can take their place as my son. But eat something first, then you can tell me what's worrying you."

I ate a little, then wiped my hands and mouth.

"May God give you a good reward, Hajj, for everything you're doing for me. But as soon as I'm married—through God's almighty power, I have to find a decent job so I can live by it and look after my family. My idea is to sell you my bookstore so I can use the money to buy part of your farm or some other tract close by. I don't like living in the city and feel claustrophobic. That's what prison has done to me, and the complaint about that needs to be directed to God. I can only see myself breathing freely in the countryside, tilling the soil, sowing seeds, and reaping the harvest that results. Something else is on my mind as well: I've completed my testimony about the prison. How can I get it published so that it gets to the people who matter?"

The shaykh gave me an affectionate look.

"Hamuda," he replied, "patience comes from God the Merciful, haste from the devil. All in good time! You'll get the piece of land you want, but not now. Your manuscript can be published with God's assistance, but not now. On the other hand, your marriage is a boon, and, as the proverb puts it, 'The best boons come the quickest.' On Friday afternoon we'll go to the farm with two witnesses, you'll be wed to Zaynab, and we'll have a reception to celebrate the happy occasion. After that, God will decide . . ."

For a moment, the shaykh fell silent and ate a little food. He then produced a sealed envelope from his pocket.

"Here's a sum of money," he said. "I'm loaning it to you with no interest, and you can return it whenever you can. Use it to buy things for yourself, but don't forget to purchase some clothes for both the bride and groom. The night before Friday you should visit the bath-house closest to my home, and until it's time to leave, you'll be staying here with me. Now go to the room you see in front of you and get what you need most: some rest and undisturbed sleep."

The only way I could see of expressing my heartfelt thanks to the shaykh was to kiss his head and hands many times before leaving him and going to the room he had indicated.

On Thursday evening I purchased various pieces of clothing and other things. I put my new set of teeth in and had the kind of wash in the bathhouse that I had not enjoyed for years. With the shaykh I prayed the evening prayer in the quarter's mosque, and we each offered our own fervent prayers. On Friday morning I brought the box of books that I had managed to save, and immediately after the noon prayer the shaykh took me and my belongings out to the farm in his truck, along with his wife and two witnesses.

Khaduj and Zaynab both welcomed us all with broad smiles, then set about preparing food and drink. No sooner had every-one gathered than the shaykh broached with Khaduj the possibil-ity of my marrying her daughter, all in accordance with the custom of God and His Prophet. Her positive response first took the form of copious prayers and blessings on God's Prophet, immediately fol-lowed by a whole chain of ululations that undoubtedly could be heard by the neighbors as well. Her daughter was overcome by emo-tions of utter joy and happiness, and she went rushing off into the fields, running and leaping into the air. She came back eventually, with tears in her eyes and flushed cheeks and responded to the two witnesses' question with a resounding 'Yes.' The wedding contract was now drawn up, and, once it was complete, the opening chapter of the Qur'an was recited and everyone prayed the afternoon prayer. The shaykh sacrificed a ram and prepared it for cooking, while the bride and her mother set about preparing an elaborate wedding banquet with the help of neighbors who contributed their own share of ululations. With God's assistance, the entire wedding went off well, and the district official and other neighbors came to join in the celebration. The women competed with each other to fill the entire neighborhood with ululations and celebratory poems, all to the accompaniment of rhythmic clapping, beating tambourines and drums, and clicking spoons and glasses on the tables and trays. All the while, other women—as far as I can tell—started washing, perfuming, and dressing the bride with appropriate clothes and expensive jewelry.

Between the sunset and evening prayers, we menfolk spent some deeply spiritual moments reciting passages from the Qur'an and chanting prophetic eulogies and Sufi litanies. I played a major part in all that and was sometimes the only one singing. During a pause, the jurist who was so responsible for my good fortune in all this leaned over and asked me where I had acquired such talents.

"God gave me such talents while I was studying," I whispered in his ear, "but such things were my spiritual sustenance and the primary source of my endurance during the long years I spent in prison."

It seems that the two witnesses and the local official were somewhat put out by their inability to participate in such religious celebrations, so, as soon as they had eaten, they rose to their feet and left, offering their thanks and good wishes to my wife and myself.

2

Oh yes, my gracious Na'ima, may God be gracious to you and comfort you!

When it came time for my bride and me to be alone, we headed for the room that had been prepared for us, each of us dressed in a pure white garment. The women who accompanied us were praising God and intoning prayers and blessings on our behalf. Once they had closed the door behind us, they all went back to start preparing the celebratory breakfast for the next day.

So here I am face to face with Zaynab, my wife. In her company I can learn again the alphabet of life. I will now start teaching her to read and write so that one day she can take my book and understand its contents.

This amazing night is the new point of beginning, the essence of a fresh outlook on life. I beg God Almighty, as far as possible, to keep it free, now and in the future, from all kinds of violence, frivolity, and sorrow.

The tears shed by my beloved wife are tears of joy as she discovers the sheer magic of married life. My tears are also those of joy, but they are also tempered by joy of another kind—the joy at being rid of the threat of death and destruction. All this is through God's good grace and yours as well, Na'ima, guardian angel over my happiness!

And it's all due to your knowledge as well, you intermediary of God the Creator in my rescue from death! Now here I am in the countryside, reading a book at times and plowing the fields at others along with my wife and mother-in-law. I am filling my lungs to their capacity with the sweet breath of my regained freedom and relishing it all in the company of Zaynab, as we use our mule to ride through valleys, streams, the Bani Sanasin hills, and the Camel's Cave. Sometimes we dismount and run races into the cave or across low-lying areas. To tell the truth, I find it easier to race a rabbit than to try to keep up with Zaynab. When the woman whom I've come to call "my gazelle" stops out of pity for me, I can assess the damage that the years in prison have wrought on my breathing and lungs. But I give praises to God that I am still alive and well and that there are many things I can still enjoy: sitting on the grass with my wife, for example, after we have been running, shading ourselves under the leafy trees and alongside a coursing brook. As we chatter, she kisses my hand and I kiss hers as we tease and touch each other and listen together to the sound of the fetus growing inside her womb.

With each passing day my period of convalescence becomes progressively shorter—what a blessing!—and all signs of my asthma disappear as though it had never really happened. My nightmarish visions gradually vanish as well, and little by little my complete recovery draws ever closer, all due to God's bounty and generosity.

My devout and generous sponsor, the jurist al-Mizati, now makes me the sole owner of the farm, with the written agreement of his surviving son. He leaves me as owner also of the bookstore in the hope that one day I'll be able to open it to my own students of religious learning, few though they may be.

I am delighted by my mother-in-law, who I hereby testify is the very best of her kind, and so is she with me. Barely a single day passed before we were sharing jokes and funny stories with each other. For example, I thought it was odd that there was no bull in her paddock. In reply she told me that it's the cow that is the more profitable by giving birth to calves and producing milk and its byproducts, so it deserves more fodder and close attention. The bull, on the other hand, she borrows without charge at particular times of the year. It impregnates her cows, and then she returns it to its owner. One of her other stories tells how one night she invited a married couple from Fez. Before breakfast the next morning, the couple were both staring in amazement at the number of chickens, cocks, and hens she had. The husband asked how that came about, and she told him that the cock has a large number of wives. "Did you hear that?" the wife whispered in her husband's ear. The husband asked my mother-in-law to explain: "Does the cock do it with just one hen and no more?" That made her laugh. "Oh no," she replied, "he not only does it with all the hens here, but even with the neighbors' hens as well." "Did you hear that?" the husband whispered in his wife's ear.

I have not yet found anyone to publish my prison narrative, except for one stupid idiot. He demanded that I pay a significant subvention, the excuse being that the book market was bad. He also asked me to remove many paragraphs and expressions because they had some savage things to say about politics and politicians and included some obscene sections that offended against public morality. I saw no point in reminding the man of the popular expression: "The person who imitates heresy is not a heretic," and applying the same principle to matters of obscenity. My mother-in-law became involved in the matter and suggested that I offer him a cow in exchange for publication. The wretched man agreed on condition that I add two rams and a hen. Even so, I refused point blank to leave out or rewrite any detail about my suffering and torture. The man turned his back on me, furious and empty-handed.

It is not in my nature or vocation to give up. Something unforeseen may come up with regard to my manuscript, including measures that I need to pursue in the capital city of Rabat and such legal foundations as are prepared to be receptive. I wonder: would I ever have escaped from my trials and tribulations if it were not for my Job-like patience and my pretense at being sick and crazy, just as you advised me to do, Na'ima? Did I ever imagine that I would be married in this locality and see Zaynab carrying my baby if it had not been for the generous help of a truly pious man? Or could I ever have used my adherence to the counsel of the Lord of all Messengers: "When you come to your womenfolk, then make love to them," to ask for the gift of a child? The whole thing is connected, Na'ima. Only time can tell . . . !

Afterword

Glossary

Afterword

The English dictionary does not contain the word *torturess*. While the feminine suffix "-ess" certainly continues to exist and be used to depict certain categories: princess, hostess, heiress, seamstress, and so on (and, in former times, a woman who wrote poetry might well be called a *poetess* rather than what seems to have become the current preference for *poet*—or even *female poet*), it might be assumed that the generally horrific functions associated with the torture of human beings has been an exclusively male preserve and thus the term *torturer* has been sufficient. In this novel by Bensalem Himmich, however, the Arabic title *Muʿadhdhabatī* is unequivocally feminine in form. It is out of a desire to underline the clear indications of the title and the fact that it consists of a single noun that I have coined the English title I have used.

This is the fourth novel written by Bensalem Himmich that I have translated into English. The first (in order of their publication in English) is *Al-ʿAllamah* (1997: *The Polymath*, 2004), which recounts the later life in Cairo of the great Arab philosopher of history, Ibn Khaldun (d. 1406)—that topic being, not coincidentally, the field of scholarly specialization of Himmich himself; the second, *Majnun al-hukm* (1990; *The Theocrat*, 2006), is devoted to the controversial life of the Fatimid Caliph, Al-Hakim bi-Amr Allah (985–1021); and thirdly, *Hadhā al-Andalusi* (2007, *A Muslim Suicide*, 2011), which follows the life and death of the controversial Andalusian Sufi physician and theologian known by the nickname, Ibn Sabʿin (1217–68)—and I need to note here that the title of the English translation is a reflection of the author's original intentions that were not reflected in the original Arabic version's title. In other words, all three of these novels in translation are narratives in which the life and career of a famous figure from the Arab-Islamic heritage are placed into a fictional context which, while based to an extent on textual accounts of the persons and periods in question, are primarily the products of the author's own imagination. One might therefore identify them as contributions in Arabic to the subgenre of the "historical novel," thus following in the path pioneered by Sir Walter Scott with his *Waverley* novels and replicated in various world literary traditions by such illustrious figures as Leo Tolstoy and Honoré de Balzac. However, Himmich himself has expressed the view—in many personal conversations and public presentations that we have done together—that he does not wish to use the term *historical novels* in connection with these works. For him, these and his other fictional works are novels (and it needs to be mentioned here that he is also a poet and, as already noted, a scholar in the field of historiography). In expressing that view he joins the great European critic, Georg Lukacs, who similarly declares that novels that utilize history in one way or another—and there are indeed many such ways—are indeed simply novels. Indeed, Lukacs goes beyond that to suggest that, in one way or another, every novel can be considered "historical"—whether it treats the topic of history and figures from the past or whether it is a reflection of the era in which it is written. In the Arabic literary context, one might suggest that Jamal al-Ghitani's (b. 1945) famous novel, *Al-Zayni Barakat*, is certainly a classic example of a novel that makes use of history to comment on the present, but that almost any novel by his compatriot, Najib Mahfuz (1911–2006), can now be considered "historical," whether we talk about the world-famous *Trilogy* of novels about Cairo in the interwar period (in the case of the novels, approximately 1917–44) or *Al-Summan wa-al-Kharif* (1962), which is set during and immediately after the 1952 Egyptian Revolution.

My Torturess is then first and foremost a novel, and yet it too fits into a particular period in history—indeed, a very recent one—the ramifications of which are still very much before us. During the period following the September 11, 2001, attacks on the World Trade Center in New York and as part of its consequences in terms of the "war on terror," the novel's primary character, a young man called Ḥamuda from the Eastern Moroccan city of Oujda, is subject to the process dubbed by the American Central Intelligence Agency (CIA) as "extraordinary rendition," involving arrest and transfer to a secret camp in one of several nations whose posture toward the use of torture was and is somewhat less punctilious than in other countries. Himmich himself has served as Minister of Culture in Morocco, and whatever information is available about these secret camps and the methods that were used to "render" those suspected of being "terrorists" suggests that Morocco may have one of those secret sites. However, the process whereby Hamuda is "rendered" to the place where he is to spend six years of his life does not indicate where the location is—whether in Morocco or another country.

Hamuda is to suffer at the hands—and other parts of the body—of the novel's title figure, a woman of apparently French origins nicknamed "Mama Ghula" (Mother Ghoul). She is the "torturess" of Himmich's and my title, and her presence in the camp and indeed the nickname coined by her victims serve to accentuate the highly unusual circumstance, it would appear, of utilizing a woman, and especially a woman's body, in the exercise of torture involving male internees. Hamuda's own statements throughout the narrative and his regular invocations and prayers make it clear that he is a devout Muslim; indeed, at one point during his lengthy incarceration he is appointed as the prisoners' mufti (religious counselor). However, it emerges during interrogation that it is the activities of his cousin, al-Husayn al-Masmudi, a member—we later learn—of a jihadist group operating in the Atlas Mountains, that appear to arouse the interest of the security forces who subject Hamuda to the process of "rendition."

Among the variety of "trials and examinations" that Hamuda is forced to endure are exposure to the treatment of a variety of guards in different segments of the prison, cellblocks subjected to intense noise, the placement of "plants"—other "prisoners" who actually are not in that category—in Hamuda's cell itself and both the exercise yard and cafeteria (when and if he is allowed access to them), and fake firing squads. However, the most direct method takes the form of cross-examinations involving two primary figures. The first is the investigating judge, a fellow Arab, it would appear from his lengthy discussions of the pedantries of correct Arabic language use and his delight in debates on literature and style—whose very pedantry is responsible for many of the cultural references that make up the entries in the glossary accompanying this translation. In justifying the methods of torture employed by the second figure, Mama Ghula (the "torturess"), the judge reveals to Hamuda and the reader exactly who those "foreign agencies" are:

> She should be punished, not merely for what she's done to you but also because, when it comes to monstrous conduct and illicit behavior, she has no peer; when it comes to terror and violence, no one else comes even close. But how can I be blamed when Uncle Sam has written her a blank check? What am I supposed to do? The Yankees have given her a green

light—in fact, it's so green that there's nothing fresher and greener. And, if you've never heard of the Yankees and Uncle Sam, then let me tell you that it's the Americans . . ."

It is only when the efforts of this judge to persuade Hamuda (and other prisoners) to reveal information about themselves, their "terrorist activities," and, in Hamuda's case, the whereabouts and activities of his cousin, fail to produce the needed results that they are consigned to Mama Ghula's ministrations. The sequence of the narrative manages to provide a terrifying accumulative picture of this fiendish woman, but the narrator's first actual view of her occurs when he participates in a vicious soccer game that she is supposedly refereeing between the prisoners and a set of thugs who essentially flatten their opposition. Soon afterwards, however, it is his turn in the torture chamber about which he has already heard so much. As one of the narrator's cell mates has warned him:

> They'll hand you over to the professional torturess, who's an expert in all kinds of degradation and torture. The worst of them, she's learned in specialized foreign centers, but she's also invented others of her own that she delights in testing on imprisoned suspects like you and me. Compared with the torture she inflicts, the torments of the grave are a joke, kid's play. I don't want you to fall prey to the woman they call Mama Ghula— and may God protect you from her barbaric madness!

Once again, the reader's attention is drawn here to the "specialized foreign centers" where Mama Ghula has received training, but it is the "other" methods of torture that inject into the narrative aspects of sexual perversion that are indeed more than liable to "upset the squeamish." Indeed, they involve "degrading" practices that are so extreme as not only to cause maximum harm and offense to those prisoners who adhere to beliefs of Islam and the norms of Arab society, but also to replicate in the reader's mind the general outrage generated by the release of the photographs taken inside the Abu Ghraib Prison in Iraq and the debates over the practice and very legitimacy of "waterboarding."[1]

---

1. A detailed investigation of the Abu Ghraib Prison is: Seymour M. Hersh, *Chain of Command: The Road from 9/11 to Abu Ghraib* (New York: HarperCollins,

It is only when these procedures fail to achieve their goals that the torturess resorts to other means of physical abuse—stubbing out lighted cigarettes on his body, hanging him upside down, thrusting a bottle into his anus, and then ruing the fact that he is too thin to scrape off parts of his flesh as she has done with other victims. Even with this, Mama Ghula is still not finished with her attempts at using forms of sexual torture in order to extract "information" from this particular victim. In a truly grotesque scene, Hamuda later finds himself in bed with his torturess. She claims that they are married and even brings in "witnesses" to corroborate her story. As if that is not enough, she enlivens the events of the night by summoning her "court jester," a midget who specializes in telling dirty jokes.

Bearing in mind the vicious and perverted ways in which Mama Ghula has utilized sexual perversion as a means of assaulting the unfortunate inmates of this detention center, it is hardly surprising—indeed, perhaps fitting—that her own demise should result from violent confrontation. At a grotesque evening entertainment organized for the prisoners by the "administration"—all of whose principals are present, an enormous, deaf-mute black guard is invited to play his drum. As his expert performance works his audience up into a frenzy of action and movement, Mama Ghula gets to her feet and rides on the black drummer's back, noting, as she does so, that she has previously been a wild-animal tamer. Suddenly, the drummer throws her to the ground and delivers a series of deadly blows before he is shot dead by guards. With that, the entertainment is brought to a rapid and chaotic close.

The narrator's "re-rendition" is brought about through the intervention of the medical authorities at the center and with the tacit support of Na'ima, one of the succession of secretaries to the investigating judge, she being a fellow Moroccan to whom the entire narrative is addressed at its beginning and end. She provides Hamuda with a vial of blood so that he can replicate the symptoms of tuberculosis in yet another interview with the judge. As the narrative reaches its conclusion, Hamuda has begun the

---

2004). The literature on waterboarding—particularly following revelations in 2007 of its use by the Central Intelligence Agency, its lengthy history as a form of torture, and its (il-)legality, is enormous.

process of resuming something approaching a normal life in the Oujda region. In fact, thanks to the good offices of a local shaykh, he is now residing in the plains outside the city at the house of an elderly widow whose daughter, Zaynab, he has married. It is in such quiet rural surroundings that he can begin his life afresh and write a record of his horrendous experiences.

In conclusion, it seems important to emphasize again that this work of Bensalem Himmich is indeed a contribution to fiction. However, that said, it clearly manages to fulfill one of the primary purposes of that particular genre of fiction that is the novel, in that, to quote Lionel Trilling's description, it serves as "an especially useful agent of the moral imagination."[2] The reader of this text encounters in its starkest form the full impact of the policies adopted by the government of the United States in its attempts to counteract the perceived threats of international terrorism in the wake of the September 2001 attacks on the World Trade Center and implemented at secret sites situated in a number of countries—apparently in both Europe and Africa. The resulting account, told from the point of view of a Moroccan who finds himself ensnared in the web of suspicion that results, is utterly shocking, and deliberately so. The novel reveals the moral depths to which humanity is capable of descending; it not only describes in painfully vivid detail the processes of torture—physical, mental, and, in this case, sexual, but also reveals all kinds of cultural biases that at times show themselves as overt racism.

The former Minister of Culture in Morocco, Bensalem Himmich, here paints an unforgettable picture of a prison camp somewhere, perhaps even in his own homeland. The period involved is six years of imprisonment— only computable at its conclusion, preceded by an apparently normal life and followed by a struggle to return to it. This novel is thus a very different contribution to its author's oeuvre available in English translation— certainly concerned with a particular and highly controversial period in twenty-first-century history, but also a major contribution to prison fiction. But, above all, a wonderful novel.

2. Lionel Trilling, *The Liberal Imagination* (New York: Scribner's, 1940/1950, vii).

I would like to thank Michael Beard and Adnan Haydar for accepting this novel in their excellent series of translations and also express my gratitude to the editorial staff at Syracuse University Press. A special word of thanks is due to the two readers of this manuscript, the majority of whose suggestions have been incorporated into the text.

Roger Allen

Glossary

'Abbas ibn Firnas (810–77): of Andalusian-Amazigh extraction, he was a polymathic scientist, engineer, musician and poet.

Abu Zayd: the hero of one of Arabic's most famous epic folk sagas, *Sirat Bani Hilal*.

'Ali ibn Abi Talib (601–61): cousin and son-in-law of the Prophet Muhammad and fourth Caliph of Islam. The Shi'ah community was founded in his name. The *Durar al-Kalim* is a collection of his short sayings and aphorisms.

'Antara ibn Shaddad al-'Absi (6th cent.): a renowned pre-Islamic poet-cavalier whose many exploits and challenges posed by the father of his beloved, 'Abla, provide the content for the multi-volume epic, *Sirat 'Antar*.

Abu Yazid al-Bistami (d. c. 877): an early ecstatic Sufi of Iranian origins.

Al-Busiri (1212–c. 1294): an Egyptian poet, best known for his "Burda" (Mantle) poem in praise of the Prophet Muhammad.

Gnaoua: the name of a tribe and language from the regions to the south of Morocco, whose musical performances are especially popular.

Hajj: the pilgrimage to Mecca; with an elongated "a" vowel, the honorific title given to a Muslim who has undertaken the pilgrimage.

Hassan ibn Thabit (7th cent.): the most famous of the poets associated with the career of the prophet Muhammad.

Hatim al-Ta'i (d. 578): a pre-Islamic Christian poet proverbial for his generosity.

Ibn Qayyim al-Jawziyya (1292–1350): a scholar of Qur'anic studies, hadith, and rhetoric, and author of *Rawdat al-muhibbin* (Lovers' Meadow).

Ibn Manzur (1233–1311), compiler of the Arabic dictionary, *Lisan al-'Arab*.

Ibn Sa'd (d. 845): a hadith scholar whose biographical dictionary, *Kitab Tabaqat al-Kabir*, details the lives of the Prophet Muhammad and of the earliest personalities in Islamic history.

Abu 'Uthman Bahr al-Jahiz (776–868): Arabic's most illustrious essayist, prose stylist, and critic.

Al-Jalalan: the title given to the two most important collections of Prophetic "hadith" termed "sahih" (authentic): those of al-Bukhari (810–70) and Muslim ibn al-Hajjaj (c. 815–75).

Muhammad al-Juzuli (d. 1465): a Moroccan Sufi scholar and author of *Dala'il al-Khayrat*, a collection of prayers to the Prophet Muhammad.

Maquis: A French word, meaning literally "scrub, bush," that was used during the Second World War to describe the French resistance forces.

Mu'allaqa: the name given to the collection of seven (or ten) long odes composed in the pre-Islamic era and much prized as early monuments in the Arabic poetic tradition.

Munkir and Nakir: the names of the two angels who will question believers following their death.

Al-Mutanabbi (915–65): Arabic's most famous premodern poet, renowned equally for his panegyrics and lampoons of rulers and patrons.

O Mu'tasim: in Arabic, "*yā mu'taṣimāh*," a proverbial cry of distress, allegedly first pronounced following the defeat of the Muslim armies in Anatolia.

Shaykh Muhammad al-Nafzawi (15th cent.): the author of *Al-Rawdat al-'Atir* (known in English as *The Perfumed Garden for the Heart's Delight*), a famous sex manual, originally prepared for a Tunisian vizier, Muhammad al-Zawawi.

Nahid: the secretary's name in Arabic means "buxom."

Fu'ad Nigm (1929–2013): a renowned Egyptian folk poet who often composed poems that were sung to music composed by Shaykh Imam.

Qays and Layla: Qays is the renowned "Majnun" of Arabic lore, the lover driven to insanity by his love for Layla and the fact that he is forever banned from seeing her.

salafi: literally, connected to one's forebears, this term now implies an adherence to the tenets of Islam in its earliest phases.

Sura of the Poets: In Sura 26 of the Qur'an, poets are said to be lost and wandering around in valleys.

Jalal al-din al-Suyuti (1445–1505): a polymathic scholar and author of over 500 works of enormous variety.

Al-Takfir wa-al-Hijra (approx. Anathema and Emigration]: the name of a radical Islamist group, an offshoot of the Muslim Brotherhood, that emerged in Egypt during the 1960s.

Abu Hayyan al-Tawhidi (c. 927–1023): major Arabic prose writer and compiler of the anecdote collection, *Kitab al-Imta' wa-al-Mu'anasah* (Book of Enjoyment and Good Company).

Al-Tifashi 1184–1253): Arabic prose writer and author, among many other works, of *Nuzhat al-albab fi-ma la yujad fi kitab* (The Hearts' Delight Concerning What Does Not Exist in Books).

Al-Tirimmah: the name of a seventh-century Arab poet who joined the group known as the Kharijites, those who "went away" from the armed forces of the fourth caliph, 'Ali, after he had agreed to arbitration following the indecisive battle of Siffin (657).

Yaqzin: the torturess is punning on the meaning of the verbal root Y-Q-Z, which is connected with the idea of "being awake."

Zarqa' al-Yamama: a legendary, blue-eyed female figure from pre-Islamic Yemen, who was gifted with such sight that she could detect enemies a long way away.